SLAYER

SLAYER

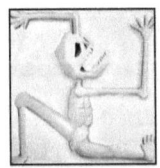

R.W. MADSON

Full Court Press
Englewood Cliffs, New Jersey

Published in the United States of America
by Full Court Press, 601 Palisade Avenue,
Englewood Cliffs, NJ 07632
fullcourtpress.com

ISBN 978-1-953728-21-0
Library of Congress Control Number: 2023922116

Cover art by the author

Editing and book design by Barry Sheinkopf

To Richard Dietz
*My husband of 53 years, legally fifteen,
who after reading Slayer worries for his safety.*

And to Anne Wennhold
Friend, teacher, and wise elder.

And to Florence Cestaro
who knows a comma when I need one.

A Word from the Author

I started my career in Sicily. Is that not some kind of cliche? Actually, Mafia killings were not needed as a cover. Those were the days when I disposed of the bodies in the Ionian Sea. Sicily has a long coastline. I kept a boat outside Taormina, my hunting grounds. Some ropes, rocks to weigh down the sacks, and a night's sail were enough to get rid of the detritus. I generally selected people passing through. Back packers. Disconnected. Ones the locals would think had left early, at dawn.

Sicilians know everybody and everything in their towns. They might never rat you out to the authorities, but they would not tolerate killing for personal fulfillment. Vendettas, financial gain, political intrigue were all acceptable, but personal need got you labeled *pazzo*. *Pazzo* is not acceptable, too unpredictable.

I escaped my own peculiar Babylonian Captivity after a year. I fled back to the mainland. Resolved some issues in Trieste, then Milan. Crossed the Alps through Switzerland. Hunted Bavaria for what felt like centuries. The hills were alive—well, dead—with my victims. Again following the same procedure, prey on passers-through. I had a life-changing experience during one of my settled residences. Moved to Bern, on to Amsterdam, through the Low Countries, Paris for a while. Following William the Conqueror, I crossed the channel to merry old England. Eventually London, being a crowded, chaotic mess, was a perfect place for this Jack the Ripper.

My ancient family was French. They hid their non-Catholicism, eventually joining without actual baptism. Just made out they were until they were. They made *miliardo* in the silk trade, which brought them to Venice. They allied their gold with banking families in Florence and Milan. Expanded with those families throughout Europe. We never outright owned a bank or were named but always held from ten to twenty-five percent of the assets. Do that over five hundred years, in fifty countries, especially Switzerland, and your fortune makes Jeff Bezos look like a middle-class relation.

Of course, such a fortune is widely invested: banks, commodities, manufacturing, arms, pharmaceuticals, international conglomerates. Many hands dip into the pot of gold—cousins, relatives I'd never heard of, some I *wish* I never had. Most in turn have created their own fortunes. We tithe one percent of our private profit back to a Swiss holding company every year. My spending a million or ten a year goes unnoticed, picayune.

After ten years in the Americas, my private current assets are astronomical. I would be counted as a near trillionaire if it were in one name. I have no public profile and no bank account larger than two hundred thousand dollars. I have many identities, social security numbers, minions, lawyers, stockbrokers, residences, and vaults in safe houses. Similarly in a few other countries. A few small manufacturing businesses of special interest in Central America. A large investment in biological research. I/we pay my fair share of taxes.

If I have holdings in a country, I master the language. Being wealthy greatly facilitates my mostly invisible mobility. I have an eidetic memory and know every account number, location, and name of my assets and who manages them. When I specialized, I knew every one of my kills' names, addresses, and the idiocy that brought them to my attention.

So here I am, an immigrant doing a job Americans were not willing to do, cleaning out their deplorable brethren.

I'm a serial killer. At least that's what the police label me. I live to eat and kill. As Ru Paul says, everything else is drag.

1

NOW, NEW YORK CITY

IN THE IMMEDIATE PAST, NOT ALL but most of my identified corpses were homosexuals and bi's. The police think those murders are being done by a homophobe. The fact is I was cleaning up the bottom feeders in the LGBTQ community, although I refer to them as homosexuals. They are the crazies, the religious fanatics, the dissatisfied, the racists, the conservatives, the Log Cabin types, the ones who see themselves as part of "normal" society—the ones who have sex in, but no identity with, the community. The Roy Cohens.

When I hunted selectively, I used a new, scientifically based method exclusively with men I would have sex with. It created the most exhilarating, lengthy, agonizing deaths. It was time-consuming. It had been perfected at my request by a distant cousin with a Ph.D. in chemistry. She took years of observation to isolate the hormones, replicate, refine, quantify and calculate. You know what Edison said about invention: two percent inspiration, ninety-eight percent perspiration. But once perfected, I gathered a small circle of enthusiasts. We practiced it with epicurean delight. Sadly, no more.

One can profile efficiently because of social media. Facebook alone has dozens if not hundreds of sites hosted for "conservative" communities. A few less for LGBTQ people. With numerous identities, I'd track them.

In reality, I am an enthusiastic supporter of total equality, an uber liberal, a libtard, a sheeple, etc., as those I seek like to call me.

I'd find a truly annoying respondent and go on the hunt. It can be very easy. When I thought they were a real person, I looked up their profile. I messaged them, tried to form an outraged relationship with them. I suggested we meet as I lived in the same vicinity. I traveled a bit when required. If a woman, I'd hint at looking for a serious dating relationship with a like-minded person.

We'd meet for drinks or coffee in a public place of their choice. I preferred coffee, as cake is usually available at those establishments. I like sweets. With men, unfortunately, it's mostly bars.

These next passages from my diary should be edited. Business and family interests have intervened. My activities are now much more circumspect. Science has been forbidden to them. I guess raw data can be tolerated; after all, it is a diary entry.

DIARY:

These ultra-conservative homosexuals love married men. I tell them I am on the down low. The illusion of passing is very reaffirming to them. I make every effort to help them feel comfortable and trusting. When I hunt someone, I flatter enough to reel him in without being unrealistic. If we hit it off and he wants to get it on, obviously it has to be at his place. This is where structure is important. If he lives with someone, the scientific method is out. Only a person who lives alone allows the time needed for that most satisfying uninterrupted production. If he suggests a tryst, I tell him my preferred role is as a top. It only works if he's a bottom. I am not a rapist in general. I want my prey to be satisfied, relaxed and aware.

A SCIENTIFIC CASE STUDY, SO TO SAY:

We met in Chelsea, New York City, at a bar on Eighth Avenue near Twentieth. He bought us drinks.

We chatted at the ledge along the back wall. I kept my back to the crowd. We compared our views on the dissolution of American society.

"Just keep your voice low," his excitement caused me to caution gently, reminding him that most of this crowd was not copacetic with our politics. "I certainly agree with you, but I don't want to attract attention."

Since he loved conspiracies, he found this an added attraction. He suggested we go to his place for drinks. He lived in a four-story walk-up on Thompson Street in the Village, a bit of a walk. He suggested getting a cab. I wanted to walk, so we could get to know each other. I assured him that I looked forward to that drink. Letting people talk about themselves is a sure key to lowering their barriers, something I learned early in my avocation.

He told me his whole dreary story, but I will spare you. Suffice it to say that neither his hard-working immigrant grandparents, nor his parents, expected anyone to give them anything. Blah, blah, blah. He worked his hump off in the office of an oriental carpet showroom and cleaning business. His bosses were "second generation Armenian immigrants who would cheat the pants off you, given the chance."

He was white (need I say), forty-ish, five feet ten inches, and had graying brown hair, a receding hairline, brown eyes, a trimmed beard hiding a not-square jaw, and weighed 180 to 185 pounds. He said he went to the gym but looked a bit soft. Not a catch, but OK enough to get me in the mood for the big time. He was dressed in brown slacks, a blue-checked button-down shirt with the neck and first button undone, and brown loafers. He wore a silver ring and a Citizen Eco-Drive watch. He was wearing a lightweight navy jacket on this cool late-spring night.

We climb to his third-floor, one-bedroom apartment. He invites me in. The living room is softly lit by two electrified glass-globed kerosene lamps.

Tells me to have a seat, indicating the overstuffed, tan-pillowed couch. He hangs his coat in the entrance closet. I lay mine on the winged forest green reading chair. The apartment is thankfully neat and lemon-fresh polished, with a good oriental rug on the floor. I note a nice antique vitrine filled with tchotchkes, many of the "Little Black Sambo" types popular before the 1960s. A large flat-screen TV is standing on a low veneered pressboard cabinet from IKEA opposite the easy chair. End tables adorned with the lamps. Generic rectangular coffee table. Pullman kitchen, a wall of the living room. Bedroom at the other end of the living room.

He asks what I'm drinking. I ask, "What are you offering?"

He gets equally coy, "Vodka and me."

I chuckle. "That's what I was hoping for—you, not necessarily the vodka. But if you feel like having a drink, let's."

He pours us drinks, offers tonic. We sit on his couch.

"Nice apartment."

"Inherited it from my parents when they moved to Florida."

We sip our drinks. I'm hungry to get on with it. I lean in and whisper in his ear, "Can I kiss you?"

"Umm," he hums.

Feeling myself becoming aggressive, I hold back. I don't want to ruin things by rushing. The longer this takes, the better the kill.

My right arm reaches across the couched pillows, fingers playing with his ear, stroking hair smelling of sandalwood shampoo. Left hand, with my simple gold wedding band, leads his face to mine, in for the kiss. He responds well. I love to kiss. Tangled tongues exploring our mouths, mine numbering his teeth, tasting quinined lips. His licking mine. Kissing his cheek, biting his ear, down his neck. Caressing his beard.

My left hand running over his chest, unbuttoning his shirt, to slide my hand under his white tee shirt. Hairy or smooth? Muscular or soft as I anticipated? My host sighs deeply.

Pulling the shirt from his pants. Hand up and under his tee, unveiling the answers to the questions. Trimmed, not abundant. Not gymmed up but natural. Off with it completely. Mirroring my action he peels my shirts off me. Our four-handed action, caressing, squeezing, pinching, licking, biting, stroking. Mutually mauling our way downward, mutually mewing. I kneaded his glutes, down his upper thighs, across the tops of his legs, returning to own his bare belly, chest, fleecy arms; measured, slow, building.

Murmured syllables. Kissing. His breath moist and warm. Leaning in, nuzzling his neck, nipping at it, restraining the desire to sink my teeth into the vibrant flesh.

Sensitive, his chest arches forward, sinking his bottom into the sofa, pulling him away from my mouth. I push him back against the couch, pausing to undress him. Shoes already gone. Socks off. Pulling his pants over his feet. Casting them aside. Sliding down his briefs. Stripped.

I roll on top of him. Wanting to begin the real performance, I sit up, urgent: "I want to be in you."

"Let's go into the bedroom." There's eagerness in his voice. I reach into my jacket pocket, securing my special condom. "Like a boy scout, always be prepared," I quip.

He leads us to his bedroom. Clicks on a small lamp. A four-poster bed . . .such possibilities. We tear off the coverlet and handmade quilt. He retrieves a bottle of lubricant from the nightstand drawer. More kissing, rubbing. He ungulates, whimpers. Flipping over, kneeling between his legs, I tear the condom wrapper with my teeth, roll it on. Towering over him, entering. Guttural sounds drive us on.

His body heat, my thrusting tearing and melting the condom. Melting the condom. What the hell? My cousin's discovery now takes precedence.

"Oh, God," he repeats in ever-intense tones.

Our breaths loud and spastic, I lift him onto his knees. I reach around, bring him to climax, timing my own to meet his. Collapsing on his smooth back. This might seem to be the perfect moment for the coup de grace but it has already occurred.

Aping the samurai bushido code, just because I am murdering him doesn't mean his last desire should not be fulfilled. I lay on him for a few moments. Lift off. He rolls onto his back. His neck in the crook of my elbow. Our lungs returning to normal. He doesn't note the missing condom.

I look around the bedroom. Spare. A black highboy dresser, the bed, two nightstands, small opaque globed lamps (an attempt at modernism), a small craftsman desk dressed with a lace doily, single drawer, matching chair, closed laptop, green glass-shaded desk lamp, American eagle-embossed coffee cup with writing implements in it. A picture of the former Pope Benedict on the wall over the desk. No cross. Thank God no mirror.

"Benedict not Francis?" I inquire.

"Francis is a goddamn pussy. Benedict knew how to keep things strict." His ire is relevant to his coming experience.

"Obviously you are Catholic."

"Church every Sunday. I substitute in the choir when called."

This postcoital conversation is an intermission as we await the next scene. I don't want him dozing. He needs to be innocently aware.

He continues proudly, "Catholic school all the way through two years of college."

Then, what I've been waiting for. "Something's wrong. I can't move."

Bingo. Act two begins. I sit up, look at him with a mixture of affection, pity, and malevolence, "I know." I wait. He can barely squirm. "I have a secret to tell you."

I whisper it in his ear. His eyes bulge cartoonishly. He struggles mightily just to lift his head. He tries to speak; soon it will be mostly gurgles and groans. His words become a hiss. "You're insane. What have you done? Why? Why me?" His head falls back, for now his asking unanswered.

After I disengage myself, I prop him up on some pillows against the headboard so he can see me and watch his own dissolution. I take the towel he brought out with the lubricant and wipe myself off, then him. Neat and clean for the show. Ensconcing myself at the bottom of the bed, I lean against a pillow at the bed post for a better view of the unfolding carnage.

Now my boyish nature takes over. Or is it feline? Anyway, I toy with him. "Let me tell you what's happening. Your body heat has activated substances that are coursing through your muscles which are slowly disconnecting from your bones. Your ligaments, too. Except for the ones attached to your spine. That's a mystery to us, but I digress. In somewhere between an hour and ninety minutes your back muscles will tighten. They will break your back, if not your neck.

"This is the best part, if I'm lucky, since it doesn't always happen, a coda in this tableau. Lucky for me but not you. If the spasm doesn't break your neck, killing you, but only snaps your spine, your eyes will explode exactly one minute after."

"Now, isn't that special," I say, quoting Emily Litella. I roar in mirth. He gurgles and moans.

He hisses, "Help me, stop this, I want to live."

Trying to soothe him: "Please relax. Think of this. You are having one of the most unique experiences on earth. Out of the six or seven billion people, there are very few who will accomplish this in any year. I will even be able to count you down to the precise moment of your demise. Truly a gift rare in this world."

"Please make it stop. Please. . . ." His wheezed praying to Jesus becomes tedious.

The muscles dissolving from the bone are maddeningly inflaming. His body temperature quickly reaches 103, topping at 110. He will be totally aware to the last moment.

I enjoy sharing this tidbit: "If I were to stop it, which I can—" a theatrical pause— "which I can, you would live like this for the rest of your life, a variation from the usual halting. Would you really want to be in this excruciatingly wondrous condition for what would be your eternity? Besides, you wouldn't want to deprive me of this joyous procession of pain."

He groans, entreats. The back muscles will begin shaping his spine into an arch precisely fifteen minutes before the spasm.

It's been about half an hour. His pleas give way to moaning groans. Soon there's a change. He exhales words.

"What's that you say? Let me come closer." I crawl over him on all fours, lean my ear close to his mouth, being careful not to press on his spongy transformation. My penis drags along his decimated leg, reminding me not to leave that detail out, although it's not likely that I would.

"Kill me. Please kill me now!"

With as much lack of irony in my voice as possible, looking lovingly into his eyes, I assure him, "My dear, that is precisely what I am doing. Patience is a virtue, you know."

I return to reclining against the bottom bedpost. Not one to hold back instruction, I continue this book of the dead. "Let me fill these last minutes with some final revelations. If you survive through your broken back, after your eyes explode there is a long moment before you die. During that time your brain with boil, fry, bake—doesn't really matter. What matters is purely for my enjoyment. Your brain will give you the apex experience of your nasty little life. It will send anguish through all of your veins, arteries, nerves, and organs, which is another mystery, as is your ability to breathe. None totally collapse until your brain is a puddle. Their parting chorus is perfection to listen to."

I take a deep breath, measured. "Sadly," I sigh, "ultimately all that is left is a skin filled with slurry and bones." Brightening, I add, "The coroners are absolutely baffled. They first attributed it to a virulent Ebola variant, but not so."

Flatly I include, "The CDC, NIH, and FBI are always notified." After a time of silence and quiet introspection, I scold, "Now, why am I doing this to you in particular, you have asked."

I go mum for dramatic effect. Disgusted, I answer, "You write—well, wrote, since you won't be doing it anymore—you write truly insulting postings on Facebook. Your politics are atrocious, and your racism appalling, as confirmed by your cabinet collections. You deny your own kind while seeking their comfort. You are an astounding hypocrite. You will be one less voice and vote for the deranged."

With unrestrained glee, I continue, "Also, as I hope I have made clear, it gives me untold pleasure. I have even given it a name, 'the von Pittasch.' Truly this is the ultimate 'von Pittasch.' If the spasm doesn't kill you, the anticipation of watching your eyes detonate induces enormous sexual stimulation, giving me a huge erection. Your exploding eyes will trigger my volcanic semen. Occasionally the same gift is granted to you, our protagonist, probably a hormonal super nova. Kind of a last hurrah. Your showstopper."

I lean over, pat him on his burning foot. Sanctimoniously I intone, "Now we will be quiet. Let us meditate on the coming finalities. I'll keep time for us so we can anticipate the best scenes in our grand comedy."

His suffering lulls me. Long minutes pass.

His back becomes a Halloween cat but in the wrong direction for a human spine, torture more acute as the reprieved muscles tighten. His babel louder, giving the lie to his dissolving vocal cords, leaving time for a goodbye. I dismount from my perch, positioning myself mid-carcass.

"From my extensive experience, I can tell from your arch that in about two minutes you will shatter." I give a small chuckle and smile at him. "Are you ready? Will this be goodbye, or will you attain otherworldly ecstasy followed by incredibly wretched agony?" My curiosity is scientifically erotic.

He would cry, if he could.

Solemnly, as befits the occasion, I muse, "Hm. We shall very shortly see."

As prophesied, his back audibly snaps, and he collapses with a slushing sound. He gurgles, utters the smallest vocalizations, no moans but audible to my preternaturally acute hearing

"Oh, wonderful. We are in communion. Look how erect I am. Aha, and a bonus for you. Delightful, a boned duet for a last mutual ejection. 1, 2. . .3. . .4. . .5. . . ." I count toward sixty, the set time.

His eyes explode at fifty-nine, a premature ejaculation, the gel squirting like crushed grapes a good two feet in every direction, his semen a stream over his ebbing right thigh.

I spew across his torso to the far side of the bed. The surprising miscount makes my orgasm tectonic. "Thank you, thank you. That was glorious," I whisper, my chest heaving, saliva leaking from my lips. Bracing on the mattress, I genuflect, resting my knee on the floor so as not to fall in the euphoria of my full body climax.

Coquettishly I inquire, "Was it as good for you as it was for me?" I guffaw at my inane jest.

Despite his total paralysis, his boiling brain's final evocation is loud, long seconds of monotoned, amplified torment. I take my bedpost pillow to muffle him enough to keep the neighbors undisturbed, being careful not to suffocate him or sacrificing the beatific choir of his collapsing viscera.

Finito. Ité missa est.

Such sacerdotal magnificence. The ritual impeccably performed. No ecclesiastic actor could have done better. I bow my head onto the bed.

Twenty or so minutes pass; my obeisance over, I arise, chronicling this altar of flawless satisfaction. No need for curtain calls.

Finding fresh towels on the storage rack over the toilet, I shower, retrieve my clothing from the living room, dress there. Fluff the couch pillows. Wash our drink glasses. I intentionally put both of them on the sink drain board. I gather his clothing. Remove the contents of his pockets and put them on the desk. Contemplate taking his cell but leave it.

Idly I look through his wallet and find an organ donor's card. I turn to the bed and congratulate him for fulfilling his bequest. I put it under his loose change.

I hang his clothes in the bedroom closet on dry cleaner's wire hangers. (I wondered where there was a bedroom mirror. He has his mounted on the inside of the closet door.) Put his loafers under the highboy with other pairs of casual footwear propped up on the cross brace. Put his day worn underwear and baby blue socks in the bathroom hamper with the towels I borrowed. Placed the lubricant in its drawer. Finding his watch and ring in there, I move them to the desk with his other accouterments. I pocket the condom wrapper.

I set the muffling pillow next to him at the headboard. Cover him with his family quilt up to where his waist once was, pick up the bedspread from the floor, fold it into a foot-wide rectangle across the foot of the bed over the tucked-in quilt.

Appreciate that he has mostly liquified.

Cross the living room. Put on my jacket, check for my kit in the inside pocket. Survey the apartment one last time—neat and polished, putrescent—and let myself out.

Adieu, Glenn Marsayas.

Time to feed this otherwise utterly satisfied being.

2

NOW, NEW YORK CITY

O K WITH BROCCOLI. See you in ten minutes." Jason put his phone on the table, palm patting the leatherette seat next to him. Victor slid in closer. They pecked each other's cheek. "Thank you for coming. How are you?"

"Good to see you. I'm doing OK."

Nervously, Jason informed him, "My sister will be here in a few minutes. She said we should order. She wants to get home in time to see her kids awake for once. This will be the second time I've seen her since she and her husband picked me up when I flew home."

Scanning the menu, Victor asked, "What's good here?" unable to think of small talk to fill the space.

"I like the eggplant parm. Anything our friends have had here has been good. Didn't we ever eat here?" Jason was as flummoxed as Victor. The pair had had an intense five months before Jason went off to New Zealand on his study research sabbatical.

"I don't remember it. I doubt it." Victor knew he damn well didn't. He remembered every date and thing they did in their previous five-month liaison.

Jason gestured to the waiter. They ordered drinks. Jason merlot, Victor Chablis. When they arrived, they ordered the food—Victor, chicken marsala; Jason, eggplant with penne.

"The third person will be here in a few minutes. She'll have the egg-plant parm also, but with broccoli, not pasta," Jason ordered for Mortana.

They sipped their wines, chatting, catching up as former lovers who parted on good terms, protective of feelings, walls with cracks, ambivalence turning to desire. Five minutes later, a ranking uniformed police officer walked past the window headed to the entrance.

"Ah, here she is." Jason jumped up to go over to his sister and hugged, kissing her cheek as she put her vaccination card back in her wallet, having shown it to the maitre d'. He had led her to their isolated booth sandwiched between a serving station and the swinging kitchen door.

"Why don't you download the NYS app?" Jason chided her. "Victor, you remember Mortana, newly promoted lieutenant," he emphasizes. "Mortana Lemures, my older sister."

"Watch the older stuff. Eighteen months. Nice to see you again. How are you?" she asked sincerely.

He stood up a bit. Since the pandemic no one shook hands. "Same here. Doing well."

"I'm famished." She slid into the booth, put her hat and jacket on the banquette next to her, and loosened her regulation collar: Victor book ended by the two siblings.

"I ordered. How are Dan, the kids?" Jason buffered her entrance with family business before his business-obsessed sister began the reason for their gathering.

"They're good. School's back full time. Dan is writing. How's getting back in the work groove?" She munched on a breadstick, realized its calories, and returned it to her bread plate.

"My classes are energizing. Can you believe my luck? On a grant in New Zealand during lockdown. I had so much time that all the writing was done months ago."

"I caught up with your ambitious brother on things the other night when he called me about this," Victor said, wiggling into the conversation. The knowledge that Jason could have returned sooner nipped at his heart.

Jason moved on to the reason for the dinner. "I told him what you told me."

The waiter stopped at the table to ask if Mortana wanted a drink. "Diet Coke," she said, "no ice, no straw. Thanks."

"While we're waiting, let's get into it." She lowered her volume. "Jason has given you some of the story. Why don't I tell you what I know? This is completely off the record, you understand. I hope you have a strong stomach, because this is not for the squeamish." She had gone full cop.

"Other than my being your brother's friend, what has this to do with a reporter for *Gay Nation Press?*" Victor made no effort to hide his distrust.

"As you know, all of the victims are Gay men. The big difference, other than the usual mayhem, is that someone is preying on them, leaving some very, very strange corpses."

"How so?" No one had shared anything unusual about murders in the press room.

"I'll get there. This is the second of these cases I'm on. The first right from the beginning. I got assigned as the liaison to the FBI during the first."

"Before I joined the Department, I was a Marine nurse and then a nurse practitioner in an infectious disease unit in Iraq. The higher-ups thought that was a good fit. You'll understand more by the time I finish."

She inhaled, readied herself to do her best not to rush through her information, a habit resulting from juggling the new level of command, the new liaison position, inter- and extra-departmental politics, twin children who were proving to be more astute than either of their parents, an attentive writer house- husband, and a quartet of delightful in-laws.

"On May 9, 911 got a call from a super on Thompson Street in the Village. He was making what he hoped was a request for a 'wellness call,' but from the smell in the hall he doesn't think so. A blue-and-white checks it out. The super opens the door. The two uniforms and the super actually run out of the building, the stench is so overwhelming. The officers call in a possible HAZMAT situation. Two of the older tenants are home. Both rush out of the building, one with her dog. The smell is pouring under their doors. The rest of the building is out to work. We get a 'bus' to take them to the hospital. The EMTs give them oxygen. The uniforms and super, too. Eight apartments, two per floor. Super lives in the building down the block." Mortana pauses, getting to her involvement.

"The sergeant and a detective from the local precinct arrived. They call their captain, who calls in the HAZMAT team from the special Terrorist Unit. He notifies the deputy inspector, who takes it up the chain."

The waiter put her un-iced Diet Coke on the table. He dropped a paper-sleeved straw next to the drink.

She hands it back to him.

"Too many turtles choking on those," she says to the men in the booth, and continues, "When HAZMAT arrives, they decide a robot should go in first. They monitor it and when they see our victim on his bed, the captain, who arrived right after the team, calls our medical examiner. Standing orders there are to call me in this specialized scenario. I call my FBI colleague.

"What they saw was one thirty-eight-year-old Mr. Glenn Marsayas, looking like a kiddy pool vaguely shaped into a human being."

"Weird," Victor says. "What does that mean? Why the special FBI set up?"

"Please remember, this is completely off the record." Answering his reporter's question, she goes on, "There've been three cases like this in three years. Two in Manhattan, and a new one recently in Bay Ridge. But they started in '16 in DC and there have been a total of thirty-one across the country."

The food arrives.

Twenty minutes later Mortana had filled Victor in on most of the details, which sound like a horror movie.

The men ordered coffees. She declined and asked for the check. "The tenants are still in hotels, waiting for relocation," she tells them. "The two at the scene spent a night in the hospital. Bio teams have completely sanitized the whole place. The stench disappeared with the removal of the body. The U.S. government is buying the tenants' apartments, all new furniture, all new clothes, with their promise of absolute silence. I think that story will last about a month after they're resettled. The neighbors have been told an exterminator had an accident and poisoned the place. The building will be kept empty until we know what we're dealing with. Then the plan is to tear it down.

"Keeping in mind that this looks medical, possibly contagious, we need to be very careful about how it's handled. You know the hysteria around AIDS at the beginning. CDC and NIH are involved."

"Yes, a long beginning of fifteen or so years, years of hysteria, hate, and victimization. Have you called GMHC and Callan-Lorde?" Victor asked, somewhat annoyed.

She had a mouth full of soda so shook her head. She swallowed. "This case is the first one to indicate that another person was present. This could be a murder. Or a Bloody Mary. Someone infected with whatever it is, not symptomatic, and giving it to our victim or possibly victims. It has become more than a health issue, we think."

"How are you sure the decay took place in such a short time, overnight?" Jason's field of study had elicited the question.

"One of the working neighbors reported running into Mr. Marsayas in the vestibule as he was getting his mail from the box on the Wednesday night around 7:00, 7:30. Marsayas was spiffed up for what could have been a date. The witness said you could smell sandalwood soap, which we found as a bottle of scented shampoo in his bathroom."

Mortana finished her Coke. "That places him leaving home around 7:00 PM, returning sometime later, and being found a bit after 11:00 AM when the super called in the wellness check."

Jason, looking green, asked, "Does this get worse?" His stomach already questionable. Two weeks home and he was still feeling the twenty-four hours of flying.

Mortana reached across the table and patted his hand, almost playfully, "Get a grip. You've handled as bad."

"Not over dinner."

The coffees were served. She looked over the bill before she returned to being a police detective. "His phone and other devices didn't have any apps to hook-up sites. No texts, no emails. We got a warrant out for his phone records. Recents on the cell had been erased. Ditto for Facebook. The team checked through those for possible leads.

"He seemed to be pretty cautious, almost closeted. A bit old-fashioned. Just the way he dressed—dress slacks, penny loafers, button-down shirts. His boss said he wore a white shirt and tie every day to a place where no one else would. He worked there for sixteen years in Brooklyn—oriental carpets, sales and cleaning.

"We've canvased the bars in the Village and Chelsea to see if anyone recognized a picture of Mr. Marsayas. We got a hit. One of the bartenders at Chelsea Generic Bar remembered him being there on the Wednesday night, going directly to meet someone in the back, then getting two vodka and tonics at the bar himself. Probably around 8:15, maybe 8:30."

Both Jason and Victor knew the long-time piano bar, the piano is on a basement level. Victor pointed out that the victim was on the younger side for its patrons, except for maybe rent boys. Most bars discouraged them. Its snide nickname was Chelsea Geriatric.

"Not enough of a description of the other guy to build a sketch on. The bartender wasn't even sure how the guy was dressed. Seems Glenn was a once-a-monther, so familiar and noticeable, but not the other guy. A couple of times our vic left with another man, usually older. The place got crowded that night, what with the lessening of restrictions. The bartender didn't see him leave with or without the possible date. The so-called bouncer didn't either. The piano player didn't see Glenn there at all. Never made it downstairs.

"The recent murder in Bay Ridge took a week to be discovered. Any clues disappeared. That's why Mr. Marsayas is our best lead." A tone of frustration appeared in her voice.

"We plan to get the groups you named, AVP, and some community leaders involved when we have a clearer picture of what we're dealing with. For now, I thought a reporter with his ear to the community could do a little checking to see if anyone got into a situation that made them uncomfortable enough to end a date before disaster hit. A Gay man, fairly well known in the community, asking questions, I hope will be given deeper consideration. Although we work with AVP, perhaps your starting there would open things up when the department asks for help."

"Now, here's the crux of the evening," Victor absorbing the scope of her story.

"Jesus, that kind of creep-out must be one in every ten dates. One in every five hook-ups. And I might point out just as common if not more in the hetero community." Victor caught his annoyance before it turned into full blown anger.

"Please don't be offended," she said. "At this point I'm holding back some troglodytes from broadcasting this. If I could get any lead, we could do a better job of narrowing it down to a perp or perps, be they sick or murderers. The scientists have zero idea of the cause. The city most certainly does not want a new AIDS stigma and hysteria against the LGBTQ community." Pointing her chin toward Jason, she added, "As you know I have personal concerns in this."

"Who were the other two victims? Did you get DNA?" Jason liked data.

"We're reworking the older one. On the new one in Bay Ridge, we've hit a wall. Only Mr. Marsayas's DNA was found whole. The other was degraded." She looked from one man to the other.

"What's in this for me?" Victor asked.

"An exclusive, before anything is given to the general press. Helping your community get free of a new predator." She sheepishly went on, "I probably could get your bar and cab bills covered. Here are my professional and personal cards."

Victor finished his coffee, Jason his Frappuccino. Mortana signaled the waiter. He brought the hand-held credit machine. She put in her expense account card, hit the twenty-percent tip, and signed, murmuring, "I will never get over those things looking like a Star Trek Tricorder."

She asked Victor, "Do you think you can be of any help? I can email you everything we just went over. I'll give you all that I can legally."

"Get me their pictures, and I'll ask around. Today is Friday. Next Wednesday will be the likeliest time to hit that bar. If you get any details on the others, include them. Let me know the day and date they were found. The regulars rarely change their days in those clubby places. Whatever you can share would be great."

She told him, "Next Monday the FBI has organized a fact-sharing conference at the Marriott in midtown. Every city where a case has occurred has been asked to send medical and law-enforcement personnel directly involved in their case or cases. Jason is invited, being an epidemiologist. I pulled strings."

"Can you get *me* invited?" Victor wanted to hear what the straights were thinking to do in his world.

"That would be very tricky. I'm making no promises." She was just being honest. She had an inkling of what Victor was looking for, even though not everyone there would necessarily be heterosexual—or Cis, for that matter.

They slipped out of the booth.

Mortana speed dialed for an Uber. Put on her jacket. Fixed her collar. Carried her hat.

Victor put her cards in his wallet. "Thanks for dinner. Here's my number. I'll get back to you in a week. If I come up with anything before, I'll text you. Try to get me an invite."

She glanced at his card.

2V or Not Too V

Asks the Right Questions

Gay Nation Press   917-220-2269

Victor Virlus   2Vornot@GNP.org

After they left, they paused in front of the restaurant: two Gay men in their mid-thirties, one tall and light, the other somewhat shorter and dark, and a female cop, slightly smaller than the blond—a less-than-usual Chelsea dinner threesome.

"Jason, where' you headed?" Victor's intonation said more than his words.

"First putting my 'older sister' in the Uber, then walking home," Jason said teasingly to them both.

"Very funny," she said. "Here's my car. Remember Dan's birthday dinner next Friday." She sounded like the older sister, reminding the baby brother.

"I'll be there with bells on. Safer for the twins now that they're vax-xed. I haven't seen them except on Zoom." They hugged, kissed each other goodbye, and Mortana slid into the car.

She lowered the window and looked at Victor. "Keep receipts. . . . "Bookkeeping, what a pain in the ass." The car pulled away.

Jason turned to Victor, eyebrow raised. "Walking with me?" Victor took his arm, exhaling the breath he had been holding in.

3

THEN, SICILY

MY UNCLE DEIMOS WAS DANGEROUS. He was my mother's brother. That whole family had mental problems. One minute he was sober, serious, the next raging, emotions phases of the moon, more cunning than intelligent. When I think of him, I see an unkempt, sun-darkened, stunted square of flesh. In truth, he was of average height and size for the island. Today they would label him bi-polar and probably a psychopath. He was a perfect Mafia Don.

When I finished my studies in Bologna, my father sent me to Riposto to live with Deimos. I had embarrassed my father and enraged my mother one summer holiday and got caught by Mama in our Tuscany villa's potting shed with the gardener's son. He was a year older than me. It wasn't love, just sex. I was a defiant seventeen-year-old reveling in my penchant for *cazzo*. This did not go down well. All my vacations and holidays from then on, I was farmed out to our family in other cities or country estates.

I turned twenty the summer of graduation, a carbon copy of my father's youthful portrait. Aristocratic, some would say disdainful, tall at five feet eleven inches, well-built tending to slim, with a fair complexion that darkened quickly in the sun, and dark hair—our Italian breeding more than the French ancestry showing through. French and Italian stubborn combined. I had entered the university at sixteen. Papa refused to have me return to Milan unless I married. I declined. We fought. Milan wasn't big enough for both him and a finocchio son.

He banished me to Sicily. That's how a well-educated scion of one of Europe's wealthiest, if shy, families ended up in a relatively little town, on a crime-ridden island that doesn't particularly care for northerners. Sent to bide my time until I turned twenty-one, when I gained my immediate share of the tontine and a yearly annuity from the ever-expanding family fortune as does every twenty-one-year-old, male or female, did in our family.

Our founder had had six daughters and one son. He'd loved each successive child more than the previous. By number seven, the only boy, he could not see favoring him over the beloved daughters. He had established a trust administered by what would become a Swiss investment and banking conglomerate. Our system of inheritance broke tradition very early on.

In addition, I would receive twenty-five pounds of gold through my grandfather's bequest. I was a grandson. Grandfather was a much more traditional man than our founder. He died when I was seven. With that inheritance, I could never be confined again. I swore to Papa I would leave the boot completely.

My mother was Nyx Tartus, whose family were centuries in Sicily. They claimed to originate from Sparta. Her parents gave all their children the most dreadful Greek gods' and goddesses' names. My grandfather, Moros, was the Don before Deimos. He wasn't as crazy as his children. He was feared, sometimes loved. He kept order in his fiefdom. Deimos wore uncertainty as a virtue.

Deimos took over his father's wine and olive oil exporting business. Through them he managed illegal substances, smuggled from Tunis, sent into Messina to be distributed to the mainland. His *piantagione*, for that was what it was, a plantation, also raised boars for the family meat-curing business. My father's family had interests in Parma, famous for ham and cheese. That's how the two families crossed paths and Papa met my mother.

In Sicily I was set to help with the butchering. Deimos thought this funny, hoping no doubt that the faggot would crumble. I flourished. Like my uncle, you might have thought I would mind cutting animals' throats, but I had no aversion to slaughtering. Over the years, my father's supervision of his enterprises brought me to many *abattoirs*. Once or twice as a child I was allowed to assist in the slaughter. It gave me a taste for blood. I found the ebbing of life from a pig or lamb calming. The smell of metal in the blood and sight of it running into a barrel or drain was fulfilling in an erotic way. I trained in Riposto for my future better than in any education I received at the University of Bologna.

As part of my rehabilitation in Riposto I was forced to be counseled by the local curate. Father Pietro Assisi was a thirty-six-year-old hulk of a man. He stood six two, very large for a Polermian, and was muscular. At first I was recalcitrant. To break my wall, he invited me on sailing excursions to various fishing villages nearby. To escape my Tartus abusers, I'd've ridden a hippopotamus to Naples. Thus, we went in a small sailboat he owned. That was how I learned to sail so well.

On our second trip, he announced we would do lunch on one of the small, isolated islands along the coast instead of in a taverna. He had had a basket packed by the cafe owner in the village we visited. After eating and sharing chianti, he suggested we go swimming. We stripped and swam in the Ionian Sea. We baked in the sun on a blanket we shared. I was impressed by his body. He complimented mine. I had grown muscular but remained svelte working on the plantation.

The following week we skipped the fishing village and went to an island with a cove where his boat would not be seen. He wanted to swim first. Returning to the blanket, he set up the lunch he brought from the rectory. We ate naked. He fed me a fine organic salami that day. We continued our trysts one place or another for the months left to us.

Speaking of confinement. I officially became a father in Milan on my fourth month of exile in Riposto. It seems I had gotten a somewhat lower-class girl pregnant. Her family dumped the almost newborn on our doorstep. In order to minimize the scandal, my parents took it in. A rich son of a fine family having a child out of wedlock, then raising the child, was considered honorable—the woman forever tainted. Milan high society was atwitter.

In truth, it was my sixteen-year-old sister Sylvie's, child. She took after my mother; she was small and thin, and she had full breasts, olive skin, wavy raven hair, blue eyes that begged you to fall into them, and lips like rose petals. Our French uncle, Loup Canne, forty-four, husband of our amazon Aunt Geraldine, impregnated her. Aunt's marriage, forced by Grandpapa, was one like my father proposed for me, except inverted.

Aunt Geraldine was a formidable woman in body and character. When she came of age, she took her fortune, decamped to Trieste, and settled in what can only be called a castle in her forest—a Lesbos in the trees. Only women were allowed inside the walls except for the occasional escorted repair men. Sylvie was sent there for the gestation. She returned to Milan when little Gaspar was six months old, having proceeded him by more than five months. He had not seen his mother since days after his birth. He, like most men in my family, shunned his mother in favor of the nanny. Gaspar adored my older brother, his other uncle, Elio, I was informed through the family grapevine. Sylvie's figure had matured.

Uncle Loup was threatened with death, of course. But he held a lot of cards. He also was well known and liked in Milan's upper crust. He was thrown out of the small business which Ottaviano, our grandfather, had enticed him with to marry his seventeen-year-old sapphist Geraldine. He extorted a nice sum for his not claiming the child as his own. Loup immediately opened a company making fine furniture and leather goods. I understand it is well known here in the New World.

Now I certainly would not return to Milan; even though father notified me that under the circumstances my manhood appeared proven. A bearded marriage would still be necessary. The last thing I wanted was a son *né* nephew.

More of that later. Back to my Mafioso uncle.

One night a little too far into his wine, Deimos began telling a story. My older cousin Vincenzo was there. He was his uncle's double. The blood runs thick in the Tartus line. Deimos had mistresses, not a wife. His sister, my Aunt Circe's, twenty-eight-year-old son was his named heir. She managed Deimos's household. Two of Uncle's flunkies were there finishing a meal with us.

Uncle began bragging about becoming a made man. He described cutting his first kill's throat, grabbing his adversary, not hesitating, using a serrated blade to tear open the esophagus, turning the arteries to fountains.

Realizing who was present, he sent his guards to bed before he continued.

He returned with details. "I'm still strong as a bull. I was seventeen. We knew Messina liked to sit by the water at the end of his early-evening meal, especially after the First Sunday horse races in Riposto. His men didn't usually join him but sat further away, on the hill. There would be no moon that late May night. So I hid in the boat house all day after swimming under water with a breathing tube. When he turned the corner and his men's view of that part of the dock was blocked by the boathouse, I grabbed him. Twisting his head back, stretching his neck, hand over his mouth. It takes strength and speed to hold a man while you slice his throat and keep him from crying out. Especially one who is always on guard.

"I slipped immediately into the water inside the boat house. Swimming into the reeds so they couldn't spot my breathing tube. Quickly out under water to the moored fishing boats about a half mile away. Up and out, into dry clothes. Into the town's tavern for a quick drink. His men didn't start shouting until I had reached there. They had been lulled by the day and the years of peace between the fiefdoms, careless in their attention to their Don."

Demos gulped the last of his wine. "I tell you my heart was near bursting. My father rewarded me with a fine horse. No one suspected me. Franco Messina was a business associate of my father's. They were on excellent terms. But my father, always greedy, thought it time to dissolve that. He folded Franco's men into his own band of soldiers, increasing his control over Riposto to leave to me.

"We set up a minor rival with a fake family grudge as the fall guy. Messina, we rumored had violated the man's daughter. An honor killing.

"Those two—" he gestured toward the closed door through which his minions had exited—"their fathers were Franco's men."

Turning to me, he asked with a smirk, "Nephew, son of Nyx, when will you be a made man?"

While I was thrilled by the thought, I knew I could not be trapped by his knowing I had killed. That would give him too much power over me. His tale reinforced my belief that neither he nor Vincenzo would be averse to cutting this nephew's throat.

"I think I'll stick to pigs and lambs." Ironic as that would prove to be.

"My sister sends me a true finocchio. Pansy."

"Our little faggot butcher," my ape-like cousin chimed in.

Their words roiled me, setting into motion my life's passion. Mulling over Deimos' story, I became sure I could easily match what he had done. I lay in bed thinking how I would kill someone and not start a Mafia war. Anything in the Riposto area would come back to my uncle or the other nephew. I did not want to be killed in the crossfire.

I thought about it for weeks until I felt I could not breathe for the desire. Necessity is the mother of invention.

4

NOW, NEW YORK CITY

L IEUTENANT MORTANA LEMURES HAD JUST finished her general overview of the conference of police, FBI, medical personnel, and some Homeland Security people, covering every location where a body had been found. Four states, Puerto Rico and the District of Columbia were represented.

"I now give you our moderator, New York City Police Commissioner Kimble Martel."

A tall, professorial, very dark man, the first Haitian-American Police Commissioner, moved to the podium. "Thank you, Lieutenant Lemures, for that succinct overview."

He picked up his copy of the material that had been supplied to the attendees. "You've all gotten the medical reports on the now thirty-one cases. Teleconferencing should have brought you up to speed on the details of each case. They should have given you a basic understanding of the science involved. We will dispense with going over them and go right to questions. Referenced photos will be projected on a screen behind us. Please identify yourself and whatever agency and city you are from. Thank you."

The commissioner recognized a woman in the center. An assistant passed her a mike. "Dr. Mae Johnson, forensic psychologist, Albuquerque, New Mexico. This is for Agent Brown. What makes you think these deaths are intentional and not the result of some new infection?"

Brown was the quintessential stereotype of the public's image of an FBI agent—tall, brown-haired, blue-eyed, solid build, square-jawed, and in his early fifties. If he had been dressed in the right color and put on reflective aviators, he could have been a Man in Black.

He was one of the five men and three women associated with the FBI's Serial Crime Unit. They were seated on the raised dais with top brass of the CDC Plague Intervention Unit, an NIH Herpetologist, Commissioner Martel, New York City Police Department Chief Wayne Lex, Lieutenant Lemures as liaison to the FBI, New York City's Chief Medical Examiner Dr. Jade Patel, and Health Commissioner Simon Eskelus.

"Three pieces of physical evidence were found at the crime scene for victim number thirty. Mr. Glenn Marsayas was reportedly a meticulous man in his home and person. We found two drink glasses on his kitchen drainboard, indicating a possible guest. More importantly, his quilt was tucked up over his hands and wrists about the height of his waist. We are sure this was staged. When the quilt was removed the forensic people found a semen stain on the interior at the height of his right thigh and penis. Knowing of his meticulousness, it is highly unlikely he would masturbate and simply throw on his handmade quilt. All indications from the ME are that the quilt ejaculation was without manipulation of any kind, no smearing from the quilt being dragged up over himself. The stream of semen was in a direct line on the inside of the quilt and body. It is noteworthy that we found a towel in the hamper with traces of his semen on it, indicating a previous ejaculation."

"What does that mean?"

"The towel is confusing in that, if he had a partner, there could have been different seminal fluid on it. Since an internal autopsy was impossible, there was no ability to test for semen in either Mr. Marsayas's mouth or anus. He could have had a second ejaculation that night. Your guess is as good as ours at this point as to how that occurred. Someone placed the quilt over him. If you look in your pack at the pictures on page. . .pages fourteen through sixteen, you can see that his hands are under the quilt. The black light pictures of the interior of the quilt, his genitalia, and thigh allow us to see that, if he had moved in any way, the semen would have been smeared. It is a clearly defined line in our photos. No smear, no spray, no black light exposure of semen on his right hand or, for that matter, his left.

"Secondly, there is the circumstantial evidence. If he'd had a drink, there would likely be only one glass on the drain board, as he lived alone. Two glasses, arm–hand positions and semen on the neatly placed quilt interior all indicate a post-mortem staging."

Many more hands arose. "The gentleman in the red bow tie."

"Thank you, Commissioner. How many cases have had eye tissue remain identifiable while other tissue has basically dissolved?"

"Please remember to identify yourselves."

"Oh, sorry, I'm Dr. Jack Coleman, ME, Peoria, Illinois. We had two cases in 2018, none since."

"NIH? CDC? Dr. Tolson, thank you." Commissioner Martel turned to a black man seated on the stage who had raised his hand slightly. He stepped to the podium and adjusted the height of the mike somewhat downward.

"Edgar Tolson, tissue, forensic specialist, CDC. Seven of the eight bodies were found before skin necrosis."

"Is there an explanation?" the ME interjected.

"The consensus is the eyes came under intense pressure—a form of super-glaucoma that built enough pressure to make the eyes explode, hurling the tissue away from the body onto the bedding. It probably happens early on in the—" he paused, looking for a word—"'event,' let's call it. Because nothing except a cocktail of mostly human chemicals, skin and bones, and in Mr. Marsayas's case semen, has been recovered."

A wave of comments crossed the room. Dr. Tolson was patient. "We've only recovered material in those seven because they apparently were found before the dissolution of the victim's skin. That took place within three hours to two days of discovery and skin collapse. In the other twenty-three, the whole area was saturated in the liquid, with bone being the only solid material remains."

"By calculating the timeline in Mr. Marsayas's case and the others' discovery times, complete necrosis occurs between eleven and fifty-seven hours after the subject died. A very wide range.

"We aren't sure why the eight had no eye tissue but believe their constituent parts dissolved like the rest of the internal tissues pre skin collapse." Tolson took his seat.

Commissioner Martel called, "Next," gesturing to a person in the front row.

"Jean Westheimer, Captain, Forensic Division, San Francisco Metropolitan Police. My pronouns are she/they. Do any of the local or national agencies have any idea what the cause of such a near total necropsy in all cases is?"

The "she/they" had caused murmurs. Martel ignored that, going on, "I think, Dr. Evangelica Russel should field this." The tall, thirty-seven-year-old brunette wonder woman authoritatively stepped to the podium.

"Good afternoon, my colleagues. Call me Viper. I'm a venom specialist with the Herpetology Department at the Universidad de Costa Rica, funded by the Mayo Clinic and on loan to the NIH. I hope that is enough ID for now.

"It is felt that whatever the causal agent is, it is so deadly and caustic that a person could not sustain a non-lethal infection. Therefore, we think the Bloody Mary hypothesis is highly unlikely.

"We feel that people are being purposefully exposed. Whatever it is most likely has been genetically engineered or is perhaps a mutation of virulence not seen before. The mechanism of infection is unknown at this juncture. When I say 'exposed,' most probably I mean 'injected,' but that is conjecture on my part."

Martel asked, "Could some kind of solvent have been injected into him?"

"It would have had to be a substantially large quantity that would be measurable in. . .in the liquid remains. Never mind the logistics of bringing a supply into a victim's apartment. The closest possible natural substance that comes near to causing the pathology we see in all the cases is snake venom, especially viper venom. Hence my being involved. My institute is the world's leading research facility in anti-venom therapies and medicinal development using venom toxins. What we think we are seeing is a massive combination of the three most studied snake venom toxins, hydrolase, phospholase A, and collagenase enzymic proteins. These toxins are called 'venins.' They play havoc with the chemistry and tissues of the human body, and the nasty consequences of being bitten by an organism that can produce one or more of these proteins are ugly to say the least.

"A snake in its natural habitat is trying to make a living catching, incapacitating, and in some cases digesting food or defending itself. In fact, the Russell's viper of Pakistan, identified and named after my distant relative, is one of the top five deadliest toxin producers in the world. It has been reported but not confirmed that, under certain circumstances, it produces a venom so noxious to breathe that that alone causes severe muscle and organ damage, especially lung disfunction. That was what almost happened to two of New York's first responders, the super and two tenants, in Mr. Marsayas's apartment building.

"We are working on the theory that one or more of these venins has been engineered into a hyper-virulent version of itself, placed in a virus shell that takes over the adrenal glands, primarily the—sorry, that would be my conjecture—one or more of the adrenal glands, inducing the production of massive replicas of those venins and, with some evidence, the hormones of those glands causing their flooding, consequential exhaustion, and finally collapse of all of the soft tissues systems, leaving only skeletal bone." While measured, her voice sounded like she had presented a dire warning.

A controlled pandemonium took over. "AIDS" was a loudly heard word. "Pandemic" and "Covid" were also.

Captain Westheimer called out over the din, "So you're saying this is snake venom married to a virus."

Dr. Russell held her hands up, gesturing for people to quiet down. "In layman's terms, so to say. That's our best working theory right now. What may be in our favor, and what we hope doesn't change, is that this seems to be a face-to-face exchange of the deadly materials—not infectious but infecting. So direct contact seems necessary. A doorknob or cough would not transmit it. Hemotoxins, blood toxins, would make the most sense as the gateway for the others. They could be introduced by injection, cutting with a knife dipped in the venom. Anything sharp." Less tremulous, Dr. Russel paused.

Another woman came to the mike, indicated to Dr. Russell to step to her right. "I am Dr. Morgana Arthur, as you know, CDC supervisor for all these incidences.

"Sexual contact has been a vector for other viruses,. but the statistics don't support that in these cases. You just heard the ME from Peoria. They had two cases in 2018 and none since. The only other city besides New York that has had any significant repeat cases but with time differentials is D.C. Four cases—two in 2016, two in 2018. All those cases were in people who had no contact with each other that has been found. The outstanding commonalities are that they are all homosexuals, all trolled social media, and all are conservative—some more right than others."

Dr. Arthur warned, "The CDC has been put in charge by the President. That information has not been shared with the LGBTQ community or the public in general. We do not want to start a panic. We saw how violence to our Asian-American communities across the country blossomed when Covid 19 was labeled the 'Chinese virus.' We cannot ignore the discrimination and violence projected at LGBTQ citizens starting in 1982 for over twenty-five years. Both forms of criminality are not gone. We live in very fragile times.

"I have more to say but will return the mike to the Commissioner now for more questions. I will finish before we break for lunch. Commissioner."

Both women turned to their seats as the New York City Commissioner stepped forward. "We have time for one more question. Let's keep it medical for now, since we have all the experts here."

Many hands went up. Martel played the hometown card.

"Jason, you have a question."

"Jason Lemures, Manhattan Kings College, University of Medicine, Epidemiologist. What about the broken spines, necks? How does that play in this snake virus theory?"

"Dr. Reginald Zao, our Nobel Prize bone man, can address that." The audience chuckled, recognizing the winner of the Nobel Prize in Medicine, 2021, for identifying the KL3 factor in osteoporosis, finding the chemical cocktail that is ninety-five percent effective in stopping progression at all stages, with an eighty-five percent restoration of bone mass and viability rate for early stage onset.

"Reggie Zao, New York City Department of Health, liaison with NIH and CDC." More than one attendee was taken by this forty-two-year-old, matinee-idol jock genius. "In twelve cases, the victims' neck vertebrae were broken. In all of those, so were the back vertebrae. In the other nineteen, only the back vertebrae were broken. If you look at the photographs on pages twenty-three and twenty-four in your booklets, you will better understand.

"In normal breaks, a common neck break, the dorsal or ventral bone edge or face will be damaged or cracked; lateral damage can also occur. If a bone fragment pierces the spinal cord, or it is severed, death is assured in minutes if not seconds. The case of the actor Christopher Reeve demonstrates how immediate medical intervention can save a person's life. A medical doctor was present and equipped at the game Reeve fell in. If medical assistance needed to be called for, he would have suffocated because his respiratory system would not have received signals from his brain. With artificial intervention, he lived a productive number of years afterward.

"In thoracic vertebrae damage, death is not as prevalent. Paralysis associated with the nerves below the damage to the spinal cord can occur. In most dislocation fractures—the most common caused by automobile accidents—death does not occur and minimal muscular impact is seen. People do recover.

"In all of our cases involving the neck, the C3 and C4 vertebrae are shattered, falling to pieces. The thoracic damage is the same to the T7 and T8 vertebrae. Total fragmentation. It is my opinion that both would cause near-instant death, precluding any other possible causes. Not having the spinal cord survive makes it a moot point.

"The rest of the skeletal mass looks pot-polished, as is seen when bone is boiled or stripped of viscera by the Dermestid beetles used by museums. Why the bone is not dissolved is not clear. But there is a high percentage of sodium, calcium, potassium, magnesium, and zinc ions found in viper venom and a still higher count found in our victims' liquid remains, which reenforces the hyper-viper venom hypothesis. All of those, except the sodium, are recommended components for healthy bone structure in cancer patients as well as healthy people.

Zao seemed finished, began to turn away, but caught himself and turned back to the mike. "A coincidental finding has been that, of our eight intact bodies at the time of discovery, only the one with the clavicle damage did not have eye tissue found. Is that chance, or does the destruction of C3 and C4 prevent the building of explosive glaucomic pressure in the eyes? Thus we have a clue to why the skeleton doesn't dissolve but none to why those specific vertebrae are shattered. Nor do we have a clue to the mechanism of assault to those specific bones. It would take a lot of force to shatter them so completely, about seven hundred pounds of pressure, and would require a very focused hit to not damage surrounding bone. Here the force must have been higher. The bones were broken into sharp, pebble-sized pieces on all sides."

Zao took his seat.

Lieutenant Lemures reclaimed the mike. "Thank you, Dr. Zao. I would like to assure everyone that all information and findings, medical or evidential, will be immediately shared, posted to our web site. I think Dr. Arthur will be adding to this line of assurance. Dr. Arthur, your closing remarks."

Arthur advanced to the podium. "Thank you. Thank you, Commissioner Martel. Thank you, all of our experts who contributed to the compilation of information distributed here and for continuing to participate over the next few days. A special thanks to our speakers, Agent Brown, Dr. Tolson, Dr. Russel and Dr. Zao.

"Lieutenant Lemures and her staff are our central command. Please see them for any professional concerns. They can filter questions or put you in contact with any one of our experts. The FBI's version of Zoom is our best friend.

"We are having this conference to map out a plan of action. You received all that material in the briefings online and the printed materials hand-delivered to you. We want all of you to compare notes, network, create relationships with a willingness to share, avoiding power politics. We have seen what that too often does to public health policy and policing," a detriment to public safety unfortunately too apparent to Arthur and her compatriots.

"Please do not discuss details outside of these premises. Lavatories, elevators, and halls are for social conversations only," she warned.

Mortana Lemures stepped to the podium., "Have a good lunch. Circulate. We will reconvene at 1:00 PM From 1:00 to 2:00, we will present some insightful and successful police investigations. Then we will move into our first planned meetings. Thank you all for taking this time from your very complex lives.

"Enjoy your meal." Lemures shut off the mike.

5

THEN, SICILY

"WHAT ARE YOU HITTING ME FOR?" I shouted at Vincenzo. Stop it! Have you gone completely nuts?"

"You faggot piece of shit, telling people I'm a drunk." *The truth often hurts* flashed across my own swelling head.

"What are you *talking* about?"

He had me by my shirt collar pulled up, my nose to his, his fist ready to smash my face again, his breath filled with his mother's cooking.

He'd grabbed me as I returned home from my duties in the orchard, waylaying me on the path behind the buildings' compound. I was late, having stopped for a quick tryst with the son of one of the laborers.

"Christo says his cousin in Taormina heard at the tavern that I was confronted by a night watchman going to my boat on the beach two weeks ago. That I was falling down *drunk!*" Vincent snorted like a bull in a Spanish ring.

"That was me. He has the story twisted. *I* was drunk. The guy asked who I was, and I told him Deimos's nephew. He must have thought it was you. Your uncle and you haven't exactly introduced me around."

Lying was so common place in that hell that, mixed with fact, it became completely believable.

"Finocchio, give your name and don't mention us again if you get into trouble. For us, you're on your own." He slammed me to the ground. I lay there while he stalked off.

"Like I didn't know," I spat, low but not low enough.

Infuriated, he returned and kicked me in the stomach. "Keep your mouth shut, pansy." He bovine-slobbered over me.

When I recovered enough to stand, I went into the kitchen for some water to wash my face and hands, and wine to kill the pain.

I was sweating. Not because of the beating as much as because I had made a beginner's mistake—almost gotten caught.

Two weeks before, I had gone in my boat up the coast to Taormina, to hunt. I had loaded the boat with empty feed sacks, ropes, and rocks from a stone beach on the way.

My uncle had stirred an unquenchable desire in me. I had planned for weeks, felt it was foolproof. But I'd miscalculated the arbitrariness of human fate.

After sailing with Father Assisi, I had decided I needed my own boat to carry out my plan. I was not without funds of my own. When I was younger, I squirreled a good deal of cash into a secret account away from my father in case what had happened happened. I had arranged access to that in Taormina, where Pietro and I were on numerous occasions. I had bought a second-hand boat and anchored it with the fishing boats in Riposto, unknown to the two cretins I lived with or the muscle they employed.

Sailing was a convenient way not to be seen traveling at night. I chose only moonless nights for kills. I knew the currents and tides. I could navigate by the stars. Pietro had taught me all those things. He had been a sailor before becoming a priest. Surviving a shipwreck made him a priest, a promise to God, one his mother had wanted him to make when he was a teen. He did not promise to give up boys, however. We laughed about that.

Taormina has a beautiful, calm bay with more than one fishing village. The town itself is a big hike up the side of a cliff to the hills it sits upon. A couple of the fishing villages below have taverns. One could identify the travelers easily, separating them from the locals. In warm months almost none of the student travelers, always low on funds, pay for rooms in the inns. They come to see the Greek and Roman ruins Sicily is famous for, and to eat inexpensive superior food. Many camp out on the beaches. The towns discourage it but tolerate a few.

I sat at a communal table. I chatted up a fellow across from me. He was rather taciturn. He began to excuse himself, being tired. Having decided he was the one, I left a tip on the table and followed him out the door.

Following my prey down to his camp, sure I could overpower him, I was a step behind him. I knew he was headed to Siracusa.

"My boat is on the beach. I'm sailing back down the coast to Riposto. You could save a day's hitchhiking." He stopped, looked at me, and declined, saying he liked seeing the countryside. I said I understood.

When we shook hands goodnight, he headed toward his tent, again a step ahead of me. I lunged and punched him as hard as I could on the side of his head with a set of brass knuckles. He melted in a heap. I dragged him to my boat, gagged him, bound his hands at the wrists, his legs at the knees and feet, his elbows against his chest, and threw the sacks over him.

I went back up the beach to wipe out the drag marks and gathered his things.

As I walked back a second time to make sure there was no evidence left there, a voice in the dark asked, "Who are you? What are you doing here?" It was a night watchman; his badge caught the light when someone opened the tavern door. His lantern threw a weak beam. Even then

I shaded my face so he couldn't really see it.

I replied, "I'm Don Deimos Tartus' nephew." I gestured to the boat. "I'm afraid my cousin Vincenzo has had too much wine in your fine tavern. I am taking him home." He lowered the light from my face.

"Why does such a peaceful town need an officer to patrol the beach?" I asked, all innocence in my questioning. Hearing my uncle's name, his tone had become more respectful. He volunteered that he was checking on the fishing boats. There had been thefts in two villas. The authorities were not happy. So night patrols had started, unbeknownst to me.

"You wouldn't know anything about that, would you?" He aimed his light toward me again.

My hand up to shade my eyes hid my face. "How could I? We only arrived in the afternoon to supply some olive oil to a business associate." I can and do lie quickly and convincingly, survival honed there but developed in Milano.

"You should stay the night. Sailing in the dark is dangerous." He started toward the boat.

Stepping in front of him, I said, "My uncle would be furious with both of us. Never mind Vincenzo's wife. Don Tartus does not like public drunkenness. We should have left earlier, but cousin likes the tavern. . .and the girl behind the bar. I hope we get home before we are missed. I have not had more than one glass. Father Assisi has been my sailing mentor. You must know him. He trained me well."

"Yes, of course, the sailor turned man of God." The watchman's reply was inflected with contempt.

My captured student moaned. "Dear God," I said, let us go. If he throws up in the boat, it will be hours of cleaning." I would muse over the contempt later; at that moment, escape was paramount.

"OK, but I don't want to be fishing you or your cousin out of the brine!" It was more of a warning about the amount of work he would have to do than concern for our well-being.

"We'll be fine. The breeze is good, the air pleasant, the waters calm. I know the stars." I walked back down the beach, shoved off, waved to the watchman, and breathed a sigh of relief.

We were past the southern hills of Taormina when my victim awakened and started to struggle. I sailed seaward. The milky way, a lighted stream across the midnight sky, reflected in the wine dark sea. When I saw no possibility of any further interruption, I lowered the sail.

"You are to have a great honor. You will be my first." My prey looked confused.

I remove his gag. He demands I let him go. "What are you talking about, first?"

"What's your name? I don't remember if you told me in the tavern," I coo amiably.

"Hans." Ah, now I get the accent. Austrian, a slight variation in his German from that in Bohemia, where I have spent a summer with relatives.

I address him in familiar German. "Well, Hans, I fear you have come to the end of your line." He almost flings himself out of the boat, correctly forecasting my intentions .

I study him, wanting to remember every detail. He, meanwhile, is giving every plea and threat possible in broken Italian and guttural German. I half listen. He has brown hair and eyes. He is slight, weighs much less than me. Probably five feet seven inches. Not my type to bed. I prefer hardier fare. But the coming sacrifice has a distinct erotic flavor to it. I even need to adjust myself.

I remove my shirt, not being sure how much splatter there may be. The air warm, silky, sensual against my bare skin, adding to the anticipated climax.

"I will try to be quick but I haven't done this before to a human." He is crying, shouting, praying to the saints, angels, Jesus, his apparently deceased parents, even the Pope, the music of predestination.

Grabbing the rope binding his arms to his chest, knife in hand, I pull him up. I'm startled as he spits at me and drop him back in the hull. His head crashes loudly. Wiping my face and chest with sea water, I splash his face, cleaning his chin, clearing his senses.

"Why do you want to make the inevitable so painful?" With that thought, I realized, I actually enjoyed that idea. "Well, maybe I am too quick."

Sitting back, thinking about what I could do to enhance my pleasure, I contemplate rape. The boat is not big enough for a comfortable, un-cooperative session. What else? I can't cut him and have him bleed in the boat. That I had planned ahead to prevent. Although his bleeding will be the best part of this act before I feel the life run out of him.

Of course.

I haul him to the gunwale and push his head under the water. When enough time has passed, I jerk him out. "How was that?" I ask more for myself than him. He is too shocked to answer. I do it again. "Where in Austria are you from?" I inquire,, not for information but to fill the void of silence while he recovers. "No answer. Well maybe this will loosen your tongue." Grabbing his hair, I plunge his face in again.

"Mercy, in the name of the most Holy Jesus, stop! You don't need to do this!" he whines, gasping for air, expelling water.

"Need, yes and no. Want, most definitely." Grabbing his shoulders, turning him toward the liquid night, another immersion raises my blood higher. I let him rally, recover his breath each time. When he can, he begs for his life.

"Why are you doing this? Please, please, please, *stop!*" he barely gur-gles through his watery breaths. Again his head goes under. I feel pos-sessed by a power thrilling through my very bones.

I realize he will drown if I continue. That would scuttle my whole voyage. I let him rest. Indeed, my arms, also, need recovery for the con-cluding performance of my masterly virtuosity of this play.

When our breathing is more even, breaking the silence I respond,

"To answer you, prolonging this has heightened my pleasure."

To amplify his terror, to drive home my omniscience, I add, "Watching your blood leave you, feeling your life run out will be a profound experience for both of us. I have done it to countless animals in other circumstances. It's time to expand my repertoire." My description intensifies my anticipation of the gratification Uncle Deimos made me so aware I desired.

"I won't give you the satisfaction." He flings himself toward the sea. Bound and bedraggled as he is, the attempt fails. He bounces off the wooden parapet, just a bit too high for his attempt.

"You certainly know how to entertain a fellow." I'm titillated. "Time is flying. I need to be back in Riposto before dawn. So it is now or never."

I again maneuver him to the side of the boat, this time on his back, shoulders well over the gunwale. I straddle his mid-section, leaning over him, my knees against the port side of our bark. The boat tips dangerously close to the water. His resistance is remarkable, considering what he has already been through. His cries escape unpitied. I grab his hair, pull his head back so the crown is below the water line. Exposing the full length of his throat, I ever so slowly cut across, his eyes fixed on the blade. The blood spills out into the water. He still breathes but not easily. I have not cut deep enough for an outright kill. He struggles in despair but I am in control.

His blood is Fra Angelico, beautiful. Driven to lick it, I restrain myself from doing so. Minutes seem to pass. Everything is in slow motion. As I feel him weakening, not wanting him to simply bleed out, our eyes meet for a moment of supernatural union. I administer a deft slice, cutting through the esophagus, through the muscles and blood vessels, into the space between two vertebrae and decapitate him. No easy task. No sound other than his blood spraying momentarily into the ocean drowning out any release from his lungs. The corpse sags. By holding him in place with my knees, the carcass is kept from falling back into the boat.

My strength at its zenith, my planning perfection, enhanced by the modifications. My barnyard training has created a true professional, my imagination that of a true artist.

Enervated, yet energized, elated, wet not just with salt water, he may not have been attractive, but the oozing, then spurting, blood and terminated life were more than sensuous.

Holding the draining head over the side, I wait for the skull to empty of blood, then place it on his chest. I choose a sack, used it for wiping my hands. Dropped the head into it, put some large stones around the gaping mouth, tie the gift for Poseidon with sailors' knots and released it over the side.

The body was more of a task than I anticipated. I conjectured it would be easier cut up for putting in the sacks, but that would have soiled the boat with blood, something I had succeeded in avoiding. I need to figure that out for future hunts. I improvised a way to fill the other sacks with all the remaining stones, placed one on his chest and tied it to his bound wrists. His body wedged between my knees, swiveling at my waist, I lean back to quickly tie the other sack to his ankles. I cut the rope holding his arms to his chest. I raise his stony arms over the side of the boat. Sliding off him to the side, somersaulting his stone tied legs over his chest, raise his buttocks a bit. . .and his torso tumbles into the Ionian Sea. It sinks in a bath of russet bubbles.

I dump his camping gear. Curiosity has me keep his knapsack until I could go through it.

I am enlarged. I feel more alive, more fulfilled, more accomplished, more exulted, than I ever have before. I wash off the bloody knife, my hands, arms, face, neck and chest. Clean up the side of the boat stained by the blood in the water. I put on my shirt, my burden lightened. The night air is cooling. Raising the sail, I hold to shore and skim homeward.

The world is entirely new. I am more than a made man, baptized in blood. Vincenzo, Uncle, beware.

6

NOW, QUEENS, NEW YORK CITY

THE BOY HUGGED HIS UNCLE TIGHTLY. Jason kissed Jeremy's cheek and forehead. He had just done the same for Calyce, the teen's twin sister.

"Fourteen. Two birthdays gone. You're giants, the two of you." The girl was five three, the boy five seven. Both had gotten the best of their parents' genes. Slightly tanned skin from their Filipino father, blue eyes from their mother, dark almost black hair from both, and smiles that were innocent and alluring at the same time. You could see in a very short time both would be beating off suiters.

Shaking Daniel's hand, Jason warmly exclaimed, "Happy birthday! How are you?" Daniel grabbed his brother-in-law and kissed his cheeks. Jason handed him a reusable bag with a present in it. "Add the bag to your daughter's collection. She lectures me about recycling every Zoom call."

"I'm good. Thanks for the present. How was your subway ride? Can I get you something? Drink, beer, white wine? Mortana's making my favorite, rack of lamb. The kids are both vegetarian now, so there will be vegetable moussaka, too." His inundation of questions and offerings was a certainty for every guest.

"Then white wine will do." Jason knew what to expect, so he had a choice ready.

Mortana came through the kitchen door into the hallway, squeezed her brother in a mama bear hug, kissing both his cheeks. Holding his face, she pulled him down to kiss his forehead. "I need to talk to you alone later, before you go anywhere," she whispered almost conspiratorially.

Daniel intervened, not quite scolding, "Let the man get settled in, eat some of your Greek specialties, before chewing his ear off with your secrets."

She put her arm around Daniel's waist, held Jason off at arm's length, happily looking him up and down. "My two most favorite men."

Jeremy chimed in, "What am I, a lamb chop?"

"You, my son, will always be my baby boy." Mortana grabbed him. "Look, Jason, he's as tall as me already. This guy is going to be a tall, dark Apollo."

"No doubt the Greek DNA is master in this house," Daniel fake soured.

"Boy," Daniel said, "take your uncle's coat, then get him a glass of white wine." To both teens, he added, "One of you grab me my drink from the dining tab."

They headed for the kitchen. "The others will be here at seven," Mortana said. "We need family time alone with you."

Jason sat at the table. Daniel began making a huge salad in a bowl Jason had sent from New Zealand the Christmas before, the ingredients laid out on the table. "This bowl is so beautiful."

"Kauri wood is stunning, isn't it?" Jason appraised his brother-in-law. About five nine, Daniel's creamy Asian skin had a hint of Spanish olive, irises almost black, made him good-looking in an unconventional way—the best mixture of Europe and Islander.

His sister and Danny had met in the Marine s. When she brought him home to meet the family, Jason'd had to remind himself of their promise not to poach each other's beaus. She had a B.A. in Nursing when she entered the Corps in 2005. Two years her senior, Dan had gone from a journalism degree to SEAL training in 2004. Both did time in Iraq and got to see each other there often, being stationed on opposite sides of Baghdad. He served ten years, she eight. They had married in 2007, and the kids had come six months later, though nobody except her mother kept count. Grandma and Auntie Eva raised the kids when deployments interfered.

The Lemures parents had split up when Jason went off to college. Dad, Georges, a man they adored, died in a car accident in Greece five years ago.

Mama, Francesca, kept (and kept still) at a distance, moved to Arizona. She had always had social difficulties. Jason and Mortana checked in with her at holidays. She sent presents to the twins but saw them rarely. She heartily disapproved of her daughter's careers and her son's sexual orientation. She was not fond of the "foreign" son-in-law even though Daniel Santos had been born in Hoboken, New Jersey.

The teens grew silent as they came into the kitchen. Calyce put her father's drink on the table. Jeremy poured the white wine, holding the wine glass by the stem while bracing the refrigerator door open with his body.

He delicately placed the glass in front of his uncle. "You know, only a barbarian would hand you a white wine. Body heat destroys the cooled bouquet. One only holds the stem."

Everyone eyed each other as Daniel quickly declared, "My son is studying to be a s. . ." and took a deep breath, all waiting for sommelier, "a snob."

All laughingly groaned; the father and son had set up this joke in one iteration or another many times. The women enjoyed it just as often as it was played.

"I would say quite successfully." Uncle Jason gave his nephew a joking jab on the arm. "God, how I've missed you all." Jason all but glowed.

Calyce leaned against her uncle as she picked up an olive from her father's accompaniments. "Tell us the best thing about New Zealand."

He put his arm around her waist, looking admiringly at her. No longer a little girl, she was wearing typical party dress-up for a teen: a blue blouse and jeans, no socks, sneakers. Her ears bore a set of green stone-and-gold earrings he'd sent from New Zealand. "Come sit down. Fill me in on school, friends, boyfriends, before I go travel guide."

The kids sat. They had the kind of conversation they'd already had on Zoom, but face-to-face felt new. The five of them caught up.

"How about you, little brother? Any new love in your life?"

Looking at his sister, Jason responded, "Victor seems interested in picking up where we left off. I'm not sure I want anything serious until I get back into the full swing of things."

Mortana and Danny exchanged looks. "What?" Jason cocked his head. Danny shyly filled the momentary silence. "We kinda thought Victor was the one. We know it was short before you left, but the two of you seemed to click."

"Besides, unlike previous strays, he was gainfully employed," the mama bear in Mortana growled.

"I know. I went through that savior stage. My therapist said it was divorce displacement. Anyway, I'm not pushing him away. In fact, we have a working date tonight. You, my dear sister, would know about that."

Mortana turned to the three others and asked them to monitor the cooking. "Set the table. Abuela is bringing some Filipino delights for appetizers. Your uncle and I have cop business to talk about. And don't ask. Let's go into Dan's office. Is that okay, Danny?"

He kissed his wife, going back to his food chores, and called after them, "Don't touch my desk or computer, please."

"Promise."

She guided her brother to the second floor. "When we got the house, I chose Astoria so we could be near Abuela and Tia but close to Manhattan on the trains. By the time the kids were ten, we knew it needed renovation. You were gone when it finally got finished two months before the lockdown. We would probably still be in Tia's house with the four of them if we hadn't been done in that January.

Juan and Abuela had tired of the commute from Hoboken. Abuela and the DiLangs bought the two-family house together but even Abuela calls it Tia Eva and Juan's. Eva, like her brother, is a writer. She, mostly for magazines. Juan was a high school math teacher up until now. Abuela had been a nurse but retired two years after the move.

Mr. Pedro Santos had returned to the Philippines years ago and had since passed away. Tia and Daniel were fifteen and eighteen when he left. They forgave him knowing how he longed for his family's farm which they had visited every summer. One of the two visited the Philippine Santos and Abuela's family there every few years. Abuela no longer went but called. She holds tight to both sides.

"We've given the kids the whole top floor. Split it into three rooms. Each has an end with a bath between and sitting area outside the bath. Second floor is ours. Danny needs a quiet space to write, so he has the back room. We really splurged and put in separate bathrooms. Danny manages our lives really well. I keep my police things mostly at the office. I have a file cabinet in here for my stuff. The basement is finished. It serves as a family room. Has a ping pong table, TV, couch, the usual. The kids bring friends down there.

"We even have a housekeeper once a week. Can you believe it? Our mother would be appalled. Dan is getting a lot of work fixing scripts. His second book has had some interest from PBS. Not huge money but recognition. Ask him about it over dinner. He never brags to his family. They will be so proud."

"They are really the American immigrant story. Not like this Italian-Greek duo." Jason took the couch.

Mortana sat in Danny's ergonomic desk chair, spinning to face Jason. "Hey, we've done pretty well. Besides, we are two generations removed from their kind of story."

Turning to business, she went on, "I want to catch you up on the conference. Victor was our undercover agent there."

"A heads-up would have kept me from nearly passing out. What was that about?"

"The conference had more to it than the stated reason." Mortana went on with details. "The organizers needed to have feedback from someone not directly involved in the police work. The people gathered were plainly divided into the scientists and law enforcement. The scientists were easier to monitor. The law knew how to be evasive.

"Brown, the FBI agent who spoke at the conference, had held a meeting with me and Commissioner Martel, cutting out my boss Chief Wayne Lex before the conference. Word was out that the Chief, through one of his lackeys, was going to let out that there was a new homosexual plague that was worse than AIDS and as contagious as Covid.

"The Chief intends to run for mayor next time around and needed an issue that was big, one that could look like his department would get it under control by advocating the closing down of all Gay establishments and forcing a register of all LGBT people in New York City."

He planned to paint the present mayor as in the pocket of the city's minorities, especially his very visible support from the Gay community, and his having a Lesbian sister and a Gay transexual son. It was also suspected that his connections in other departments would not be averse to a little homophobic hustling to take the pressure off them from the Black Lives Matter and Defund the Police movements. Putting everyone back in their proper place, so to speak.

The FBI informed the Chief of the rumor they heard and hoped he would help them make sure no one caused a pogrom. He got the message, but no one can say for how long, with power being too attractive for too many people these days to care about who got hurt in the battle.

It was imperative that Victor do his best to get a lead on the perpetrator. The coordinated units were pursuing other avenues also. Other cities weren't having much luck either.

She clapped her hands together. "There you go. I guess your date tonight is fortuitous. Sorry to lay this on you, little brother, but I need you to be safe. Knowledge is power and we need to get this under control. Now! We plan to have that conference of LGBTQ groups in a few weeks. We would like you to be there and spearhead it. It's better they hear it from someone they respect and mostly know. We would love to be able to announce that we caught the perp or at least had a lead, but the community needs a heads-up as soon as we can organize it."

Jason frowned. "Really, am I the best one? When and where do you want this to happen?"

"Two weeks from today. The same hotel—we can do security checks there. Dr. Arnold will organize it with New York and D.C. experts."

"Sooner. Can it be moved to this week, say Friday? Give me a list of everybody you'll have on the panel. Lambda Legal needs to be called, seeing how this could be a civil rights nightmare. They'll know who needs inclusion. Set up a meeting for me with them—Monday afternoon, if you will. Can you be there? Get me a list of who you want from our side, so they can make suggestions. Also, be open to our people having opinions about who you're bringing. Victor will have something to say about this, I'm sure."

"He is already aware, been helpful already in who would be a wrecking ball on both sides. He didn't get anything yet at any of the bars. I'm afraid you're headed to Bay Ridge tonight."

A voice called from below, "Mama, Uncle Jason, Abuela and Tia's family are here."

Mortana opened the door, called to Calyce, "We're almost done. Be right down."

"Can you get me your panel names and info ASAP?" he asked. "Set up the Monday thing. Call all the organizations you already want there. We need to get this contained." Jason looked worried.

"Brother, you are the number-one priority with those people downstairs. Put on your party face. It's birthday time."

By the time they got to the bottom of the stairs, Mortana looked like she hadn't a care in the world. Jason took more time to shake off what he has been told. Jeremy met them at the bottom of the stairs, an apron over his NYU tee shirt and jeans, socks with Snoopy, no shoes. Around his neck he had a green stone amulet carved into a Maori symbol of authority on a braided cord of human hair. He asked, eyes on his uncle, "What's up?"

His mom, sounding annoyed, said, "No fair—I told you not to ask."

Jason, soothing, slid in, "Your mom asked to borrow a million. I told her I can only lend her seven dollars."

"Well, that's two more than I have," giggled Jeremy.

"Get your poor uncle another white wine, please. Stem held only," Jason ordered, admiring his glib nephew.

"Hello, Mrs. Santos, Eva, Juan—oh, my God, David! You're all grown up," he greeted the five-year-old.

"Jason." Eva kissed his cheek. Juan Di Lang shook his hand. David hugged his legs as Jason bent to hug him back.

"This boy loves everyone," his grandmother observed. "Come give Abuela a kiss! None of that 'Mrs. Santos' stuff."

They piled into the kitchen. "Abuela, I missed you and your wonderful cooking."

"The lumpia are vegetarian now," gesturing toward the twins.

"I'll live. I'm sure they are just as wonderful." He used his fingers to rescue one from the platter. "Crisp and tasty. Adopt me."

She half joked back, "I already have."

"Okay, folks," Mortana called out, shooing them out of the kitchen. "Take Mama's platters inside. I need to get this food out of the kitchen. Go sit at the table."

"Mama, stay, talk." The older, rounder version of Eva rested at the table. "Eva, Calyce, help put things in bowls."

Jeremy arranged drinks, looked toward his mom.

" I'll have white wine."

"Same," Tia said.

"Abuela?"

"Red."

"Calyce, you want iced tea or soda?"

"Iced tea, Jere." He got the men's orders, shuttled back and forth dining room to kitchen and back, and found the juice box cooling on the refrigerator door for David.

In a few minutes the women started bringing steaming, wonderfully fragrant delights to the table. Tia bent to David's ear and said, in a stage whisper, "Next to Abuela, your Tia Mortana makes the best dinners. Well, expect for your mama." The boy eyed the food with obvious relish.

Daniel objected, "Juan has been known to dazzle us."

"True." Eva and Juan kissed even though Juan had a mouth full of wine.

Jason noted, "No one can out-rival me for an appetite. Any man I marry better be a good cook, or we will need to perfect ordering in." Abuela offered a space at the cooking lessons the children had once a month, when everyone went to Tia and Tio's house for Sunday dinner, something introduced after the Marines were no longer deployed.

The family used Spanish honorifics even though English is their primary language, a nod back to the Spanish conquest and Christianization before the American takeover of the Philippines. David at five years old was fluent in the three languages used by the family.

They filled their plates.

Abuela checked that everyone had a bit of everything except for the lamb-less teens. Compliments were given, nuances noted. The family members shared their news. Juan had applied for a position with the Guidance Department in his school. His fluent Spanish would fill a big need. Tia Eva was getting a short story published in a Philippine magazine similar to the now-defunct *Look* used to be here, about being a first-generation American, with photos. David had started kindergarten. Abuela helped at the local food bank.

Jason asked Daniel about the PBS offer. Daniel filled them in. Abuela chastised him for not saying something before. Eva added, "He was always like that. Never toots his own horn. I sometimes wonder where he came from."

Calyce teased, "The stork brought him. Forgot the big ego the rest of us got."

Juan asked Mortana, "What can't you tell us about?"

"Oh, I can tell you that the mayor is not laying the vaccination checks on the Department. He is going to have other agencies do that. Like how they grade restaurants." This deftly moved the conversation away from her.

Jason answered their questions about New Zealand and his return to work.

Dinner done, they retired to the living room. The teens volunteered to do clean up. David was asked to help. Daniel, in mock shock, asked, "Who died?"

The teens in practiced unison, "Don't get used to it."

"It's part of your birthday present," Calyce added, pecking her father's forehead.

After much rattling they reappeared with a candle-lit birthday cake.

Not forty-two candles but two wax numbers. Everyone sang "Happy Birthday" around the reset dining table. Jeremy insisted Danny make a wish. "Jeez, you're old," his snarky son declared. His dad poked him, tickling him, until he bent over, wiggling.

Coffee and cake done, presents ooh-ed and aah-ed over, Jason excused himself to go meet Victor, kissed and hugged each one in turn. He called Victor to say he was leaving. "Okay, meet me at the Fourteenth Street R station." He listened for a few seconds, "I forgot—she's paying. Well, the Department is. We'll take an Uber."

"OK, I should be at your place by nine forty-five."

Danny and Mortana escorted him to the door. They both kissed him as they hugged goodbye. "Thank you for the job you're doing with those two. They are a delight. I love you guys and my adopted family, too." He pointed his chin toward the living room, and was then out the door and down the street with no more delay. Mortana leaned out, waving and watching until he rounded the corner, hoping he and Victor would find the perp. . .and each other.

7

THEN, SICILY

NICE DRAWINGS: HANS VON PITTASCH HAD recorded his travels in Sicily in sketches, none signed; I decided to keep them. His diary, however, I would have to destroy after reading it. He was quite a ladies' man, unless he was writing fiction.

The knapsack was sunk with his clothes and trinkets in the water off Riposto days after my return. I was not a thief and cared nothing about his paltry funds. All of his banking information sank with the backpack. There was a coin from Charlemagne, or as the Austrians called him, Carl die Grosse, which is historically important although there are hundreds, if not thousands, that float around Europe. Safe to keep—that is, on display in a glass case in my safe house in Bern.

I debriefed myself over the next week as I lay in bed recounting in my mind the handling of the departure of Herr von Pittasch. The plan was perfect in concept. For the most part I had anticipated the sequence of events very well. The major danger was the watchman hired by the town for the fishing boats. That was a twist I had not expected. My skilled deceit prevented an unplanned murder. In the future I would need to be armed with more than a set of brass knuckles and a blade.

Next time, I would also need to balance the boat better. Before hunting, after landing, I would load the stones to one side of the boat so that lying on prey on the other would not bring the gunwale so close to the water when I mounted them.

The terror of the water torture was brilliant. It made the play so much fuller. The extended eroticism edged me to a near- mystical climax, one only repeated in the new scientific method I'd used. Hans, I will always be grateful to you for that. I would refer to any extended torture I improvised as a "von Pittasch" from now on. This one exhausted him so that when I made the first cut his thrashing about was minimal, which probably prevented blood from getting inside the boat. The little that got on me, other than on my hands and arms, was manageable.

The sight of his blood on my limbs created a desire to smear it over my body, like a fine body creme. I was a bit disturbed by the desire to lick it. Blood-borne diseases were a concern. My life was too precious to chance that. The thought of cutting up a carcass was intriguing but not viable for a boat the size I had or the time frame I worked in.

My improvisations assured me that any future unforeseen occurences would be handled with aplomb. All in all, a brilliant first success of quite a few to come.

Those nights of intellectual and physical reflection were relieved by readings from my Viennese companion's journal. Actually, I don't know if Hans came from Vienna, only that the identification I gave to Neptune was issued there. It was the town he noted as the place his pilgrimage commenced from.

In a few of the entries he mentions messages to and from his parents, so I had misconstrued his entreaties to them during his von Pittasching. They were quite alive. I wondered how long it would take them to seek his whereabouts. He had made a virtual pilgrimage to all the saintly places across the Alps into Italy and down the boot, crossing the Apennines to Sicily. He kept count of the days he traveled, noting the date he made a stop, each day spent there, and his total on the road. So Udine was recorded as May 15, Udine Day 1/18.

> *Day 4/21: My companions from Udine would leave me in Venice shortly after we arrive, so we planned a meal on the canal north of the Ponte Vecchio where they knew a cook of superior skill.*

> *Day 4/28 (Venice): Last night we feasted on a dish new to me of pasta shaped like seashells covered in a boar's meat sauce that was superior to any had in Austria. The vegetable, eggplant, was slightly charred and covered in their best parmesan and olive oil which made it creamy without a touch of liquid dairy. We had a moderately priced red that held its own with the strongly flavored sauce. I could have eaten double. My companions went on their way to Rome this morning. I will be in Venice for two more days at least. Fredo introduced me to a former mistress, Angela, who agreed to give me a bed for a bit of money. I think if I play my cards right, I will be sharing hers tonight. She is not so old, probably twenty-nine, that I would need to close my eyes to do the deed.*

I would say Hans was nineteen or twenty at most.

> *Day 6/30: I was at the ferry dock to Merino when a group of refugees, driven out of Anatolia by the Turks, were brought in to be processed. They looked miserable and the Venetian authorities were not happy to have these indigents land as they were rejected from shore to shore. The unscrupulous middlemen were practically bidding on them like slaves for lowest wage ateliers.*

> *Day 2/38 (Bologna): Three days of travel, too tired to write last night. When we bid each other goodbye after I stayed three more days than planned. Kissing me on my cheeks Angela said, 'Gigolo, my ragazzo,*

when you return bring me something nice from Siracusa.' She was a realist
without sentiment which made our goodbyes free of the drama I had with
Gretel. I made many bad sketches in St. Marks and on the canals but
three really good ones that I have kept separate. I'll use the back of the
bad ones for better in time.

And so it went. The last entry was Taormina Day 2/69. As I said, Hans seemed to be a ladies' man. I noted five women in June alone, many like Angela putting him up and into their beds. He must have had a good line. His short descriptions of the food he ingested say he was a budding gourmet with a potential for being a gourmand.

After committing to memory the parts that interested me, I burned the book in the trash pile we had in the orchard for reducing olive tree trimmings.

Our days proceeded like the day before. My times with Father Assisi kept me satisfied mostly. If the opportunity arose, a side encounter was none of his business. We became more discrete, taking separate boats to rendezvous. I no longer visited the rectory but occasionally attended mass with Vincenzo's wife, Lucia, and Deimos's sister, my Aunt Circe.

I went to Taormina at least once a week. I killed another four times during my last few months in Sicily, all planned essentially the same way. One a female runaway, two more students, and one a foreign sailor cast ashore for causing problems on his ship. None known to the town. Another was business, so I don't count it.

One night as I washed up for dinner, I heard Lucia screaming in the house she, Vincenzo, and their baby Nyxos occupied in the plantation compound. Normally she would be in Deimos's kitchen, but he was away to Palermo on Mafia business. Some disgruntlement between two Dons needed refereeing to prevent a bloodbath. Circe was making a meal just for the two of us. Vincenzo and Lucia rarely ate alone.

Grabbing the door frame in both hands, I stopped my rush into the house. Vincenzo was assaulting his wife on the table. Raping was more accurate. Circe pushed past me and started beating her son about the head. He pushed her to the floor. She got up, picked up a wooden kitchen chair and bashed it on his back. "You fucking animal. I didn't birth you to do this to any woman." The cursing on both sides was epic.

Needless to say, he had withdrawn and was now facing his mother with clenched fists. Four foot eleven inch Circe held the chair in battle form, not broken apart but no longer useful to sit upon. He spotted me in the doorway. I confess I was smirking. He came rushing toward me. His mother deftly held out her foot and tripped him. As he lay prone on the floor, she and Lucia fell on him, kicking and punching. After a long time, I could see they were tiring so it was safe to lift them off.

Vincenzo was bloodied and chastened. The women looked at me. Still incensed, Circe looked at Lucia for approval. That was willingly given. "Take that son of a pig and put him in the barn. Lock him in," they ordered me, Circe spitting, "Deimos will deal with you."

I dragged and helped my rag doll cousin up and out of the house. I have to say his falling down a few times on our way to his new residence was preventable. I got him onto a pile of loose hay, took a bucket of water to him, resisted drenching him and washed him up a bit, gave him a drink of water and urged him to stay put. I told him I would lock him in as much to protect him as to do the women's bidding.

"What were you thinking, man?" I asked, feigning an interest that I did not have.

"She hasn't put out in a month."

"I hope Tartus sympathizes with you. You know, he listens to his sister like the Holy Mother."

"Thanks." He begrudgingly acknowledged the trouble he had brought on his head. Deimos will cut your eyes out without a blink, but if Circe says word one, he is a lap dog.

"Here's a fresh bucket of water. Clean up. Sleep in here. I'll try to head off Deimos before they get to him when he returns tomorrow. If not, I'll do my best to assuage him. The two harpies might cool off by tomorrow." Fat chance, I was thinking.

In truth, I couldn't care less what Deimos or Circe did. I liked Lucia, who was the only sane one in the whole enterprise. Physically she was quite like my sister Sylvie, only eight years older, taller and darker skinned. But if I could get Vincenzo to back off his constant bullying and begin to trust me, I'd have made an investment in the future—one ruinous to him and ultimately to Deimos. If I failed, Vincenzo would get beaten to a bloody pulp. Either was a win-win as far as I was concerned.

8

NOW, NEW YORK CITY

THE NUMBER COULD BE AS HIGH AS TWO THOUSAND," Agent Brown answered. "We publish a much lower number, but some independent researchers say that would be conservative—and it could be more than double, triple that number if we include Canada and Mexico."

Mortana was almost sorry she'd asked. She had no idea there could be so many serial killers working in the United States and most of North America. She shuddered to think of the number in the world.

"The really scary part is that many of them are pillars of the community. The majority are loners. Most are never suspect. You hear it all the time: 'He was such a nice person. Quiet. Kept to himself,' or 'He was my son's scout leader, church elder. . . .' You never know.

"Some disappear for years, then start killing again. Others just stop. Some begin with animals when they're kids. Others begin for no explainable reason other than opportunity. Some crave publicity. Others have a thing about outsmarting, taunting the police. Some have political or social grievances. Thrills, attention seeking, sexual pleasure, control, dominance, even brain damage, are factors. There are occasionally women, but not nearly as many as men. The vast majority are white men in their thirties through fifties. Usually they get caught because they get overconfident or careless. At least forty percent are never caught."

"It sounds like we're looking for a needle in a haystack the size of New York City," Mortana speculated.

Agent Brown put down his fork and smiled at her. "That's why we're setting a trap. If this doesn't work, we're back to square one. And don't get upset, but there are at least three others identified working in New York City right now that we know of besides our Bio-Killer—a female sex-worker murderer, a guy who stages his victims and another homophobe. Which means there are at least four, possibly up to ten.

"The prostitute murderer works Staten Island, Bay Ridge, and Dyker Heights. The NYPD has a line on him. They think they have it narrowed down to two suspects. We call that type 'a guy with a mission.' His hatred of women shows up as cleaning up society's transgressive types. They're obviously easy to prey on. Usually the perp is made to feel inadequate by a mother, girlfriend, wife. You get the picture. The other homophobe is preying on men on the down low, which probably is who he is, too. Any number of psychological reasons for his motive," Brown continued.

Despite her background, Mortana was stunned. "I know I asked for a short course in profiling but this is really a lot." She had stopped eating.

Brown looked at her in a big brother kind of way. "I'll stop."

"No, no. I just need to toughen up. I did two tours in Iraq. I've let myself get too involved because of my brother."

Brown raised a questioning eyebrow.

"I thought you knew. Jason's Gay. He's my only sibling. We're extremely close."

"I didn't register that as causing you a problem. You're going to need your objective toughness. If the Bio-Killer strikes again, you'll be first command on the scene with me." He reminded her that emotional involvement can cloud the minds of even the best trained officers.

"Up until the last killing," she told him, "I had no concerns. Jason was away, out of the country, out of danger. Now that we are talking about it, I can see where I haven't been acting like a professional. Emotionally, I mean. . . . That is over. Correction noted." She wanted his respect, and getting it would not be enhanced by emotions gone amok.

"This steak is excellent," he said. "How's your dinner?"

"I'm full. The appetizers filled me up. I can't eat any more."

"Well, if you're not going to eat those, can I?"

Mortana nodded. "Feel free."

He had no problem appropriating her French fries. As he picked at them, he went on, "I come from a big family. Nothing went to waste at the dinner table. Money was tight. My granddad raised me and my three siblings. He was a machinist most of his life, worked for a company that made printing presses for the *New York Times.* 'Line-o-type machines,' the guys called them. They used hot lead to make the copy rollers. All that went away when computers came in. He continued with another division as middle management until '96.

"In fact, I grew up in Ridgewood, Queens. He worked in Brooklyn, at the foot of Atlantic Avenue. Died in 2000. I was just starting at the Bureau then after a stint in the NYPD. I moved to Virginia when I got my position in the Bureau."

Brown was unusually talkative about the past. Nothing about the present. Nothing about why his granddad raised him. No mention of a wife, kids.

Up until then he was all business, decidedly stand-offish. Talking this way put him in the category of human, not just agent. But there were large gaps and questions Mortana would normally have asked a dinner partner. She wasn't sure if she should probe. He was tough to read. She figured it was best not to.

He knew she had a husband and twin kids. When she became liaison, the Bureau had done a complete check on the Lemures and Santos lines. Despite her *mea culpa*, he had no concerns about her abilities. Her record had been outstanding in both the Department and the military.

She decided to talk a bit about herself. Her father, Georges Maximillian Lemures, was a military man. Twenty-five years in the Marines. Staff sergeant in the motor pool, then ambulance corps in Viet Nam. Ambulance corps meant helicopters. Loved his kids, who adored him. Didn't care that his son was Gay, unlike their mother, the religious—she almost said "nut," but caught herself—"devout Catholic," she said instead. They divorced when her brother left for college. She filled in her life in the corps. "Dad died a few years back in a car accident. I'm happy the kids got to know him for as long as they did. Jason looks a lot like him—both blond, both tall. Jeremy got my black hair, but when I look at his face, I see my dad. Our daughter Calyce takes after Danny's side."

Brown (or "Agent Brown" when appropriate) is how he asked to be addresses, never by his first name. He finished her fries. "Sorry about your dad."

"Thanks," she replied, leaving that hurt where it sat.

"I need a coffee. Want anything?" He gestured for the young woman who was their server to come over.

"Black coffee. Mortana?"

"Yes, make it two. Milk, please."

Handing them the dessert menu, the server said, "Our pies and cakes are made on the premises. I'm partial to the Key lime, but everything's good. Le me know if you want anything. I'll be right back with the coffees."

Mortana shook her head. "Not for me."

Agent Brown read the menu, "Looks great, but I shouldn't have had the rest of your fries. No for me, too. Anyway," he said when the server had left, back to the profiles, if you want."

"Definitely. Staged how?"

"The NYPD and the Hoboken Police have reported four cases. Three in Jersey, one in Manhattan, in Chelsea. Two men, two women. The murderer slit the throats. Their hands, feet, knees and arms were duct-taped. Not quite mummies. They were naked. One woman must have been stripped before he bound her. The others, their clothes were cut off them after he bound them. Shreds caught under the tape.

"They were propped up in their own bathtubs. Head toward the drain, feet elevated against the back of the tub up onto the wall. They bled out into the tub. Pretty much all identical."

"Were their mouths taped?" Mortana asked, trying to piece together the killer's selection process. "Were there any similarities in the victims? Race, coloring, size? Associations like work or social? Social media?"

"No, and the mouths showed no sign of being taped. No neighbors heard anything either."

"Were they drugged? What does the autopsy show?"

"No drugs, according to the tox report. Exsanguination cause of death in all four.

"Three were met in different bars. Two bars in the Thirties, west side near the PATH train. The other, a bar in Hoboken. One at a coffee shop, the big one on Fourteenth/Fifteenth Streets and Ninth Avenue. Three on a Friday after work. One on a Saturday. Those were the last places any of them were seen.

"They were all office workers for different companies in Manhattan. None knew each other that we can find. The largest weighed 180, the smallest, a Gay white man, 125, thirty-three years old. Three whites, one Asian, Chinese-American woman, forty; she was the Chelsea victim. The other two were the naked woman, twenty-nine, and our thirty-five-year-old, 180-pound weightlifter. I'd need to look at the notes for the other stats. Our murderer must be strong.

"The weightlifter was an avid baseball fan who told his brother the

killer thought their mutual love of the Yankees called for a drink together. He was the Saturday victim, met in the Jersey bar. The brother
thought our perp must have special persuasive powers—his brother almost never had friends.

"The perp must have worked quickly once inside the apartments.
He must have known the two women had roommates. The baseball guy
lived with a girl who was just a roommate. She didn't like him, but he
paid his half of the bills on time. The roommates were all out on dates
when the killings took place. How he convinced the baseball guy to take
him to his apartment is a mystery—possibly to show a collection of
memorabilia. Had a collection of baseball cards worth in the ten-thou-
sand-dollar range. Not stolen.

"The two women had texted to find out when their roommates were
going to come home. They said they needed privacy; one used a winking
emoji. The roommates found the bodies when they got home. The Gay
guy was found by his cleaning lady the Monday after his murder."

The waitress brought the coffees, milk, and sweeteners on a tray.
"Well, did I tempt you?" She smiled professionally.

Mortana looked up. "It all sounds good, but not tonight. We'll have
the check in a while," she added, implying that they weren't ready to
leave.

Brown picked up his thread of thought. "The bartenders and a bar-
ista remembered the victims. They gave different descriptions of the
perpetrator. The MO is too exact, though, for the perp to be a different
person, unless we have a group of people working together. Disguise is
more likely.

"None of the victims was overly social. Their friends, more like ac-
quaintances from work, and roommates referred to the women as opin-
ionated, strong personalities, rubbed people the wrong way. The baseball
guy was a loner, closest to his family; the others not so. The Gay guy
was active in the Log Cabin Republicans.

"The FBI is involved in this case because the killer has crossed state lines."

"What about surveillance tapes?" Mortana asked.

"They're useless. First, they are so grainy I almost couldn't identify myself. Secondly—and this is really odd—the PATH train station cameras didn't catch any of the victims with anyone. The Gay guy and Hoboken woman were talking on their cells while they stood waiting for the train. Yet the phone records didn't register the calls. We caught the Asian woman on a bank camera; she was alone, also on her phone. No record there either. All of them seem to be using Bluetooth earpieces, but only the Gay victim had them in his home when we searched. Very strange."

"I wonder what that's about?" Mortana went on to note how the internet played into both the Bio-Killer and the bathtub killer's MO. "Any commonality there?"

"Some. The victims were fans of the last president's twitter feeds, two of them on the same Facebook pages."

"That's really close to the Bio-Killer's selection process. What do you think? One and the same?" Mortana speculated.

"Could be. Probably not. Never say never." Agent Brown sipped at his coffee, which was by then barely warm.

"Only one was Gay in this case. And of course, the startling difference in MOs and the resulting corpses. There have been a string of murders of liberals in the Atlanta and Dallas areas we think are serial. Miami, Tampa, and Kansas City, too. Jesus, a lot of cities are looking into possibilities on both sides. Especially the ones with bio-killings. The two sides may have a mutual feeding frenzy going on. All of them are mixed up in different ways on social media. Our conference has made a big difference in the quick sharing of commonalities," Brown concluded.

He called the waitress over and handed her a credit card. "FBI business dinner," he told Mortana, who had started to take out her wallet as they got ready to return to Police Plaza to prep for the LGBTQ conference the next day.

"I need to monitor my kids better," she mumbled to no one in particular.

9

NOW, NEW YORK CITY

"COME ON, OLD MAN. LET'S GET YOU TO BED." Victor pushed Jason playfully out the elevator door. Jason leaned on the wall next to his apartment door and handed the keys to him.

"Watch the old-man stuff. It's been a long day. How long did I sleep in the car?"

"About a half hour." Victor locked the two door locks behind them.

"Work, party, detective bar-hopping. Way too much for a thirty-seven-year-old intellectual."

"That's your new title, Intellectual?"

"That's what the Maori nicknamed me. It's a bit embarrassing. I can see I'll regret letting *that* cat out of the bag." Jason yawned, flung his arms over Victor's shoulders and gave him a peck on the lips.

"I hope you're staying. No hanky-panky. Just sleep. I need a shower."

Victor called to him from the kitchen. "Water or seltzer? You need to hydrate."

"Seltzer, please." Jason had taken his clothes off and called from the bathroom as he regulated the shower temperature. Victor came in with two glasses with a lemon wedge in each. "Put it on the night table, please."

"Yes, Mr. Intellectual, master of his domain."

"Give me a break," Jason laughed as he closed the shower door.

Two minutes later, Victor opened the sliding glass door and stepped into the shower. Jason, glad for having replaced the tub with this large walk-in shower, hugged him. "No hanky-panky. Save it for the morning."

"Let me massage your back." Victor craved the touch of Jason's flesh.

"Whatever your ploy, this boy is too tired to get it up. Let's finish washing and cuddle in bed."

"You are such a tease." Frowning, Victor had hoped to encourage more intimacy with his massage.

In bed they drank their lemon seltzer and discussed the night's bar crawl. Two bartenders didn't recognize the photos they showed them. The third remembered the one victim as a local. "Didn't come in often. But I haven't seen him since I got back from Key West. Have you ever been there? Fun town."

Victor said, "No, haven't been there. Unfortunately, the guy you recognize, he's deceased."

"Gee, he couldn't have been more than forty-five. What happened?" The barkeep was more curious than concerned.

"The cops think he may have been murdered." Victor laid out his information.

"That's terrible. How?"

"They aren't saying, but since I'm with the *Gay Nation Press*, they tipped me off. Figure I could do some checking, make a column out of it. Didn't they speak to you?"

"I was on vacation all last month. The day guy, Bill, handled my shift. We had a sub for days, now permanent. Bill left for Oregon last week after I got back. Family stuff."

It'd been their second Bay Ridge bar that night. Cheers To All was a dance bar with a mix of men, women, and gender-fluid types. Victor handed Gary his card, holding his hand out to shake the bartender's. "Victor or V2."

"Gary." The bartender grasped Victor's hand a few seconds too long.

"Gary, this is my date, Jason." They shook. "Do you ever remember seeing John Gerrard with a date or meet someone here?"

"That's his name? He never introduced himself. Drank gin and tonic. Once or twice I saw him chatting with a few fellows. Saw him leave with a couple. Older men in their sixties. I think one was Hank. If you hang around, Hank is a Friday night regular. He usually comes in around 11:30. He might be more helpful."

"We'll do that. Anything will help."

Jason was fading by 11:00. They sipped the alcohol they ordered. At 11:45, the bartender, talking with a guy of sixty or so, gestured toward the couple hanging out at the ledge near the window.

"Hank?" Victor asked as the man approached. He went to shake hands.

"Sorry, I don't shake. Covid, you know. Vaccinated but careful at my age."

"I surely understand. I've gotten a bit lax lately."

"What can I do for you? Gary said I might be able to help you. Who are you? What's this about?"

After Victor filled him in and asked what he knew about Gerrard, Hank said, "Yes, he came home with me last spring. We had a decent time. I didn't realize how right wing he was until we talked later. I wasn't interested after that."

"Did you ever see him meet anyone here about two, three weeks ago?"

"I did see him with a guy around forty. A few years younger than him. Unusual in that he seemed to like us older daddies."

"Can you describe this guy?"

"Not much, other than he was real good looking. Near six feet or so. Fair completion. Dark hair. Dark eyes. No facial hair. Casual slacks and tee shirt that said San Francisco on it. Built in a natural way, not a weightlifter body. Is that enough detail?"

Jackpot! Victor almost saw slot machine lights go off. "Hank, you are a gem."

"Who couldn't remember him? Guy was way out of John's league. Way out of Brooklyn's types. Stood out like a toned rent boy. . .well, rent man. Definitely not from around here, and I never saw him again."

"Did Mr. Gerrard leave with him?"

"He might have. I don't remember. I got caught up in a conversation with Ben, another bartender who was telling me about his father having heart surgery. I had the same procedure, so I tried to help him be better informed and less frazzled by it."

"Do you mean Bill?"

"Yeah, Bill. Well, I got the 'B' right." Hank sighed; his memory had gotten loose—age and isolation could do that, he was thinking.

Victor asked, "Do you know who else might have seen him?"

"Sorry, my memory is not usually accurate when I've been drinking. John with that hunk was so unusual that who could forget him?"

"You've been a big help. Let me describe him back to you, so you can see if you left anything out." Victor repeated his description.

". . .I didn't mention his hair. Longish, like a Renaissance painting. You know the one of the young aristocrat in the Morgan library? Full, cut really well. Framed his face nicely. Dark, could have been brown, maybe black. The lights were lower, and I'd had more to drink than I have tonight. 'Aristocrat' is a good word. He projected that feeling. That just jumped right out of my mouth," Hank observed.

"Hank, I think the police will want to talk to you. Can I give you our contact's telephone number? She is Lieutenant Lemures, Mortana Lemures. She'd be very interested in hearing what you remember."

"I don't want to get involved." Men his age shunned the police. Too many still saw faggots, not men.

"Well, she's Jason's sister. My boyfriend here will vouch that she is more than Gay-friendly. She wants this guy off the streets if he's the perp. She has a personal stake in this." Victor put his arm around Jason.

Jason chimed in, "Hank, I'm not with the police and not a reporter. I do know that they think this guy has done more than one murder in our backyard. Please call Mortana."

Victor, taking out a card, wrote Mortana's number on the back, handed it to him. "If you have any hesitation or questions call me. V2. It would really help if she could get in touch with you."

Hank looked at the two earnest, relatively young men. "OK. Give me a pen and one of your cards." He wrote his name and number on it.

"You too are too cute for your own good." They'd both giggled. Not the most mature thing two thirty-somethings could do. And the conversation had ended on that note.

"I'll call Mortana first—well, *second* thing in the morning." Victor yawned.

"You called me your boyfriend. Are we at that stage?" Jason sounded serious.

Victor treaded lightly. In his head, it was all *yes, yes!* but out loud, he said, "That would be nice. We had a good thing going until you left. I know you were honest right from the beginning that you would be away for a long time." Victor stopped, the air thick with concern.

"I'm not saying I haven't thought of us that way," Jason said. "I just got back and haven't settled into a routine. I don't want to start something serious and the two of us getting hurt if we've been too quick. You know we aren't Lesbians." He has fallen back on that cliché to lighten the atmosphere.

"You'll *wish* I was a Lesbian when our car breaks down." Victor smiled.

Jason frowned, reached over him and pulled back the covers, "Out," he commanded. "Out! Nobody tells me I need to own a car."

Victor's look blossomed from shock to amusement. He grabbed Jason to him, kissing deeply. Jason eased out of the kiss.

"Buddy, turn off the light. I said hanky-panky in the morning."

Victor leaned over and turned out the bedstand light. Jason did the same, turned to him, and kissed him again. He rolled Victor onto his side with his back toward him, putting his arm across his chest.

"Cuddle time. Good night, baby." Victor held the "baby" his Intellectual Old Man had just given him.

10

THEN, SICILY

I WAS THINKING YOU WEREN'T COMING," I said, my tone peevishly annoyed.

"I have wonderful news! I have been appointed chief priest for the district. I will be raised to Monseigneur. A step closer to Bishop!" Pietro practically shouted.

I had been on our secret island for almost an hour.

The last two days had been nerve-wracking. When Deimos got home, Circe had flown at him like a fly to shit. She'd spat out her rage over Vincenzo. I still had the key to the barn, so he needed to deal with me.

Quietly, I spoke to him outside of anyone's hearing. "Uncle, what my aunt has told you is all true. Can I ask your indulgence and tell you what Vincenzo told me?"

"Finocchio, give me the key." Deimos was loud but seemed reluctant.

"Uncle, a moment of your time to act as a mediator, the way you have just done."

"You have nothing to do with the judgements I create." His self-esteem would never tolerate my comparing myself to him. My nature could barely tolerate his inferiority to me.

"Absolutely true. But everyone involved is a person you love. I am simply the advocate for my cousin. I can give you the key, but he has need for your ear before you dispense your rightful justice." I almost got sick from laying it on so thick. "Let's walk down to the water. I'll be quick. You'll decide your sentence in the time it takes to walk there and back."

I was surprised that he agreed.

We headed down the water trail to our dock. I had finally begun securing my boat there, as I used it to transport slaughtered boars to Taormina's butcher. Convenient for other trips also.

"Well?" he snorted.

"Vincenzo has been thoroughly chastised."

"That is for me to decide," Uncle snapped.

"Of course. I only wish to report what I saw and have been asked to tell. The ladies beat him badly. Aunt Circe hit him with one of his own chairs. Believe me, that delicate lady was a lioness last evening. The two of them punched and kicked Vincenzo so hard I thought for sure he would have broken bones. I could hardly pull them off when I feared I heard his ribs break."

"Well deserved. No man in my household can rape a woman under my protection." Especially when Circe had witnessed it.

"Justly true. However, Vincenzo told me that Lucia has not performed her wifely duties for over a month. He thought she was flirting. Things got out of control. He couldn't stop himself for want of her, his wife."

I paused for that to settle in, having emphasized the word "wife."

"He begs your forgiveness. He begs Aunt's forgiveness. He begs you to help him seek Lucia's forgiveness. He knows his mother would eventually forgive him if Lucia and you take up his cause." I was nauseated by acting like such a sycophant.

"Circe demands punishment. She rules the hearth in our household. She has every right to demand it. As does Lucia." Uncle was obviously pondering how to get out of this situation without making everyone angry with him—and without having to beat his heir.

I chanced a suggestion I had plotted all night, hoping for the opportunity. He and Vincenzo were little more than dumb peasants. With honied words I hoped to manipulate him under those difficult circumstances. "Perhaps a time of banishment? Everyone can cool off. He can do penance elsewhere. Buy fine things to send to Lucia. Give her money to redecorate their house. You know how women love that. Especially to get rid of the table that would remind her of the mismatched chair. . . . Get Aunt Circe presents, too. Send you a gift to ask your forgiveness. A month or two in Siracusa or even over to Naples would punish him for his ugliness to his wife." Again, I made "wife" a title of duty. I went on, "You have the wisdom to decide what is best. You love Vincenzo, Circe, Nyxos, and Lucia. Find a middle ground that will satisfy punishment and show a modicum of mercy. All will be obliged to you for it." One thing Deimos loved was people obligated to him.

We stopped at the water. Uncle stared at it. Ten minutes passed while he devised his own scenario.

"This is what I have decided," he finally told me. "Vincenzo will go to Siracusa. He will go to our cousin Philo, who will set him to work on his farm, like any common laborer (which is no different than his role in Riposto most days). He will ask his wife to redecorate their home, expand it for more children. Send presents to his child. He will buy a fine silver rosary for Circe and a new long gun for me. He will pay for all this from his own purse. He will give you his communion rosary as a sign of contrition and thankfulness for your intercession.

"This is how it will be done. You will not unlock the barn. I will chastise him through the door. I will tell him I am afraid to see him, that I may kill him. I will shout all of the things I just decided through the door, so all can hear. The workers will think me just. The women will see my rage. I will order you to gather his travel needs. I will order you to arrange his passage to Siracusa. You will get him fed and ready to leave in the morning. Vincenzo will suffer no more physical harm. Until then you will protect him from my wrath by holding the barn door key.

"Now we know why you were called to Palermo. Excellent. Let me go ahead and disappear until I hear you call me. Everyone will know that Don Tartus is a man of justice and peace." My flattery had not been too much, I concluded, for his balloon of an ego.

Deimos put on a great act. He pounded on the doors of the barn, which almost came off the hinges. All of his rants were exactly as he had said. I got busy doing as ordered.

While he was at his supper with the ladies and baby Nyxos, I went to Vincenzo. He had obviously been crying. "Vincenzo, it will be a month. Some money. All will be forgiven. Accept it all graciously. Deimos truly loves you. Anyone else would be mashed like a beetle under a hobnailed boot." I enjoyed that image.

"Cousin," he said, "I am in your debt. I can hear your voice in his decision. You have not wasted your time being educated in Bologna."

I was floored by this ape actually acknowledging my help. "Well, in a month you will return to a house in the turmoil of renovation. Believe me, having lived through my mother's many renovations, you will wish to be back in Siracusa. What shall I pack for you?"

He gave me his keys. I gathered his things, made the necessary transportation arrangements. Telling him I would unlock his door at six in the morning, I shook his hand, the first time that hand has not delivered a blow or gesture of disdain. I had the spring ready for my trap.

AT 6:00 AM, HIS PRISON SWINGS OPEN. He is off to his purgatory. I am off, later, to my own heavenly choir of lust. To what proves to be a day that gifts me with life-changing potential.

After breakfast, I tell Aunt I need to sail to recover from these trials. She smiles and calls me her blessed finocchio. That was a good deal more affection than I have seen in this house over the last eight months, except maybe for Lucia, who has a truly kind heart. She suffers in this place. She deserved a better education than she has. She has a first-class mind. I have had occasion to read to her from my classical books, and she was astute in her questions. Maybe when I spring my trap, she will be liberated from hers.

I arrived on our island around noon. I laid a blanket under our favorite fragrant oleander. Set the basket of wine and cheese in the shade.

The better part of a long hour passed. I was despairing of Pietro until he arrived with his wonderful news about being raised to Monseigneur, put in charge of three parishes.

In Sicily the church outranks the government and the Mafia most times. He announces that his path to bishop looks assured. I certainly hope so. He is a kind if rough man. When he makes love, it is very physical. Delicacy and subtlety are not in his repertoire. He is totally versatile and does not demand fixed roles. I call him my Admiral. I am his sweet Sailor.

"Admiral, what does this mean for us?"

"My sweet Sailor, we will continue as we are until you depart in a few months. I will not leave the parish. It will be my Vatican. The curates at the two other churches under my authority have been there for a few years. They know, as I rise, so will they. I will find a new curate for my position, although I think I will bring Tomaso from St. Basil to me. He is like- minded as you and I. I would send the new curate there after some training. Tomaso is well equipped to see to my success. He is also well equipped."

"You are such a quipster." Not mockingly, I ask, "Should I be jealous?" I slap him playfully.

He goes on to say how he plans to expand and enrich his churches.

The Cardinal is always looking for men who can feed his coffers. Being intelligent and driven, I can see Pietro in that high office someday.

"Come eat. I have waited so long, I am famished. I need to tell you about the goings on at the plantation."

While we eat, I replay all of my maneuverings in the chess game of my Mafia household. I leave out my setting of the wheels to crush the Tartus men. Pietro has no idea of my lust for blood. He knows me for who I am to the unknowing world, a self-centered rich boy who has carnal desires not in keeping with my family's image.

We finish lunch. Swim. Two lusty seamen triumphantly mate, nap.

When we awake, he is obviously contemplating something. I tell him to speak it, thinking it was something I could advise him with.

"Sailor, I have a great secret to share with you about your family." We are naked, lying in the sun, hidden in our sandy cove. I play with the hair on his chest.

"Do tell."

"This will give you power, but it can also put you in danger."

I sit up. "Let me open another bottle of wine." I, stage performer, declare, "I need to fortify myself for this onslaught." I pour us two cups. I'm making light of this, thinking I know nearly everything about the Tartus cabal.

"When Father Cordia passed away, I was tasked with going through his room and arranging the distribution of his belongings. He was fairly humble and left few things of value except for a book. The book is a baptismal register. But I keep the baptismal register for our church and the two others under his control. I couldn't understand why he had a second. I opened it to find it started over two hundred years ago, and the newest entry was seven months ago. It is a book of the dark secrets of the families in the three parishes."

"Wonderful! Secrets—I love them." I rub my hand over his sun-heated thigh.

"Stop, maybe later. You are insatiable. Come kiss me, my young sailor." We kiss passionately. He pushes me off. "Later. Listen. This is the gift of knowledge. The Spanish say, 'Knowledge is power.'"

I pout, though not really, for I would not be my parent's son if I did not lust after power. "Proceed."

"Many families have illegitimate children in the eyes of the church. Often they are covered up with a quick marriage to a bought or tricked father. Over the two hundred years of the secret baptismal, every holder of the book records the true paternity of those otherwise illegitimate waifs. Some have detailed notes recording more facts around the events. I imagine blackmail was sometimes used when a priest needed funds.

"In your family, I have found a few notations over those two hundred years. The most recent is the seven-month one. The previous, twenty-eight years ago, both concerning your despicable cousin Vincenzo."

I am acutely attentive. I sit up.

"Have you ever wondered about Circe's dead husband?" Father Assisi asks.

"In passing. Not of deep concern to me." Maybe I should have asked my father more. He was not overly fond of the Tartus brood.

"There was never a husband. Vincenzo is Deimos' son."

I choked on my wine. "Shit! Don't tease me. This is too delicious." My mind is creating channels of revenge faster than the words come out of Pietro's mouth.

"I'm not teasing. The note from Father Pano, the then-holder of the book, says that it wasn't even rape. Under close examination, Circe and Deimos confessed to being lovers. Their father threatened to kill them. Circe went off to Milan, to I presume your mother, for her confinement. Deimos threatened to kill his father if he could not raise his son. Moros knew his son and feared him." Pietro grew silent.

"So much explained. I could never understand why I was sent here.

I had been farmed out to better places after they found out about me. But this was a place no one would dare refuse me for a full year. Deimos's fanatical devotion and submission to Circe—so obvious. I wonder if they are still lovers." I think about how I can spy on them. "But wait, you said there is a note from seven months ago. That would be about the time of Nyxos' baptism. I came here two months later. The child was four months old."

"Yes, Father Cordia's last entry. There is no note, just an entry. "Nyxos Paulino Tartus. The Paulino has a line through it, and Vincenzo is written above it. I looked up the public baptismal records I am in charge of. Nyxos Vincenzo Tartus is listed officially, Lucia Torred Dume as mother and Vincenzo Moros Tartus Dume as father. So who is Paulino, my son? What made Lucia seek counsel and wisely change the child's name? Father Cordia was cryptic about this, unlike other entries in the secret baptismal."

"Pietro. . .the only Paulino I know is possibly Paulo, one of Deimos' henchmen. Is he? Oh, God, the possibility is beyond delicious. Vincenzo a cuckold. Be still my heart!" I rub my hands in glee.

Lucia has more depth than merely being a suffering beauty. What does the Bible say? "Vengeance is mine saith the Lord." I think the Lord has a stand-in in the house next to where I suffer.

"Holy Father, you have made a day of triumph incredibly unique. I will carefully preserve this knowledge. I can see the obvious danger." Who knows when I will use it to my advantage?

"Sweet Sailor, what is my reward?"

"Lie back, Admiral. Your ship has come in." My imagination has been unleashed. I hang any inhibitions I ever had on the limbs of our flowering arbor. I will devour his body and offer mine in a consummation we had never experienced before, my ecstasy of body matching the ecstasy of knowledge.

11

NOW, NEW YORK CITY

"WE'RE TESTING OUT A NUMBER OF facial-sketch programs before the Department commits. From what we hear from others, human sketch artists still need to add subtleties the programs can't yet provide. Our experience, too." Officer Collins was enthusiastic as he turned on the program. "This one is 'Sketch Cop'. We tested 'Faces' last week. Good results, but we still need the artist."

Collins explained the basics of what they were going to be doing for the preliminary face, kind of a rough sketch. "I'm going to call up different templates for the major parts of a human face. Then we will get into the real fun part. This program is good at subtle things like uneven eyes, wrinkles, and so forth. Mr. Hilton, you just need to point at the templates as we go through. Tell me anything that needs changing. After we're done, Detective Holiwell will do the finishing touches. You're talking about the changes will help you remember more details when Holiwell gets to work with you. We've done this together before, and it helps revive witnesses' memories.

"Mr. Hilton, look at the screen and choose a face shape."

Hilton pointed to the more oval one, noting, "But the jaw would be squarer."

Collins did some adjusting.

"Too much. . . . Pretty good."

"OK, let me call up the nose templates. . . . Which is closest? Classic Roman nose, real aristocratic. . . ."

And so they went through the various eyes, ears, cheeks available.

Hank Hilton was seated at the console with Collins. Mortana, Brown, and Victor stood behind them. They were fascinated by how lifelike the rough sketch was already. Hank noted, "That is very, very close to how I remember him."

Collins saved the results, printed out a copy. All of the settings were printed in a column next to the face. "This is so we never have to redo the basics," he said. "If the artist wanted to actually pencil draw on it we can obviously make numerous prints. But our expert over there is a genius with the stylus. He's training me. Today you need the master, not the apprentice."

"Brian, you're up." Collins was speaking over the cubby to a man in civilian clothes sporting a badge in an ID case hanging over his chest.

The group had introduced themselves before Collins did the grunt work. Holiwell was on a sister monitor, seeing the work Hank and Collins had been doing.

Holiwell was one of the best sketch artists in the Department. He specialized in portraiture. Most police artists specialized: crime scenes, court cases, and other aspects of criminal investigations where photos and written descriptions missed the subtleties of the study. It's amazing what a trained eye can clarify in a photo that might not show through the gore of a crime scene. It was why medical books contain sketches as well as photos.

Holiwell took Collins's seat. Collins joined the others. "Mr. Hilton, as Officer Collins already said, we like you to just keep talking. I'll guide you with some questions. I'll adjust the drawing as you answer them. Stop me when I'm closest to what you remember. Now let's save time by talking about what most obviously needs adjusting."

Hank talked about the lighting in the bar and how it caught the man's cheek bones. They began by adjusting shadows and highlights. After twenty minutes of questioning, erasing, and adjusting with the drawing pad stylus, the computer sketch was done.

Hitting save, Holwell printed out a copy of the face on the screen. "Sometimes the print looks different than the screen, so take a good look at the copy in your hands."

"You guys are amazing," said Hank, pleased with himself. "This is as good a likeness as I remember."

He turned to Victor. "It's the way I remember him. Like I told you the other night, I had had a few drinks and it was across about fifteen feet. But this is really accurate." Holiwell printed out six copies, which had the case number, date, and time stamp at the top.

Mortana was almost gleeful. Brown, ever serious, clapped a hand on Hank's shoulder, saying, "This is the best and only lead we have. I'd say you, Officer Collins, and Detective Holiwell have done this case an outstanding service."

Each studied a printout—looking at a man thirty-seven to forty-two years old, handsome, light-skinned, with well-set dark eyes, a Roman nose, an aristocratic bearing, not quite but almost a haughty look more Gregory Peck than Peter Fonda, and dark wavy hair that feathered around his face exactly as Hank had said. Hank had brought a book with the Botticelli self-portrait that he alluded to. It did not belong to the Morgan.

"NOW YOU HAVE THE FULL BACKGROUND." Jason was addressing the gathered LGBTQI participants. "We can take questions in a minute. I just want to personally thank Mr. Hank Hilton, who has given us the only concrete lead in this case. His description of the man you see in the police drawing is a tribute to community cooperation. Let's give a hand to Hank." The crowd applauded.

They were in the same Hilton Hotel conference room as the CDC gathering. Crystal chandeliers, long tables with cushioned chairs, yellow-damasked walls, yellow–beige indecipherably patterned carpeting on the floor, and a dais up front ready for a banquet or murder conference. The room was big enough for 150 people. The CDC had fifty-something professionals attending. Also in attendance, more than a hundred activists, care workers, and representatives from community organizations.

Jason continued, "All of the materials you have already been shared with all the cities in which attacks have occurred. The FBI has provided them to the major LGBTQI community organizations in them. Most of you got them over the last three days as PDFs. We hope to contact a wider audience on a website that the AVP, GMHC, Callan-Lorde, and Lambda Legal have coordinated. That has been funded by the mayor's office, the Health and Hospitals Corporation, NYPD, and the CDC. This is a national concern. As we said, we do not think this is contagious. We think that the perpetrator or perpetrators are injecting the victims.

"Let's have questions."

Hands shot up. Jason called on seven or eight. Most questions were not too different from those at the CDC conference. Many asked for details on how the victims might have come into contact with the killer, some medical, some policing.

Jason pointed to Victor. They felt this needed exposure. Mortana and Brown knew nothing about their setup. Mortana had shared information about this serial killer when Victor told her the good news about finding Hank.

"V2 *Gay National Press*, he, him. What about the murders in Hoboken and Chelsea?"

Brown stepped up to the mike. He gave Victor a stare-down, thinking it was just a monkey wrench and off topic. Victor was unimpressed. Jason was nervous his sister would be pissed. Brown described the facts as they were known, concluding, "The FBI is involved because the murders are in two different states."

"Carol Chou, LGBTQ Asians of America. My pronouns are she and her. Why did this get left out of the presentation?" Angry murmurs could be heard across the room.

"AIDS. Considering this is a biological assault, we are concerned with getting ahead of what some have already tried to equate to an AIDS-like maelstrom. So far we have been able to squelch that, but we won't be able to for much longer. So it's important for your community organizations to have specific information to help keep things fact-based in these alternate fact times we live in. We were not hiding these murders. Their MO is obvious and does not feed into a new plague scare."

That does not satisfy the crowd. Jason asked for quiet and calm. Turning to the police commissioner, he asked, "Mr. Commissioner, can you explain how the police are working these cases?"

"Kimbel Martel, New York City Police Commissioner. My pronouns are he, him. We've pretty much covered the Bio-Killer work. These other murders are a serious matter. The Hoboken and New Jersey State police have the lead but we are fully involved in the investigation. The murders were definitely committed by the same individual. The Hudson River is a notoriously fluid barrier to criminals who haunt our respective cities and states.

"Agent Brown has given you all the information publicly available. The fact that only one of the victims is Gay, and the general circumstances surrounding the victim's death, did not seem to pertain to the reasons for this conference. We have made complete profiles for our victims. Interviewed hundreds of family members, friends, personnel where they were last seen. We've gone through Public CCC tapes. We've asked community help. We've done the same for our Bio-Killer cases. That's how we found Mr. Hilton. As of now, the Bathtub Killer investigation hasn't turned up solid leads. If anyone has any information, you can contact the Department at Chief Lex's number in your resource packet."

Noting the lateness of the hour, Jason began to wrap up. "Can we return to a final question. Since time will make this our last one before closing, please keep it to the Bio-Killer cases. We will then have closing comments from our Lambda Legal web coordinator, Dr. George Whiska."

People were being less attentive, some already leaving.

Calling on a man he had known professionally and dated at one time, Jason was clearer on why he had been asked to chair this conference. After ten years of activism, before he got the grant to New Zealand, he had personal and professional contact with at least fifty percent of those attending, who led important community organizations.

"Dr. Babatunde Ali, arachnologist, Bronx Zoo: Men of African Heritage, Bronx. Have the people at the CDC and NIH considered the possibility that this injectable may be spider venom and digestive-juices based? Viper venom does all the things you say, but none are, to my knowledge, digestive of internal organs in the manner you've described, whereas all spiders accomplish their food ingestion in that way, liquifying the internal structures of their kills."

The head of Health and Hospitals answered, "Dr. Helena Perez— you all know me. My pronouns are they. In truth, the CDC and NIH have both been approached about that. As of now the possibility of such differing animals being the origin of the injectable materials is being seriously considered. With a little money, relatively speaking, splicing machinery resulting in the acronym CRISPR is readily available, so putting together a genetic sequence of such hideous consequences is not impossible. Difficult but not impossible."

She took a sip of water from her metal sports bottle.

" It's the delivery system that is mysterious. I'm not sure if it was stated, but a virus shell containing the genetic hybrid would be a likely conductor to penetrate the cell walls so thoroughly throughout the body. The extremely short time from injection to total transformation indicates a massive invasion of an unusually small viral shell. That virus would simply be extremely fragile because of its tiny size and would not survive outside controlled conditions. So it would not be infectious in generally contagious models."

"So they say," someone shouts. An uproar broke out.

Another conference participant shouted, "They have all been MAGAs, so who cares?"

Perez barked, "*We* care, because they are *human beings*. They may not fit *our* definition of community members but do share our orientations. And suppose someone from another hate group gets hold of it? We will have an epidemic of cruelty and murder. That is not what we do in this country." She was greeted with boos and derisive calls.

Jason returned to the podium. "You're right, and so is the good doctor. History makes us cautious. Right now, friends, what matters is that *our community is under threat*. You've heard from our community leaders. You've heard from government and health leaders. Now it is up to us to help ourselves, like we did during the first fifteen years of the AIDS health crisis. It was our community working together that got us through to today. And *this* time the government actually *wants* to help."

He ran his eye slowly over the crowd. "Please listen to our closing speaker, Dr. George Whiska, Ph.D., Coordinator for the LGBTQ Bio-Killer website."

A late middle-aged man came to the podium. "George Whiska, Standing Rock Lakota, Lambda Legal Defense Fund, Senior Council, Coordinator LBGTQ Bio-Killer website. I use he and him.

"This is a state of emergency. We are under attack. This could easily turn into a human rights struggle again.

"Our best defense is knowledge. Knowledge can only come from the scientists and community cooperation that is shared with all agencies, especially law enforcement, as already mentioned. We can defend ourselves by being willing to look out for even our worst neighbors. There are fliers in your packets that will give the website address. Please post yours to your organizations' sites. Send it to your friends."

"Follow best safety practices. All LGBTQI people need to be aware. Don't feel safe because up until now all of the victims have been men and MAGA. Our best defense is to make sure your date, new friend, trick, is seen and knows they have been seen with you by a bartender, friend, or acquaintance. Dating before taking or being taken home is a good idea. Follow your gut. You can always find another date but not another life. Google the person, not just their Tinder profile, before you go out. That may sound creepy, but dead is permanent. And these deaths are horror movie, sci fi, psychosis-inducing horrific."

He waited for the murmuring to die down, adding assurances of confidentiality. "Ladies and gentlemen, contact numbers for any information you can share are on the site. If you are wary of being involved, all contacts are confidential. Also, the admins of the website will supply any contact judged viable with an escort to the agency that can use your information. Please use the website. Please keep yourself accurately informed by checking the website. Medical and law enforcement information from their closed site will also be posted as available.

"Let us take care of each other. Lives saved are lives that can grow and become better members of our community.

Jason returned to the podium, drawing the conference to a close. "Thank you, George. Thank you all. Your questions and skepticism are well noted. Make sure you have the packets and other materials before you leave. Let's be safe. Love yourself and each other. In health. Get home safely." He shut off the mike.

Victor mounted the dais to give him a kiss.

Mortana came over and congratulated him. She punched Victor in the arm. "Was that Hoboken thing necessary?"

"You know I feel they could be the same guy. Brown and Martel handled it well. Please try to understand."

Brown had been standing behind Victor the whole time. "You know the FBI is like lawyers. We want to know what the questions and answers will be before we go to trial. I'll forgive you this once. In the future, a heads-up, even one I don't want to hear, is better than a sucker punch."

Mortana pulled her brother aside, scolding him by assuring him the law enforcers were on the community's side.

"Tough crowd," Brown told Dr. Perez and Commissioner Martel, who had joined their circle.

Victor answered, "Regular. Kind of like the old story about putting a question to two rabbis, you get three opinions. Here you get five conspiracies and six unanswerable questions screamed back at you. Our community has too many wounds and not enough Band-Aids."

Whiska asked Brown and Martel for an ear. Brown pulled Mortana into the circle, "Lieutenant Lemures is always part of the discussions."

Whiska blushed deeply. "I apologize. I thought you went off with your brother." The five pulled chairs together to have a tête-à-tête.

Victor, Jason, and Baba hung out, talking in the lobby, waiting for Mortana and Brown.

12

THEN, SICILY

P AULO, WHAT ARE YOU DOING HERE?" We are in one of my
Taormina beach taverns. Thank goodness I'm here having just
completed butcher business, not hunting.

My uncle's henchman is a bit drunk. "I needed to get away. Time
to think away from Don Tartus."

I hadn't seen Paulo for almost a week since Vincenzo left. I was
keen to see how he and Lucia might interact. Now here he is, alone and
perhaps as melancholy as his face seems to suggest. "I haven't seen you
in a while. What was that about? You are uncle's constant companion."

He looks at me. "Your uncle thinks I am his dog."

Wait. Discontent: Let's see how I can use this. "Paulo, he doesn't
appreciate that you have your own life to lead. How did you get away
tonight?"

"Joseph is guarding the compound gate, Mario the dock entrance.
Normally that is the only time I have to myself. Besides, it's usually when
Deimos and your aunt have one of their secret meetings. Kid, I think
your aunt really runs this show."

As though that could be a revelation. Circe is the brighter of the two by miles.

Paulo orders another gin. "The Dutch are good gin makers. Wine is for food. Gin is for getting drunk."

"Ah, drunk is your aim. I can't. The last time I did, I was sick for a week. Now, a little high is enough. Besides, there are other pleasures I enjoy more."

He looks me up and down. Looks between my legs. "So I hear," he murmurs, and laughs—with irony, not derision. I wonder, Is he coming on to me?

But he, as most drunks eventually do, begins sharing his miseries. "You're not such a bad fellow. You get treated much worse than me by your cousin and uncle. Your uncle drags me to Palermo, where I'm holed up for five days while the Dons hash out who has to pay who and what territory is going where. The minute we're back, he sends me to babysit Vincenzo on the trip to Siracusa. I didn't even have time to see my own. . .mother." "Mother," I'm sure is a stand in for "child"; there was a real hesitation while his addled brain realized what he could not say.

"Vincenzo carried on like a blubbering baby. How he would miss Circe. How his uncle was unfair. How Lucia was a bitch. Never mentioned his own child. Such a wonderful boy," he sighs in a longing voice. "I was happy to ditch him at Philo's. I hope they work him like a dog. I'm sure he will do his best to avoid that, like he does here." Paulo's voice is conspiratorially low.

"I have noticed that you seem to have many tasks around the plantation." Showing sympathy to him will not hurt my cause.

"Except, except for Lucia. The lovely Lucia!" he suddenly says out of nowhere, but realizes he has just overstepped a boundary.

"God, yes, she is lovely. How she ever got into this family is a crime. Lovely, sweet, kind, smart. . .and tall. I personally like tall women. Aesthetically, of course," I smoothly inject. He laughs, relaxes.

"She *is* smart. And watch her with the child—so good. Circe must have raised Vincenzo like her namesake. One monster to another." Now he is letting go. I buy him another gin. The tavern owner says it's closing time.

Drat. Maybe I'll buy a bottle, and we can sit on the beach while he talks. But he stands up. Downs his drink.

"My mother lives up in the town. It's a hike, and I'm drunk. I need to be careful going up. Only thing working this late are my legs. Even those I'm not so sure of." He shrugs his shoulders like a little boy.

"Can I help you?"

"No, I'll be all right. I've managed my life for thirty-four years. I'll mange the climb."

We leave together. He steadies himself as we walk the gravel path to the road.

I point to the beach. "My boat is down here."

"You sail a lot. Good for you. Get away from those people as often as you can. Don't get trapped like I have." Nothing more bitter than a bitter drunk.

"Be safe getting up the hill. Will you be back tomorrow?" I ask. He staggers away answering, but I can't understand him.

Knowing how drunks can have regrets, I think the sooner I see him and reassure him that his talk was the rambling of a tired man who had drunk a bit too much of the Low Country's brew, the more likely I can cultivate my plan, in which he is shaping up as a central figure. Originally, I had hoped to start a Mafia war between my uncle's fief and his neighboring Don's. I would time it to be heating up just about the week I would be leaving. I hadn't worked out the full details. Some murders, I imagined. But my Admiral delivered such knowledge on our last outing that, tonight, I saw how I could destroy both Tartus men, shame my aunt into submission, and advance Lucia's standing.

I saw it all as Paulo poured out his woes. His son came first before

Lucia in our conversation, so that baby's future became a key to my plan. A man measures his success by what he leaves for his son.

Paulo was not stupid. I had heard him in conversation with the Don over meals. He had good insights and was clever in steering the Don into less drastic behaviors. Vincenzo and Deimos were brutes. Paulo was brutal when ordered, or needed, to be but seemed to want a less fatal engagement with the Sicilian populace.

It was a fine sunny day the next noon when I saw Paulo. Lucia returned to the kitchen after supervising the workers' meal preparation. Circe was making the family's meal. I rang the bell, as Lucia had requested, notifying the workers to go to the cantina next to the orchard. I had asked her if I could bring Nyxos out into the yard. We sat under the almond tree that grew there, waiting, knowing that Deimos and his family of henchmen would follow shortly.

The chickens were doing what chickens do. The two dogs, Hades and Pluto, lay in the shade near us. I was singing a lullaby to Nyxos when the men arrived for lunch. Paulo came over to me and the baby while the others went in to wash up. His face brightened. "Hello, Paulo. How's your head?" I said in a low voice.

He scrunched down to scratch black Hades behind the ears. Tawny Pluto pushed in for attention. Paulo put his hand out to Nyxos who grabbed a finger. Paulo cooed to the baby. "I hardly remember last night."

"It was nice getting to know you a bit. How was your mama?"

"Mama is fine."

"Right now I need some water. So does Nyxos." Water to lubricate the plan I have into action.

"I'll get it," Paulo is quick to offer.

"Why don't you take my seat and hold the little one. I'll get a nice cool cup for us to share."

"Are you sure?" He glances apprehensively toward the kitchen.

"It will be okay." I   assure him as I hand him the unwritten contract to our futures. "Lunch is a few minutes away."

I bring Paulo a cup of fresh spring water. I have my own. He begins to get up, offering me the baby. I put my hand on his shoulder and gently push him back against the chair. The man is as solid as a mountain. Definitely Sicilian. Olive skin, black hair, dark eyes, square, muscled. No facial hair, very *un*-Sicilian. Pleasant to look at. Under other circumstances I'd do him in a minute. Here I'd end up slop for the boars.

"Why disturb the child? He seems very happy in your arms. Hold the cup to his lips. Don't drown him. Lucia would never forgive us." I smile inwardly and outwardly.

"I have about three more months here. I can't tell you how I count the days."   I stare toward the water and begin my weaving. "I hope saving Vincenzo from the beating he deserved will get him off my back."

Paulo breathes out, "Pig," through clenched teeth.

"You should have been there. Those women were hell cats. I only stopped them when I thought they would break his ribs. Otherwise, I would not have stepped in. He was going to beat me for having yelled at him to stop violating Lucia."   Little lies make big knots. "Circe tripped him. The women fell on him. I pray I never get Circe angry. She was quicker than my fencing teacher." A truth easily shared.

Lucia appears in the door. "Food is hot." She broadly smiles when she sees Paulo holding their son. I take Nyxos from Paulo and carry him the few feet to the door, exclaiming, "Momma, we males do not have the means to feed this growing little man." Everyone at the table laughs. Lucia takes him from me, walks to the end of the kitchen away from the stove, and loosens her blouse to feed the child. Paulo does everything not to look their way. Circe serves.

Every day I try to get the boy into Paulo's arms. I thread talk of all our futures into our sometimes-long conversations, always mildly diminishing the Tartuses, speculating how such an angelic child as Nyxos deserved a better future than to be the son of a rather inadequate father and feared grandfather. I bemoaned how bright Lucia is, noting how a book was not in the house until I brought mine. Nyxos needs a fine education.

"My family could not afford a good education for me but the good Father Pano saw to it that the children in this parish could read and write. I was an altar boy, so he taught me some other things. He let me read all his books. We would have what he liked to call 'Aristotelian conversations.' Such a fancy word for figuring out the best solutions. It was almost a game. We both enjoyed it. I didn't know a man could be so kind. Father Pano was a fine man. Not like most other priests. Suck the bread right from your mouth."

I feel the need to defend my Admiral. "You know Father Assisi. He has helped me to control my anger. He explained to me that the way I am is not an offense to God, only man. How could my God-given nature be a sin before God? He taught me."

"I really don't care. God this, God that. The church and the law make it up to get you by the balls." I hear my head think, *Paulo, do tell.*

"Father Assisi was a sailor. I think being a man of the world made him a good priest. He has his eyes open to the tricks of his church. He has a good heart. Not far from your Father Pano, I would think. Besides, he taught me to sail and mapped the coast to Taormina in my heart. The sea speaks lovingly to me. I leave her presents." I divulge no further. "Soon I will go back to a city, not Milano. Up until Riposto, small places were vacation visits. It has been most instructive to live here."

"Don't let this compound be what you take from here. It screws your thinking up. I settled my mother in Taormina years ago. The people there are much less suspicious of other people than the compound has made me. When Old Messina died my father moved here. Here I was born. And here I've lived all my life. When my father was killed, Don Deimos moved me into his position and finally as his per-sonal bodyguard," Paulo reflected emptily.

THAT NIGHT I GAVE MY FOURTH OFFERING TO IONA, just before dawn. I had not yet docked. The sky was less dark when, from the sea, I saw a figure climb out the back window of Vincenzo's house. Ah. Paulo, you horny bastard. Good, taking advantage of Vincenzo. Another thread in my tapestry.

13

NOW, BROOKLYN, NEW YORK

BROTHER, I NEED TO SEE YOU." It's Elio, a voice I haven't heard in years. I'd rather face the cops than see him. "What is this about?"

"Not on the phone."

"How did you get my number?"

"Such a ridiculous question. You haven't been a member of this family, have you? Follow the money, all roads go through the expenditures. Enough—invite me to your present lair."

Elio has played this game before. Being head of the family required reining in the recalcitrant and vile. Over six hundred years of anonymity cannot be thrown away because of a bunch of apparent psychotics. Elio was sure there were many in our past, but he did not much like research. This was not something he wanted to have the family business librarians poking around in.

Bowing to the inevitable, I gave him my latest address in Brooklyn Heights. Three years ago, I bought and renovated a home in the landmarked district. Three buildings, in fact, plus a carriage house. The early nineteenth-century buildings were completely gutted and only their historic shells maintained. My builder assured me you could burn them down and the new buildings beneath would stand unharmed.

The interiors are totally modern. Each room soundproofed. The carriage house and the two buildings next to it were combined into one home, meeting my special requirements. The third building's top two floors are for staff. We are solar paneled with storage batteries in the ground under the driveway, enough for a sunless week, I'm assured. Bribes for quick permits were enormous. I moved in three months after construction ended.

The important feature that is incredibly luxurious for this village is the carriage house, which is set back on a cobbled drive with an underground tunnel between the three houses connected to it. It was a station on the Underground Railroad before the Civil War.

"Make it 8:00 PM. Sunset is at 7:00. Bring sweets if you want to be invited in." My time in Bavaria made me a pastry addict.

I know why he's coming. The police have gotten a good sketch of me well advertised. One of the family agents must have seen it and contacted Bern, family central. I'm pleased and annoyed at the same time. It means that I will either need to disguise myself or suspend my current attack on the LGBTQ bottom feeders.

My own agents have been able to identify the culprit who gave them my description. One slip-up, and there you go. Back tracking from him, I learned that two men were responsible for his being found. Jason Lemures, Gay activist, epidemiologist, professor, and Victor Virlus, newspaper reporter.

I'm toying with the idea of contacting the reporter. One of the reasons I left subtle clues at Marsayas's was a desire to make the game more interesting. I just didn't think someone in Bay Ridge would be so aware. I'm a twelve, out there was a sea of sevens. That's mean—there *were* one or two nines. Why wouldn't I stand out? I mean, I am the perfection from a long line of selective breeding.

I am the dark result, Elio the light.

My brother is six feet, an inch taller than me, solidly svelte, blue-eyed. He has skin like satin, a regal nose, silky blond hair curled to perfection, lips so kissable that they glow. Even his ears are perfect. Our French ancestry abounds in him. He is five years older than me but looks five younger.

When we were growing up, I had an enormous crush on him. He was not below using that to his advantage in every way possible. I was not the only one under his spell. His friends, and our family, fell all over themselves to gain his favor. My father could not hide his adoration of him. Mother was less caring; when Sylvie arrived, she was her favorite. I, like most middle children, got lost. Being Gay made it easier for them to overlook me.

Luckily for the world, I am the one with the peculiar drive. I do have the superior intelligence. Don't get me wrong, Elio is very intelligent but misses the cunning I have. I think Deimos and Vincenzo were my teachers there. If Elio had my proclivities, people would be fighting to submit to his fatal torture.

I'M OUTSIDE, HIS TEXT READ. Opening the door, there he was, almost a ghost on my top step in the dim carriage lamp lights. Pale in a light gray suit, paisley gray on gray vest, pale blue shirt, pink tie, large-brimmed matching fedora half hiding his face, tan shoes, his hair as curly as ever, cut in a fashion similar to mine. Could he be more perfect? I thought. Then, Be on guard.

"Did you bring sweets?"

"Bavarian cream puffs, your favorite, made by my host's housekeeper. Here." He offered me a fabric bag with a box inside. I almost snatched it.

"Okay, come in." I stepped aside, ushered him past the public rooms to my elevator, took us to the sitting room on the second floor with greenhouse attached atop the carriage house. The master suite is the whole top of the second house, the two rooms connected by hidden set of double doors behind a bookcase.

A guest bedroom is off the kitchen in the third building on the first floor. My office–library is in the back there. The entrance we have come through is an open plan dining-living room. The basement has a laundry, a gym, and other underground rooms. I dug out the carriage house floor for a potting cellar.

All the glass windows are filtering UV, tempered to withstand small-caliber gunfire or 140-mile-an hour winds. Instead of shades, the glass in my combined residence goes opaque in numerous colors or to natural scenes when electrified. The exterior has appropriate faux-wood steel shutters for all the windows. Having lived in war-torn circumstances, I take no chances. The total cost was staggering.

I took his hat, lay it on the sofa. My sitting room has a wall of glass doors facing the garden and terrace. There is fine outdoor furniture from Neiman Marcus, purchased before they closed, on the wide terrace across the sitting room.

"Can I get you something?" Being cordial does not temper my caution.

"Do you have our special red?"

"It will need to warm. I'll let it breathe." Our family has dealt in red for as long as Elio has been in charge.

I slid open a panel next to the fireplace, revealing a wet bar, shelves of beverages, and a refrigerator. Conveniently there is a vitrine of fine glassware and pottery on the adjoining wall.

I open the creampuff box and put them on a plate made by a Japanese national treasure potter, place it on the glass coffee table. Elio idly observes, "Nori Sashida. I have a cup by him."

"Shall we sit outside?" My eyes go to the terrace.

"I think we need more privacy to comfortably discuss what I've come about."

"Okay. Have a seat. Why don't you take off your jacket? Get comfortable."

He did. I find this very encouraging. If he was angry, he would remain formal right up to keeping the suit jacket buttoned. I took his coat and gestured to his vest. He took that off also. I put them on a hanger and placed them and the hat in the closet.

He smelled of lavender, wool, and his own personal musk. I had forgotten how it enhanced his beauty. Only one other person has ever come close to his enticement, my admiral.

We lowered ourselves onto two French chairs in an Egyptian revival style from the last century that I love. Brought to America via England ten years ago.

I moved the creampuffs between us. I placed my chair to his right so I could enjoy his profile and be nearer him.

My pale 1930s Finnish rug with Erté's ladies staring up through the table unifies this intimate area. The base is swirled glass so as much of the rug as possible will show through. The chairs square the sides of the glass table in front of a modern green-marble gas fireplace. At the other end of the room near the terrace are a cream-colored chaise and the piano, a sliding panel to the half bath in the wall next to it. A large, low, soft-pillowed ecru sofa occupies the center of the room, facing a Jean-Michel Basquiat painting. A low Japanese folding screen reflective of the season stands on the floor below it. The four seasons I own were once used by a shogun for his sleeping privacy when on campaign. A low glass table in front of the sofa sits on a Picasso rug.

A Broadway theatrical lighting designer planned all the recessed lighting. I have a genius interior design woman who finds the furnishings I have in mind if I don't already own them. She can work from my sketches. I have decorated many houses.

The sight line is unobstructed across the room except for the light cherry-colored baby grand piano and some lamps. I favor French deco wood side tables and cabinets. The room reflects my taste with guidance from those I trust. It is spare and homey at the same time. Classical while modern. Warmer than its owner.

He complimented some furnishings. "Father's Botticelli looks handsomer than I remember him. Works well where you hung him."

After a moment of silence, I went to the bar, poured his drink.

Handing him the glass, I sank back into my chair. "Well, Elio, let's have it."

"Brother, how could you be so careless?" Elio has switched to Milanese.

"Elio, I know. You tolerate my peculiarities. I never thought that I would be so well observed."

"The family wants you to stop the killing."

"Shall I starve to death? Killing is my life. . . . Which family?"

"Let's not be dramatic. You know perfectly well we tolerate a lot from you, but you can't continue in this city. Move to another country. Go to Africa for a while. Cameroon is semi-chaotic. A good place for you."

"Africa. Don't be crazy. I like air-conditioning too much. You haven't answered me—which family?"

"The Eternal Family."

Turning his chair to me, he reached over for my hand, held it between both of his. Stroking it. "You know I love you and always will. I need you to be safe. The family does not need to hear about everything. You know how to be discreet."

He freed my hand. Leaned back. Took a deep breath. We both went silent. I knew what was coming.

"These are the words the council told me to say exactly. 'Tell your brother he is to stop his terrorizing that has been labeled Bio-Killer. Also, the bathtub killings. We cannot have exposure. He will suffer the worst consequences possible if there is one more from him in either style. There are places in Switzerland with caves deeper than Hell. He does not want his coffin sealed in one.'"

"Well, that's blunt." How the hell did they connect me to the staged killings? Was I to have no fun? Not wishing to show my anxiety, I ate a puff. "Delicious. My compliments to the housekeeper."

"Brother, brother, do not trifle with the council. They are deadly serious. You endanger the family. For love of me, back off." His eyes actually glistened with possible tears. I needed to reconsider my blustering.

Going to the bar, I brought the carafe of red to the coffee table. I had my own glass in hand. Holding up the carafe, I asked, "More?"

"Yes, please." Poured into both glasses; a little was left. "Sip your glass, so I can top you off." Elio smiled at me, his top lip a bit redder, anointed with his wine. He sipped then held the glass out to me. Bled out, I went to the bar and rinsed the carafe.

"Don't you have staff?"

"He lives next door. I see him more often than I used to now that the windows are UV filtered glass. You met him a decade ago. Henri?"

"Ah, yes, the butler's butler." Henri gave that appearance but was more relaxed when not playing the part. We have a healthy familiarity.

Reseated, Elio and I shared recent events in our lives. We talked company business. Discussed the tithe's possible increase to two percent. The corporate family has expanded, and new investments need capital.

"Let me ask you, Elio. If I do as the council asks, would my 'von Pittasching' be tolerated if they were random?"

"Not the bag of bones. I can assure you they are done with that. Barbara had no right to bring you six together and provide you with those condoms. She has been warned to turn her research into something profitable. That witch will get us all burned at the stake. I have

been ordered to find the other five and give them the same warning."
His dislike for Barbara is a personal offense in a long semi-feud.

"Your need to terrorize your prey is up to you. Just do not get publicity. Cease these repetitive acts." Elio sipped at his drink, sizing me up so to speak. He seemed more relaxed now that I had the formal warning and his brotherly cautions.

"Damn, brother, they were so spectacular. The last one was exquisite. I ejaculated so intensely that I fell to my knees."

"You were always sexual even as a little boy. Seven years old, the day after your first communion, you tried to molest me in my own bed."

"Helping you masturbate is not molesting." Elio began to laugh, leaned over, grabbed the back of my neck and kissed me full on the lips. Elio caught me entirely by surprise.

"We haven't done that in years." He breathed out his words slowly, like smoke from a fine cigar. "My bad boy brother. You can be intoxicating." He breathed me in.

He rose from the low chair in liquid motion. He wandered the room, absorbing my psyche in my possessions. I know how insightful he is. Every item a piece to my puzzle.

He stared out the terrace into a row of tall cypress trees that form a screen around my property. Settling onto the chaise lounge opposite the piano, he removed his tie, laid it neatly on the marble-topped side table next to his empty glass, unbuttoned his shirt, back to the terrace, caressed the chaise's slanting support, patted the space next to him. "Come here," the demigod intoned.

I command my house. "Lao Tzu, Admiral." Yoyo Ma began playing softly, lights dimmed to candle power, some flicker for effect, the windows electrified to an Ionian night.

I was at his side not knowing how I got there. As I said, all do the Sun God's bidding. His name isn't Elio, for no reason.

14

NOW, QUEENS, NEW YORK

Uncle Jason, what's it feel like to be Gay?" Calyce was in an AP Psych class, looking for a topic for her next paper.

"Now, that is like me asking you what it feels like to be a fourteen-year-old twin. I have no basis of comparison. But I'm sure Victor would chance an answer."

Victor rolled the dice on the Monopoly board, looked at the niece, then the uncle, and winked. "It makes you feel pretty, oh, so pretty." Jason joined in the song, arm over Victor's shoulders matching his, swaying to their singing, "I feel pretty and witty and Gay. And I pity any girl who isn't me today."

Calyce fell vaudeville-prat on the floor. The men continued to hang onto each other, laughing. Jeremy looked puzzled. "It's a show tune. *West Side Story*," his sister giggled as she leaned her elbows on the chair seat.

"Oh, some young people, no culture. Well. . .we know you're not Gay," Victor declared to Jeremy.

Calyce had regained her seat. "You guys are no help. Fun but no help."

Jeremy defensively retorted, "I can quote the New York Mets stats for the last five years."

"Touché," Jason chuckled. "He has us there."

Victor partnered Jeremy's revelation: "Actually, I love baseball. I can give *you* last year's stats."

"Ow! That hurts. Let's see your Gay card." Jason elbowed Victor. Jeremy asked, "Who rolls?"

"Still my turn, Jeremy. I just rolled a seven. Let me move." Victor moved his shoe seven spaces. "Jail. Bummer."

Calyce announced, "Ice cream break! What do we have here?" She had opened the freezer door. Jason put out bowls. They had been playing in the hearth of the home, the kitchen, a Greek, Italian, immigrant-Filipino kitchen. Except that, in the renovation, it had been modernized and a door to a back deck added. A large window of square panes covered half of that wall.

Jeremy looked at Victor, his only seated companion. "Are we done?" Victor nodded as he rose. "I think so."

"Then I'm the winner. You all left the field of battle." Jeremy declared.

Victor chanted, "Jeremy, Jeremy!" The others joined in weakly. He put the game in the box and put it in the bottom cupboard with a bunch of others.

Calyce laid the cartons of ice cream Jason had brought on the table. "Chocolate, cherry vanilla, pistachio, and rocky road," she read aloud. "Dad will be so jealous." Victor got the spoons. "Do you have a scoop?" he called over his shoulder, scavenging the flatware drawer.

"No scoop—use serving spoons," Jeremy responded.

Victor grabbed the paper towels and put the roll next to the spoons. Jason, looking inside the refrigerator, asked, "Vic, you brought whipped cream?"

"On the door. Chocolate sprinkles on the counter."

Jeremy improvised a parody of the tune he had just learned, "I feel Ben's, I feel Jerry's, I feel oh so creamy and Gay. I pity the poor slob who isn't us today."

"Good try, cigarillo and a lighter." Jason declared. They high-fived.

The cartons passed, whipped cream fired from the can, chocolate sprinkles star-lighting the top. Quiet descended while they enjoyed the party.

Jeremy resurrected his phone, forbidden during pizza and the game. "Mom and Dad are at the hotel. Text time fifteen minutes ago."

Calyce, "Tell them you won by default."

Victor added, "And I know the Mets stats for 2020." Jeremy wrote that. Danny responded with a shocked emoji. All their phones had the same texts from both parents: love hearts, four times.

Dan and Mortana were in Connecticut for the wedding of one of Danny's cousins. They thought they would make it a three-day weekend and wouldn't be back until Monday afternoon or evening. Victor and Jason volunteered to house sit. As Danny put it, "Seeing the house doesn't get burned down."

So far it'd been homework, pizza, Monopoly, and ice cream. The game was a favor to Jason. The kids wanted a TV festival. Victor stayed out of it. Game over, the agreement was anything until 11:00 PM on TV. Friday night was an hour past official weekday bedtime. The twins cleared the table, put the dishes in the dishwasher, and turned it on.

"The longest movie can be two hours." Jason noted the time as they settled in the living room to watch the fifty-six-inch TV, which even Mortana felt was a necessity when they renovated. The one in the basement was as large. They agreed on what the men thought was a hijack movie that turned into a vampire movie, *Blood Red Skies*. Double bloody, double violence. The teens knew about it from school friends and had neglected to inform their uncle, nor their semi-uncle.

"Don't tell your parents we let you watch that," Victor warned.

"Big guy, we're fourteen. We won't go bananas," Calyce conspiratorially reassured him.

"OK! Get yourselves to bed. What happens with your uncles stays with your uncles," Jason announced in an indulgent grandparent way.

"You could sleep in our parents' bed instead of the fold-out." Jeremy reminded them that Dan had insisted, but they felt more comfortable in his office. They both felt a couple's bed was something too personal. Jason declined again.

"Give us a few minutes we'll get you set up," Calyce announced. "Everything is out. Towels are in Dad's bathroom,"

Jason yawned. "Okay, thanks. We'll watch the news. Then get to bed."

Calyce gave them each a hug and a kiss on the cheek. "Sleep well."

Jeremy came back down after he and Calyce set up the men's sleeping quarters. "Good night, uncles. I'm really happy you're here." They hugged him at the same time. Jeremy kissed them just as Calyce did.

They responded in kind. "Good night."

He bounded up the stairs, stopped half way, said, "Don't do anything I wouldn't do," and quickly disappeared.

His uncle mused internally from his own fourteen-year-old's memories, the year of beginning to find his maturing self.

The eleven o'clock news was on. During the commercial Vic speculated, "They could almost make you want to have kids."

"No, thanks. I'd be fifty-one, you'd be forty-seven, when they got to fourteen, if we had some right away. Being an uncle is more fun. Shake them up and hand them back."

Something Jason always told his dad when he pressed for more grandkids. "Find a husband. You could adopt. Have a surrogate." Dad had offered to help pay.

"You'd make a good father." Victor was serious.

"What about you? You seem a natural with these two." Jason had glowed in the growing affection the twins had for Vic.

"No, I'm way too undisciplined to raise kids. They would be feral."

"Undisciplined, you who never misses a deadline?"

"That's about me. The cat I had was left to raise himself. I treated Nikki like he was a roommate with benefits. Loved each other but he would steal food right out of my plate, no respect."

Victor had had a hard childhood until his now-deceased aunt took him in. Other than a general outline, he shared very few details with Jason. Jason knew that Victor needed to feel ready to talk about his past life; pressing him was not going to get anything but silence. He dropped a headline on occasion that might allow for some expanding, but not often. "In due time," was a thing dad always said. "In due time" it had to be.

After half an hour Jason heard the second shower end followed by a toilet flush, a bathroom door being opened. He waited a few minutes, called up to both of them. "I'll check on you when I go to bed. I'll close your doors. No cheating. Lights out. By the way, we love you."

"Love you too," from Calyce.

"Ditto," from Jeremy.

Waiting a few seconds, Jason, knowing his niece, called up, "Calyce, put the book away."

"Okay, Grandpa!"

"More TV or bed?" Jason questioned.

"Bed. I hope we haven't made a mistake. Mortana told me they bought a special mattress because Filipino families always have people flying in. They have had a few spill over from Eva's. It's a queen size for us queens, if that's any comfort."

Jason came in on cat's feet after checking on the teens. "They're sound asleep."

"They leave their doors open?" Victor was incredulous.

"Only when I stay over to babysit. Oops, excuse me, house sit. I need to be sure they're safe in their beds. When they were little, I was allowed to tuck them in. Now I get to close their doors for them." He turned out the light.

"Aren't they a little old to need house sitters?" Victor reflected on being mostly on his own after his mom died before his aunt got him out of the system.

"I know, but military. . .you know," Jason explained. "Also, Mortana shared some of the horrors she saw happen to teens in particular over there. Made her super-protective."

"Well, they need to loosen up pretty soon or they'll have a full blown rebellion." Victor leaned over to kiss his lover.

"I know. I've been hinting. Anyway, Jeremy gave 'Uncles' a really nice sound," Jason shared his happiness with Jeremy's easy adoption of the title. Victor purred agreement. They discussed possibilities and have-to's for the next two days.

"First thing tomorrow, we need to check they have all their work prepared for school on Monday," Victor added to the list.

"Talk about helicopter parents." Jason chuckled. "Love you. Good night"

"Ditto." They folded into each other like people who have been to-gether years, not months.

* * *

Dan led Mortana down St. Francis of Assisi's steps. They had just congratulated the bride and groom. Mrs. Santos and the DiLangs joined them. Danny petted his nephew's hair. Mortana kissed Dan while they waited to throw the confetti from little paper bags some children were handing out. "So much like ours."

"Not at all, we had crossed swords," Dan pointed out.

"Not that. The *service*." Mortana thought, *His is a military memory* even of our wedding, not knowing whether to be annoyed or amused.

"Yes, of course. How do we get your brother and Victor to do this?"
Dan ever wanting to share his first greatest joy, being married to his Lemures.

"In due time, my dear, in due time," quoted the daughter of another
military man.

15

NOW, VIDEO CONFERENCE

AGENT BROWN AND MORTANA COULD hardly believe it. He had expected everyone to be at the online meeting promptly. No one needed to be at the FBI offices. It was either a break in the case or a huge disappointment.

At 2:00 PM, he dialed in and opened the session. "Hello, people." Mortana, Police Commissioner Martel, Police Chief Lex, and Victor were visible. "We are waiting for Dr. Whiska and Dr. Arthur. There's Morgana."

"Hello, Agent Brown. I see we're all here."

"No, Lambda's Dr. Whiska...is signing in. Hello, Dr. Whiska. Now we're all here." Whiska nodded hello.

Brown was wearing his stoic FBI face. "We have been contacted by the person in our sketch." He let that settle in. A number of raised heads and eyebrows were visible. Attention will be paid. "Or so he claims," Brown continued. "Actually, his lawyer called our Bio-Killer contact number. They patched him through immediately when they verified the caller."

"Byron Hall, a founding partner of Hall, Strickland, and Bush Law Partners, one of the leading firms on the East Coast with international businesses, called to set up a meeting between us and their client. Mr. Hall and two of the firm's defense attorneys—one civil, one criminal, I was clearly told—would like to accompany their client to a meeting this evening around 7:30. That is PM. I told him that was most unusual. They say their client has a skin condition that keeps him from feeling safe even momentarily in the sun. They said, if the evening meeting cannot be done, their client would need to be assured that, wherever our meeting was, he could meet in an interior room and be admitted to a door as close to the curb as possible. Or at their law offices. I have a return call with Mr. Hall at 4:00 PM."

Lex broke in to ask, "Why all these people? Especially Virlus?" Brown didn't like interruptions but couldn't do anything about the high-level ones. Politics.

"If he is the real thing, frankly, I'd invite my grandson." Mortana noted that revelation. "Mr. Virlus's op-ed in the *New York Times* about police inadequacies in solving LGBTQI murder cases caught his eye. He tracked down the original piece in Mr. Virlus's paper. Saw his own face in our sketch. His lawyers say he is both astounded and concerned. The client assures them he has no involvement other than being in that bar. They knew nothing else except his naming all of you to be at a meeting."

"How do we know he isn't one of the usual attention seekers?" Lex sounded annoyed—probably because it seemed that Virlus kept one-upping him.

"I truly doubt that so prestigious a firm would allow a client, no matter how rich, to play hide and seek with the FBI." Brown had lost some of his patience. Lex was showboating, and Brown, like most of the Chief's own department, didn't like or trust him.

Dr. Arthur returned to the subject at hand. "Agent Brown, what do you think about this meeting that's been proposed?"

"We always like interviews to be on our turf. We like to control as much of the meeting as possible, have as much information as possible before we even *return* a call. Everyone here knows we have hit the proverbial brick wall." He called on Lieutenant Lemures, who knew her role.

"We have had no killings in this case in two months now. The trail is ice cold. I know everyone here, and certainly in Mr. Virlus's community, would like us to say we caught the person. If we have to rule out the man in our sketch, so be it. Transparency goes a long way to build community trust. And that has waned seriously in this case."

Knowing her brother's and his boyfriend's pressing for action, she tried her best to clarify further. "Charging an innocent man, even just saying he's a person of interest, gets us nowhere. Better to say we had a good lead that simply didn't pan out. Remember, none of the barkeeps who remembered the victims could identify our man in the sketch. We even checked out the bathtub killer victims' last sites. Clear the man on the flier, say he is not of interest any longer if that proves true. If he remains of interest, we now have physical contact and all the possibilities that implies."

Agent Brown explained that he would like consensus in the requested group so everyone could be unified at the meeting. Going in with different aims would be destructive to the investigation—and justice.

Commissioner Martel asked the person's name and what information the FBI or New York City police had on him. Chief Lex was fuming; his neck had literally reddened even though his face was a blank. Martel loathed Lex, and the loathing was mutual. Brown was not happy with the answers he had to give but knew the questions were logically inevitable.

"We know nothing about him, not even his name. His lawyer would only refer to him as Mr. Willow, admittedly a pseudonym. They say all would be above board and revealed at the meeting."

Victor urged, not hiding his annoyance, "Accommodate him tonight."

Whiska spoke up, "I would like a resolution of this case as soon as anyone. The truth and the law do not get served if we are barking up the wrong tree. I say accommodate him as far as his safety goes."

Brown asked Whiska to clarify what he was saying. "On your turf," Whiska said flatly, "during the day. If he is as wealthy as his law firm indicates, the press would not be kind if we treated him to a time or place of his choosing. People will only accept health needs to a point."

Victor was not as enthusiastic, wanting to move faster, but understood Whiska's point. He acceded, unhappily, to the meeting for the following day.

The Commissioner and CDC coordinator, Arthur, agreed.

Lex was the holdout. He enjoyed being the stuck cog in the wheel. Morgana tried to sooth his feathers by re-explaining the dangers of this bio weapon, pointing out that, if the arrest of the perpetrator, whoever it was, happened in New York City, the NYPD would get a huge share of the credit.

Lex was hoping, not before April. Primaries in June, election in November. People didn't remember last year, barely last month. He reluctantly agreed after losing the argument to hold the meeting at Police Plaza. Knowing he could figure out how to slow the case at any time, he decided it was better to play along. Play it long.

Brown and Mortana had hoped for this outcome. "I'll call for a meeting at FBI headquarters tomorrow," Brown concluded. "There's a parking garage in the building. This Mr. Willow and his lawyers can be driven directly inside. We will figure out the room and hallways as soon as they agree. Everyone, I will propose 10:00 AM." The 1950s FBI building, though upgraded, did not have a huge atrium with glass elevators, common by the end of the twentieth century.

Dr. Arthur had a problem. "I have a meeting with the Vice President at 8:00 AM here in D.C. I could be there by 1:00 PM. Two o'clock guaranteed."

Brown asked, "Anyone else? . . . So I will propose 2:00 PM New York time, tomorrow, Friday, October 8 at the FBI offices in Manhattan. You all know the address. You will be met at the desk by agents and escorted to the meeting room. Masks and metal detector checks are required. The meeting agents will explain firearm regulations when you arrive. They keep evolving.

"I'll text your official numbers with confirmation as soon as I have them. Thank you for being so flexible and prompt today. We have an interesting afternoon ahead. Be safe." He shut down the video feed. "Wait 'til they find out they'll need to give me their weapons to use a restroom." He smiled at the blank screen, remembering Lex's ruddy neck.

16

NOW, NEW YORK CITY

WHAT WAS THAT?" JASON RESENTED THE DIVERTING of attention from his planned evening.

"Agent Brown confirming tomorrow."

If we had land lines, they couldn't track us down, he thought, annoyed that their dinner was interrupted. First Victor's editor, then Mortana to Victor followed to himself, now Brown. All texts—at least that was a saving grace. "Shut the damn thing off."

"Hon, you know I needed to get that." Victor was not happy with having to placate him. He knew how important the meeting the next day was.

"I know. I'm shutting mine off—do yours." Jason was piqued.

"OK, don't get your panties all in a twist." Vic, who tried to play annoyed, wasn't sure it was playing.

Jason pulled himself together. He didn't want to be a cause for further tension tonight. "I'm nervous for you tomorrow. This guy could be dangerous."

Victor stopped him. "In the FBI office. Surrounded by cops and lawyers, please." Victor felt drama creeping into their supposedly romantic dinner.

They were at their favorite neighborhood tablecloth bistro. A table in a niche. Both facing outward, diamond-angled table for four, backs to the wall. Dark red walls, stenciled beams, brick pizza oven at the back. Long bar on the opposite wall, a row of tables between them and it. Italian movie stars framed on the walls. The doors fronting Eighth Avenue were open to the balmy fall night.

"Well, afterwards, when you're on your own." Almost sulking Jason continued, "I'm sorry. This has really gotten weird. I worry about you and Mortana."

"Baby, relax. Let's finish our dinner, and you can tuck me into bed. I may even let you stay over and do nasty things to me." Victor smiled at his own proposal.

"Don't make promises you can't keep."

"In that case, have I ever disappointed?"

"We'll have to set the alarm—I have an 8:00 AM class tomorrow. Psychology and Epidemiology."

"What does *that* mean?" Vic was doing his best to follow Jason's career's jargon.

"Well, for one thing, overcoming vaccine resistance in a population. Like the present mess in this country."

Jason brought the conversation back to their current third month anniversary, or eighth month if you included three years ago. "I have a toast. C'mon!" He poured a bit more wine in Victor's glass, "To us. The blond and the brunette, the salt and the pepper, the romantic and the realist."

"To us!" Victor sipped and asked, "Who's the romantic?"

"Why, me, of course, not the hard-boiled, crack news reporter."

"You don't think I'm romantic?" Victor sounded pissed.

Jason heard the edge in his voice. "Victor, why are we sniping?"

"I guess tomorrow has us both a bit more wound up than usual. I'm nervous, not about meeting the guy but about the outcome. Why so many of us? Why so secretive? Is this going to blow up or blow open the case? I'm sorry if I'm not being good company." Hesitating, he added, "I'm just *nervous*."

"Well, I have two people to worry about here. You and Mortana are deep in this. I always worry about Mortana. She picks dangerous occupations. I hadn't thought that yours could be too, but it can."

"Jason, honey, you are too sweet. You're right in some ways, but we are big kids and have a good handle on what we do. For Chrissake, your sis and brother-in-law survived a war twice —or was it three tours. I promise you, if there is any shooting or slashing, I'm the first under the table. I'm a proud coward."

"You're no coward. You played Monopoly with Calyce, my cut-throat niece."

Victor pounced on that perfect opening. "How would you like to make that 'our' cutthroat niece?" His face was nervous for the answer.

Jason slowly lowered his fork. Swallowed. Sipped his wine. "Victor Virlus, did you just propose to me?"

Victor produced a box out of his backpack, ceremonially folded back the cover, and cleared his throat, "I'm not kneeling down. But yes, Jason Patton Lemures, will you marry me?"

Eyes filling, choking on his words, Jason whispered, "I thought I was the romantic. You've ruined my reputation. Yes, Yes, of course!"

Victor put the black-diamond David Jurman ring on Jason's left ring finger.

Looking into his eyes, Jason said, "I love you so much."

"To quote my soon-to-be nephew, 'Ditto,' and more, so much more."

Victor secured the candle well away, not wanting any marring of the moment, and leaned in for a kiss—one slightly less intense than both were feeling, conscious they were being observed.

The table of three next to them applauded, shouted, "Congratulations!" then turned away so they could have their privacy.

"How did you know my size?" Jason was no longer fighting his tears—Victor either, as their happiness moistened their faces.

"The twins. I put them on the case."

"That's why Calyce was playing with my ring last Saturday. That girl is devious."

"Well, you did call her cutthroat."

"We need to get you one," Jason wanted them to announce their union without having to explain.

Victor reached into his pocket, then raised his hand wearing the identical ring, having maneuvered it onto his finger. Jason kissed him again.

"Let's pay the bill, Uncle Victor. We have people to call," Jason urged, anxious to share their news.

"And a bed to be fucked in," Victor cooed hungrily.

"ARE YOU ALL THERE?" DANNY, PREPARED FOR BED, assured him they were all assembled. "We are on my phone, speaker turned on."

The twins had been vibrating since their dad got them from their beds, explaining Jason and Victor had exciting news they wanted to share with them. Danny had more than an inkling. Mortana had finished showering and was brushing her hair. He called her through the door to come out of the bathroom. She had heard Danny's phone ring and thought it might be Abuela. Her hair was wrapped in a towel, and she had on her matching big bath robe they had bought from the Connecticut hotel their weekend away.

Mortana was surprised to see the kids on their bed. "Who's on the phone?"

"Sis, Jason and Vic here."

"Yes, Sis," Vic warbled.

"Are you two drunk?" Mortana asked.

"Sis, he asked me to marry him! I said yes!"

And then everybody was talking at once. Congratulations. What, when, where. . .no need for why. Answers were brief.

Vic was trying to be heard. "Mortana, your threesome there did this. Danny put the bug in my ear, and the kids helped with the ring."

Danny looked at the kids, hugged them, whispered, "You two are too good."

"Are you two sure?" Mortana asked, unsettled by the rapidity of it. "I mean, it's only a few months, maybe near a year counting before New Zealand."

"*I* certainly have never been so sure," Vic nervous for her approval.

"Sis, you know, everything in due time. Well, it do be time. The minute I saw him that night at our bistro, I felt he should be mine. He just beat me to the punch. . . . Sunday, family dinner so we can tell you everything. We have friends we need to call."

"Okay, but we cook—come here. We'll invite Abuela and the family, OK?" Mortana sniffed.

"That would be wonderful." Jason squeezed Vic's arm and pulled him in for a kiss. They were naked in Victor's bed, wrapped in his king size quilt, having rushed to his studio apartment, calls be damned. Lovemaking came first.

"We really have to go. It's getting late. We already have to violate Ron and Rich's 9:00 PM curfew."

"Future Sis, see you tomorrow. Love you! Love you all!" Vic sang out.

Jason added brightly, "I'll call you tomorrow night, Sis. Kids, Danny, you don't know how happy I am that you made this happen. We love you all."

"See you Sunday. We love you, *our* uncles." The twins had practiced that *our* just for this moment.

"Bye."

"Bye."

The phone went quiet. The twins were besides themselves. Danny was holding back tears. Mortana could not.

"Just wonderful, just wonderful." Danny was happily self-satisfied. What he hoped he'd set in motion when he cornered Vic in his office the month before had happened.

He looked at Mortana. "They never said they were helping Vic. Excellent secret keepers." He was squeezing the twins.

"I should be mad at the three of you that I wasn't in on this." Mortana wiped her eyes, sitting on the edge of her bed.

"You said 'in due time.' Jason said 'in due time.' Well, it do be the time," Danny joked.

Jeremy laughed. "We both thought we'd bust. But a promise is a promise. Vic, Uncle Vic, swore us to secrecy."

"We raised them well." Danny proudly eyed his recovering wife before he turned to the twins. "Give us a kiss, and off to bed, you two."

"Good night. You can cry now, Dad," Calyce teased. The twins closed their parents' bedroom door as they left.

Mortana secured the door lock; taking off her robe, she shook out her dark hair, long and sleek. "You deserve more than a kiss," she murmured as she slid naked into the bed next to him.

17

THEN, SICILY

P AULO TELLS ME I AM NEEDED to unload a boat arriving tonight or tomorrow night. I can't go sailing to drink in Taormina
or disappear during the day. Luckily I had a rendezvous with
the Admiral a day ago. I'm curious: This is the first time I have been
asked to help. Unless this is the first smuggling since I got here.

"Tunisia has shipped. The barrels will need handling. It all must be
done in one night." Paulo is managing this. Don Deimos has business
in Messina before these goods arrive there by our land transfer. Vincenzo is two weeks more in Siracusa's whore houses.

I'm curious what is coming in. Paulo tells me it is better not to know
sometimes. I think he is concerned that I might want a cut. I know
that bills of lading are often doctored to give the dock manager a cut.
The Don always expects the smugglers to be shady, padding, or stealing.
He is at their mercy. This Don doesn't have enough power to take on
the Tunis mob. He thinks his men would fear cheating him, but insults
and physical assaults eventually get paid back.

Currently, it will be in goods. Later, I hope to arrange a different bill.

I have been in on such schemes in my father's warehouses. I've witnessed it. His trusted chief manager, Jackolore, was skimming on boar carcasses. Jackolore saw I was going over the paperwork while I was laboring one summer in the butcher business. "So you will know honest men's toil," was my father's order.

Jackolore took me aside and said this was the way of the world. If I revealed his skimming to my father, many people who depended on him would be harmed. "Riches pour into your father's hands every day. He is not overly generous in our pay." He knew where my father was doing his own cheating. Italians expect vigorish, but the recent enterprises in Switzerland would be severely compromised. The Swiss have no concept of "go along to get along."

Jackolore offered me a cut. Being wise to the world and expecting to be the butt of my father's anger for something eventually, I had by then wisely started my secret money account to get me through to twenty-one. This cut would go a long way to fatten that. Future slices would enrich me more than Jackolore could because, while I was still fifteen years of age, my father paid all my bills—reluctantly. Reluctantly for my sister also. Happily for Elio.

I did not press Paulo. Before supper, I was playing with Nyxos under our almond tree. He had begun to try walking. I had him holding onto my fingers. He was bouncing more than taking steps. I made sure Paulo got to comfort his son, who began to cry. Pinching has that effect on babies.

It is starting to approach first light when we are done. I see one barrel being carted off by two of Paolo's henchmen. Yes, of course Paulo would need them. He had the ability to hide the loss but needed help transporting the goods to the fence. He would put money in their pockets. It bound them to him. Obligations are the net that traps everyone in this world.

Everyone is gone. He has opened a bottle of port and offers me a cup. I don't usually drink anything but red wine but I need to make progress with him tonight. We sit on an overturned rowboat near the dock.

"You must think me stupid."

I'm not surprise by this. I was expecting something sooner than later. No, I most certainly have seen that he is not.

"Paulo, I was waiting for you to say something. I have no intention of trying to play innocent. Nyxos belongs in your arms, correct?" I am cautious, noting his leonine expression, fierce, almost frightening.

"What you're saying can make shark chum. Be careful, finocchio."

"Paulo, no need to be rude. You are better than that."

"Is the chopping into shark bait less concerning than name calling?"

"Plain talk it is. I have zero intention of harming you, Nyxos, or Lucia. I know the secret and think you are far superior than the father and grandfather recognized by the church."

"What do you want?" Direct. Now or never.

"It's very simple: to destroy Vincenzo and my uncle. End the Tartus rein of moronic cruelty, their casual terror. Vincenzo and Deimos treat me like a soccer ball. Kick it whenever, wherever. Vincenzo makes my life hell. His father thinks it's funny. I escape in my boat when I can.

"Deimos is quick with his hands to the workers. Vincenzo apes him at every opportunity. But fear makes vinegar, not wine. You know this. Worse, a Don should care about his fief's prosperity, not bleed it dry only for his own."

"Don Deimos doesn't do that." It was an assessment, not an expression of loyalty. True, Deimos had expanded his fiefdom, made it prosper. Small farm holders supplied grapes for wine, olives for oil, raised his boars, for a fee. Discontent met with brass knuckles or the knife and the Ionian. I was not the only one making offerings to our deep mistress.

"Vincenzo has only the skill to give Nyxos rubble." Though I was voicing my honest opinion, I hesitated to let Paulo think of his child's future.

"Vincenzo is a brute. He diminishes the lives around him merely by his presence. If he suspected for a minute that Lucia was anything more than a submissive pet, he would march her naked through Riposto and gut her on Assisi's altar like a boar in the abattoir. Like Chronos, he would eat his own child. *Your* child."

Paulo's face emits light for a moment. Loyalty to your chief is a thing of great weight in Sicily. I have made his conundrum clear.

Paulo calls me a fool. Vincenzo can only be deposed of over Deimos's body. Vincenzo was as good as Deimos's son, not just his nephew. Augustus to his Julius. "Easy to kill, but Deimos has soldiers quick to vengeance. Even quicker to ravage the country to become the new Don if your double desire were achieved. The Colosseum would never have seen the likes of *that* extravaganza."

"Stop. Are you never to recover your family's fortune?" I had rehearsed this hundreds of times on my pillow.

"What are you talking about?"

"Franko Messina was your grandmother's brother. Your mother's uncle."

Paulo gives me a sidelong glance. I can feel him absorbing this. "How do you know Messina was mama's uncle?"

"Priests know everything. A bit of money on a collection plate can uncover many forgotten relationships without a name being spoken. Father Assisi once alluded to Old Father Pano, wryly laughed at Califo's daughter's seduction. Pano said you can't seduce a cat in heat. . . . Deimos drunk revealed that a few of his men were Messina's men's grandchildren. Two plus two needs proof to be four. So I asked Father Pietro how one could find out who from our compound was related to Franko Messina. He said, 'Baptism.'

"Three baptismal registers later, your mama is uncovered. As well as Sebastione Colon, Benedicto Adolpho, and Antonio Calabria, distant cousins."

"I'm running out of patience. Our family keeps track of our kin.

You already know too much about me. Where is your two plus two going? Get to your point. We will see if you breathe in the sunlight."

"My Paulo, dear Paulo, Deimos killed Messina. He said so to Vincenzo and me a few weeks after I arrived. I can repeat the details, but why hurt you further? I have heard that, for Sicilians, forgiveness is found under a headstone."

I press these olives, oiling the gears I've set in motion. "Seeing who took an orphaned barrel on the road toward Catania away from Messina, I would say Benedicto and Antonio may be allies in erecting that headstone. If anyone would be a superior Don, Messina's great-nephew Paulo Garaldi could not be a better choice. The means will be to build deeper obligations to you before any moves could be made. Blood requires blood in strong muscles and pliant minds."

Paulo is silent. I can see sparks flaring behind his dark eyes as the stolen barrel turns into a keg of gun powder. He takes the cup from his mouth. Tosses out the thick port. Already clear eyed, his words squeeze from tight lips: "Hold your tongue. Sharks live by blood. I need sleep and a head not afloat in Portuguese Madeira." Rising from our barnacled bench, he instructs me as he starts towards his bed, "Meet me in the olive orchard near the pruning pile after the mid-day meal. It may be time to burn that down."

WHEN I ENTER THE KITCHEN FOR LUNCH, Circe and Lorenzo are at the table. Lorenzo is a senior gardener, one of Circe's many informants. They keep Circe abreast of Deimos's and Vincenzo's shenanigans when her antenna are too far away. Some are women. All report what is taking place on the plantation. Only the Vatican has a better spy system. I put more names on my list to discuss at the wood pile.

Circe gets up and begins stirring the fish stew that perfumes the compound. I hope it is not shark.

Lucia rushes in with the baby. "He needed changing. Even octopus would not cover his smell." I laugh, taking him in my arms. There is no time to go outside and have Paulo walk his son. Paulo comes into the kitchen, eyes the attendees, and sits near Lorenzo, not me and Nyxos. On the worn farm table, Nyxos is banging the spoon I have given him. His mother comes over and takes it from him. She puts a crust of the fine bread she is known for in his little fist. He chews happily. "Banging gives everyone a headache. He has two teeth coming in. The bread will help him." I like the way she has communicated to Paulo.

Hearty soup and bread, cheese, some slices of cured boar, a little wine, water, and back to work. Paulo leaves before me. I linger, using the outhouse near the fields before following to the orchard. Paulo is chopping up some larger tree trunks. When I greet him, he asks that I take over the chopping while he gathers the bunches of tied branches that have been brought in from last fall's trimming. He piles them in the pit. I drag the logs in, stacking them over the faggots into a church spire.

We stand a bit apart, surveying the areas behind our companion guarding its emptiness. Paulo speaks first. "What makes you think I would take part in a plan to wreck the man who has shown me much favor? I am his chief bodyguard. He trusts me to manage the plantation when he is gone. I would be consigliere if Vincenzo weren't around. The past is buried."

"As you will be if either figures out Nyxos's paternity. Circe's consigliere always will be. Her spies are everywhere. Lorenzo isn't just an expert gardener. Those women who cook in the cantina, the ones in the fields, a few other men, they all seek her favor with tidbits of gossip that are as accurate as the baptismals I used. Just because a person wears skirts doesn't mean she isn't dangerous."

"This is pointless. Let me light this fire and walk away. Circe will be the chief no matter who is Don. We both know that. The road you propose is extremely dangerous. I plan to die an old man in my bed, not bleeding out as my body is pushed overboard."

I didn't expect this. In my head he was supposed to jump at the opportunity to raise himself higher than he thought possible. I will play my best card now or all is lost.

"Circe can be blunted."

"How?"

"What I tell you will give you a good deal of power over her. It will depend on how disgraced she feels if her secret is known. If she doesn't care, then her fate is tied to the two Beasts. It would serve you better to appear to have her blessing. Still, you will need to send her away either way because she is one who is totally Sicilian. I have the woman's sister for my mother, remember. . . . What I am going to tell you is absolutely true. There is no way to prove it that I can give you. Circe and Deimos are more than sister and brother. They are lovers."

"Stop! Enough of your fabrications. You have gone too far." The lion looks like he will roast me on our unlit pyre.

"Think harder. Vincenzo is a brute, lacking the cunning of his uncle. Why does his uncle dote on him so? Deimos tolerates more foolishness and inadequacy from Vincenzo than he would from DeAngelos's brain-damaged daughter. Take a moment, think."

"Are you saying the unthinkable?" Paulo's face squeezes in disgust.

"You have your Aristotelian argument in front of you. Lovers. Utter devotion from Deimos to Circe. Vincenzo's incredible favoritism. Now, *there* is a two plus two you cannot miss." The family tree I have just pruned had more than a little rot in its roots.

"Dear God. That is a pact with hell."

"I care nothing about their bedding and breeding habits. It is the hate they pour into the world that is their true crime. You can and will be a better Don and a finer father." I spit this out with vehemence. I do not reveal how this will repay my mother's lack of love, her vile expression of repulsion for my nature, and my father's very marrying into this cesspool, condemning me to a year of misery.

"You just want vengeance."

"Most assuredly. I could just do them myself and would. I could escape easily. I will have more money than Deimos will ever have in just a few months. But that would leave chaos. I care too much for Nyxos and Lucia. Father Assisi has been so kind to me that I would not like his parishes to turn into a charnel ground. I hope to see him bishop or cardinal someday. He has been my only friend until now. With proper planning, some money spread around, your building on the good graces of the soldiers who already trust you, we can get you the roles you are so better born to play in this fiefdom. In your son's life."

"The flaw in your little speech is money. I don't have that much," he scoffs, leaving an opening as wide as the channel between Messina and Naples. He knows I have assets.

"No, but Vincenzo does. Deimos does. They keep huge amounts locked in their houses. I have the means to get to it unseen. If necessary, I could finance this business with that knowledge as a guarantee of repayment. There would still be enough left. And you would have the Don's income."

Lorenzo comes down the path. I signal to Paulo, whose back is to him. Paulo orders me to light the pile, acting as though no one else is present. I go for a flame from the lamp he brought for the purpose. Lighting a pile of wood with a constant breeze from the ocean can be difficult. Lorenzo makes himself known, stepping next to me as I get the flames going.

Paulo acknowledges him. "I'll leave this to you two, now that Lorenzo is here, if he can spare the time. I could be doing something more useful than tending a fire." Lorenzo nods, silent as ever, always listening for the chink in the armor that would buy him Circe's gratitude.

As he turns to leave, Paolo directs these words to me: "When you light a fire, feeding it is easy, but you better be ready to contain it."

My gut burns. Destiny in the flames.

18

NOW, NEW YORK CITY

B YRON HALL, ESQ. WAS THE LAST TO SIT after one of the
other lawyers with him took the chair to the left of their client.
"First, thank you for accommodating my client. His allergy to
sunlight causes him to develop symptoms that can be disfiguring, definitely painful. It is called solar urticaria, so the stenographer can record
the name of his affliction." He gestured to the man typing on a stenographer's machine to the side of the room.

He introduced himself and each of the others, hand outstretched:
"William James and Nebu Wilson are junior partners of Hall, Strickland,
and Bush. We represent our client, Mr. Jonathan Beyer. His use of the
name 'Willow' was cautious on my part. Mr. Beyer is a very reclusive
man who cherishes his anonymity. He is an international financier. If
you want a list of the corporations he holds, we have it with us. We
would like to avoid any shred of publicity. The seriousness of this case
has Mr. Beyer's complete attention. He wishes to clear himself of any
connection to it other than happenstance."

Agent Brown informed the gathering that Dr. Arthur could not attend. "The weather has closed down Reagan International. There are tornado warnings. The train or driving would not get her here until past four. She sends her apologies."

Hall murmured, "No need for apologies. We appreciate that Dr. Arthur was willing to come."

The remaining introductions took place at the large curved rectangular table—in an interior room as had been requested. Water bottles sat at each seat. Two microphones on each side of the table were attached to a small recorder at Mortana's station. The three lawyers and their client occupied one side, and the others the opposite, with Brown and Lemures in the center of the New York team.

Agent Brown said, "OK. For the record." He nodded to the stenographer, and Mortana turns on the recording device. "Today is Friday, October 8, 2021. It is 2:00 PM, EDT. We are meeting at the FBI Offices in New York City. We are recording on both electronic and written devices." He gave the names and titles of all present for the record.

Agent Brown looked at Beyer. "State your full name for the record, please."

"Johnathan Augustus Beyer, III." He gave a home address on Riverside Drive the on Upper West Side.

"Mr. Beyer, we have assembled at your request. As you know, we are investigating the death of John Gerrard. We are working from a sketch we have made from a description given by a patron of the Cheers For All, Dance Bar at 75 Ridge Boulevard, in Bay Ridge, Brooklyn, New York City. Mr. Gerrard was last seen there having a conversation with the person in the sketch. Seeing you here, there is no doubt that the likeness is uncannily yours or a person who could be your twin."

"Mr. Beyer, where were you on the night of Wednesday, August 3, 2021, from approximately 9:00 PM until midnight?"

"I believe I arrived at the bar you named around 10:00 PM. I had driven there from my home to. . .shall we say, find companionship. I have a liking for men who are not. . .not seeking to be masters of the universe."

"How can you be sure of the date?"

"I completed and signed the paperwork for the purchase of a holding in Switzerland the next day. I checked my calendar and confirmed it with my accountant, as I knew it would be important to you. We did this all on closed-circuit TV. I am not about to fly to Europe these days. Two of my employees had tested positive upon their return when they flew to transport papers that had to have original signatures."

"Could you describe your time at the bar? What you did?" Brown identified himself for the recording to keep it clear who was talking.

"I ordered a seltzer. Watched the dancing. Spoke to a fellow whom I did not feel comfortable with. Had a young man approach me. Too young for me. Spoke with someone a bit older, more my type. Decided 'not tonight' and left."

"Could you describe the men you met?"

"The first one was shorter than me, rather nondescript, five foot eight or nine. He had brown hair, a beard, a mustache. Jeans, maybe a button shirt. Yes, a button shirt. I remember because he was a bit forward and ran his hand over my San Francisco tee, expressing a desire to try it on. He was trying too hard too soon. The young fellow, I shooed away ASAP. The third was in khakis, blue button-down shirt. He was clean shaven. Blondish. Wore glasses. He was two or three inches smaller than me, five foot eight or nine. About forty-five. We spoke for a while. I felt he was a bit disdainful of the place we were in. If anyone is going to be a snob, I would think it should be me." He chuckled slightly.

"Really, gentleman and madam, I know this is a serious matter, but I cannot take myself or anyone else seriously when our sole purpose at such a place is carnal. I guess I was there a little over an hour. Maybe ninety minutes."

"Did you go anywhere else afterward?" Again, Brown identified himself.

"No. I drove directly home. I was in bed by 1:00 AM. I have my own garage, so there would be no record of the exact time of entering—or leaving, for that matter, as a condo garage would." He turned to one of the lawyers, "Mr. Willow, could you have your secretary call my butler and ask him to arrange an electronics device to do that. When my nephew visits, I think I need to know his comings and goings a little better.

"Excuse me, I'm so self-centered. I didn't want to forget to do that now that its usefulness has presented itself. Please, next question."

"Can anyone testify to the time of your return to your home?"

"No, my servants don't usually live on the premises. I think people should have their own space away from work. I grew up with servants who lived in. They seemed to have no lives except my family's. I cannot think of a worse condition to subject a person to. I own an apartment a few blocks away that my man servant and his companion live in. If needed he can be at my service in an hour's time. The other servants are not at my call as he is. They have duties and fixed times, like any other job."

"If you had found a companion, would you have gone to their home or taken them to yours?"

"Neither. Most definitely not mine. There are three or four motels nearby. I Googled them. I would have taken the gentleman to one of them. I would have paid cash. I want to leave as few trails as possible. I had an incident of attempted blackmail in my younger days. I keep my carnal life isolated from the rest of it. I am very uncomfortable discussing all this, but I swore to be honest. It is better for me if we can conclude this business today and I can leave it all behind me."

"A few more questions, please." Brown looked at some notes.

Chief Lex cleared his throat; Brown acknowledged him. "I hope you don't mind, but our attendees may have questions. I'm sure Chief Lex does. And I presume you might have some for them, as you requested their presence. First let's finish these.

Lex asked, "Had you been to this bar before?"

"No, in fact it was my first visit to Bay Ridge, except perhaps for driving through. If I can be frank, I usually pay for companionship. Meeting at a convenient boutique hotel. This was an experiment in breaking out of my shell. That is why I have as good a memory of those men as I do. It did not go to my liking—now *doubly* not to my liking. I think this turtle is done with that. I feel totally exposed. What else?" He looked at the others, his voice slightly exasperated.

Hall asked, "Mr. Beyer, do you need a break?"

"I'm not a wilting flower. Thank you, though. Let's continue."

Lex went on, "Why are the rest of us here?"

"Chief Lex, correct?" Beyer looked for confirmation. Lex nodded.

"The fact that you, all highly ranking people, were willing to come today speaks to how serious this matter is. If catching this killer can bring you to a meeting with a suspect, think how I feel being sketched as a person of interest. Being a recluse does not mean I'm a hermit. I would like to go to dinner and the theatre without having whispers about me because someone recognizes a supposed criminal.

"You are chief of police so your role here is obviously the same as that of the other law enforcement agents. I prefer to deal with the heads of corporations, so it is logical that the head of New York's Finest would be a person I feel comfortable having present while solving this dilemma. It is totally within your ability to make certain I am eliminated from any future dragnets. I'm jesting, of course, but only a little.

"Commissioner Martel, again head of your department but on the political front. Not to diminish your importance, for me the mayor would seem more a more likely choice, but that would be, shall we say, pushing it. Besides, Mr. Martel, I think you have a bright future in politics in this city. It doesn't hurt to have had a face-to-face, so we have established a contact if one of my companies has to have dealings with the government of this city in the near future. By the way, a city I have come to love.

"I should say the same to Chief Lex. I think police chiefs often enter politics when they leave that powerful position."

Beyer stopped, had a drink of the spring water in front of him. "Plastic is going to eat this planet," he said to no one in particular.

Turning to Dr. Whiska, he went on, "Lambda has been on my radar for a long time. I donate through my corporations. I asked that you be here because I trust that you would care that a member of your community not be subjected to bias. My lawyers here are experts in matters I want them to be expert in but do not live our lives, no matter how different my economic situation is from yours and Mr. Virlus's. I trusted that you would speak up to a subtlety they might not catch—although I think Mr. Wilson has a good track record in identifying micro- aggressions." He acknowledged the African American lawyer to his left.

Returning to Whiska, he said, "I looked up your resume and curriculum vitae and was most impressed.

"Last, Mr. Virlus. 2V." He smiled at Victor, his first actual facial expression that afternoon. "Your op ed and article about the murders and police bafflement were admirably written. Your tracking me down was well done, however misplaced. I think you have a knack for presenting the community's anger and concern without stirring up unreasonable hostility for the police in this case and elsewhere. I have read some of your past essays in the GNP. If anyone is able to see that I am publicly exonerated with as much honesty and anonymity as possible, I believe it would be well within your skill set.

"As for Agent Brown and Lieutenant Lemures, their presence is beyond logic. I hope in the future I never see either again unless, it is totally social."

"I haven't asked the most important question, Mr. Beyer." Brown paused. "Did you or anyone you know have anything to do with Mr. Gerrard's death?"

Hall raised his hand slightly and leaned over to his client. They turned away from the table and had a short conversation inaudible to the rest. Hall looked to his colleagues. Some signal had been sent. Chief Lex wished they had filmed this so he could discover what it was. Wilson, then James, nodded. Apparently a go-ahead.

Beyer answered, "I have no reason not to answer. No, I had nothing to do with his passing. I have no knowledge of anyone else being involved."

Brown followed up, "Do you know anything about his death?"

"Cliche as it is, only what I have read in the newspapers."

Brown looked around. "More questions?"

There were none.

"Mr. Beyer, do you have any questions?"

"Just this—when will I be exonerated? I would very much like Mr. Virlus to publish that the person of interest has been removed from any suspicion."

James pointed out, "As Mr. Beyer's criminal lawyer, since our client has no reason to be charged, we would like that statement as soon as possible."

Brown had no comment about that. "As of now, Mr. Beyer, we appreciate your candid remarks. Thank you for stepping up."

To the lawyers, he added, "Thank you, gentlemen. If we need to speak to your client in the future, we will let you know."

"Well, my lawyers were mostly silent. I guess you didn't compromise my civil rights. Thank you all. Good afternoon." Beyer proceeded to the door.

Hall stopped to confirm with Agent Brown, "You have my direct number. My secretary will have instructions to put you right through."

"Your escorts are at the door. They will see you to the garage. Again, thank you." Brown held the door open for the four men and waited until the elevator indicator showed the number of the floor below.

To the New York team, he said, "A short break. If you leave this room, please put your firearms on the table at your seat. Rest rooms are to the right. Code four three one men's, five seven four ladies'."

Lex began to leave, thought better of it, and laid his pistol on the table.

TEN MINUTES LATER THEY WERE IN THEIR SEATS. Brown had sent out for coffee and tea. One of the escorts brought it in while they were getting back together. Brown began, "Well, what do you think?"

"Now that we know where he lives," said Lex, "I'll order surveillance. We don't have enough on him to convince a judge for a wiretap."

"Could you put the team under Lemures' command?" Brown asked. "It will make things simpler. I also don't see us getting a wiretap. I'll contact legal after we finish, just in case."

Lex was unusually cooperative. "I'll be happy to give the lieutenant command."

"Opinions." Brown looked from one to the other.

Martel felt he was probably telling the truth, although he had never heard of Mr. Beyer. He thanked Lex for putting the surveillance team in motion and wondered what businesses the man was involved in, the size of his wealth. They only had his word. Wait and see was the Commissioner's standard approach in most things.

Brown, holding the corporate list that Wilson took out of his brief case, said, "Half the companies on here are Swiss headquartered. I wonder if he is a member of that Beyer family. I'll get one of our researchers on it. I should have the information you're asking by tomorrow afternoon. We'll dig up as much about him as we can find.

"Let's see what our departments can find out about him. Does he have social connections that are traceable or would be helpful?" Brown conjectured. "Dr. Whiska, does Lambda share information about donors?"

"As much as the law requires."

"I guess you could save my people a little time. I'll have this list sent to you. Just let us know what you are allowed to."

"Send it to all of us," Lex asked. Looking at Victor, he added, "Him, too."

Whiska agreed, adding his opinion: "Typical of my experience of some corporate types. Not quite in the closet. Not quite open. Definitely finds it easier to buy sex than to spend time looking. If he's not our killer, then this attempt to put himself out there that he described indicates a lack of some basic LGBTI social skills. He does not seem to be a man who tolerates failure. If the attempted blackmail is true, his closet door is more closed than open. That is usually a psychologically damaging position."

Victor agreed. "I think he was telling the truth about the bar and his—what did he call it?—his carnal life. I haven't known any super-rich people, but his whole rent boy story is common among the Wall Street types that I know. If Amazon listed them, they would order escorts on there. He certainly sees to it that he is well protected. Three lawyers—the boss, a criminal, and a civil one to cover all bases. I'm curious about his wealth. I'm not one hundred percent sold he is definitely not our guy."

Mortana cautioned, "While he was up front, we still have him as the last contact with Gerrard. Surveillance is our best option, but he will surely be advised by his lawyers that he will be watched." She asked Chief Lex, "Will you pick the team?"

"I'll get you a list of the best, and you can figure out the duty roster."

"Anyone else?" Brown looked about him.

Victor raised his eyebrows. "What about you, Agent Brown?"

"He came across as honest."

"There's a but in there."

"Surveillance will tell. If he's the killer, time will tell. Remember, the killer is using a biological agent. Beyer is drugs, if he has connections there. Even if not, he seems to have the means to purchase almost anything. Typically, serial killers get arrogant and therefore sloppy. Any mistake, we will be at the door knocking."

Everyone agreed he was smart enough to expect to be watched with or without the three lawyers at his sides.

Brown opened the door, and they started to leave.

He gestured to the two agents sitting in chairs lining the hall. "Ben, Mack, you're on duty. Don't let our guests get lost."

"Goodbye. We will keep each other informed." As Victor passed him, he murmured, "Mr. Virlus, thanks for your help. You know this is all off the record. When we have a final opinion, you get the story first as promised."

Mortana grabbed Victor and kissed his cheek. "See you Sunday. This guy is going to be my brother-in-law. Sooner than later, I hope."

Brown smiled. "Congratulations, I guess. Been there, done that." Mortana added that to her Brown notebook.

"All will be revealed. See you Sunday." Victor beamed.

"Mortana, stay." Brown waited for the elevator to leave. He closed the door to the conference room and indicated for her to sit. He took the plastic top off his paper cup. Drank. Tossed the empty cup into the waste basket at the door.

Mortana offered her cup. "I haven't touched it. It's black. I like with milk."

"Pass it over. . . . The surveillance teams need to be extra careful. This Beyer is smarter than our average cop. He knows we'll have him tailed. We may be in for the long haul."

"Lex was unusually generous. I wonder what's up with his nod to

Victor. You know, of course, the teams will be reporting to Lex first."

Brown gave her a look. "And holding back. We'll go over Lex's list. I'll get an FBI plant on those teams."

Mortana was not entirely surprised.

I THANKED MY LAWYERS BEFORE I LEFT the black SUV. We had pulled under the *porte-cochère* to the mansion. "Please, relax. I have told the truth. We will leave them to what they need to do. Good evening, thank you." I entered the door held open by my butler.

The gates to the cobbled driveway closed, locking automatically. "Good evening, Henri. Did you put out my red?"

"Yes, sir. Shall I pour it?"

"No, I'll get comfortable first. You're free until tomorrow afternoon, say four. I'll take care of myself for the rest of the evening."

"Very good, sir. May I ask, how did it go?"

"As well as can be expected. I didn't like using the Beyer identity, but it has the best provenance for this case. The paper trail is nice and full. It will do. I have an important call to make. Thank you for getting the drapes. I really like the new windows in Brooklyn so much better than these. Good night."

"I'll be in the Ninety-fifth Street apartment, sir."

"Yes, near enough. Turn the exterior lights on low. Set the alarm. Thank you."

Henri bowed very slightly and left.

I went to my bedroom, stripped, and put on a heavy robe. I heard the front door being locked. Returning to my sitting room, I placed the crystal decanter on the side table near my overstuffed chair, put my feet up on the hassock, and pressed my nephew's speed dial number in Albuquerque.

"Gaspar. . .yes, it's done. Your turn now. You have it arranged for tonight? Good. Please, that is not funny. You know I hate it when you call me that."

Listening to him complain, I said, "Your reward is you get to do the last one. Elio will find you shortly. No, he will. He has amazing powers in that way. . . . Yes, I know I had the most. I paid for the research. I helped Barbara form The Six. We've had our adventure. Be patient, Barbara is the incarnation of a Hollywood mad scientist. . . . The Six is over for now. It is fortuitous that production spread our games out, no overlapping. I have warned the others. Barbara is reigned in, as are we. Lie low after this. Your success tonight will get their surveillance teams removed from my door. Mr. Beyer will be exonerated. He can fly to Bern, and I will resume my life on Willow Place for a while longer. Have fun tonight. I want a full description tomorrow. Make sure he is discovered by the morning.

"Nephew, I love you like a son, but you most definitely are not." I hit end. Beyer, for a moment more, being Beyer, poured himself more red.

19

NOW, QUEENS, NEW YORK

BEWARE OF WEDDING-ZILLA. Are you sure you want them to do the planning?"

"Jay, your sister, Abuela, and Eva will burst into flames if we don't. You heard their minds spinning, tongues wagging, the minute I brought it up. We'll control the service. Well, Ron will, he's the pastor. Rich will control him." These last two were The Boys, their best couple friends.

"What about Calyce?"

"I already have a deal with her and Jeremy to spy on the planning blitzkrieg. They will let us know the machinations that we need to nix. Those kids can manipulate those women. You know how they dote on them."

"Juan will stay out of it. He's busy with his new job." Jason was watching Astoria pass by the car window. "Danny is the wild card. Now that he takes credit for all this, he is not about to sit back."

"Let him plan our bachelor party." Victor was not joking.

"Our Gay friends will kill us. What do straight guys know about bachelor parties except bar hopping?"

"Like we're so wild. I'll ask Bill if he could team with Danny. Bill has four straight brothers-in-law. He goes out with them occasionally."

The duo were in an Uber being driven from the Santos's Sunday engagement dinner to Jason's Chelsea apartment.

They stopped at a light. The driver turned to them. "Get the fuck out. I don't have fags in my car. Diseased sinners."

". . .What? Victor, did I hear him right?" Jason was dumfounded.

"You heard me, get the fuck out. You're going to burn in hell. Get out." More than a little rage was rising in the voice.

Victor took a "make us" stand. Jason tried reason. Victor threatened the guy's job. The guy threatened violence with a machete he pulled out from a sleeve stuffed next to the passenger seat. They fled, jumping out of their closest doors. Victor grabbed Jason's arm and ran a short distance, around a corner. The car sped off.

Shaken, they Googled the nearest subway closest to get them to Chelsea.

Jason called Uber as soon as they were safely behind his locked door. They were assured the company took such accusations seriously. Had they been physically harmed? Had they called the police? Please do. They would take that car out of rotation immediately. The person he spoke to guaranteed they would get back to him by tomorrow.

Victor called the Anti-Violence Project. Since it was Sunday night, they weren't physically harmed, and had each other, they decided not to go in. The intake person asked them if they could come in first thing in the morning, Monday. "We open at eight-thirty. We can accompany you to the police." They were shaken but agreed.

Jason tried to minimize what had happened. "Look, we're okay. Nobody got hurt."

Victor was livid, his body physically shaking. Jason got them both a glass of wine, the strongest thing he had in the house.

Victor asked, shouldn't they call Mortana? Jason needed for them both to calm themselves before that. Victor decided to call George Whiska. They both knew him. Jason was hesitant. It's Sunday, they were all right.

Victor was adamant. "You are in denial. We need to call out the baying hounds."

"OK. OK. I know you're right. That fuck really rained on our parade. A fucking machete. . . ."

"Well, I'm glad Babs is still with us." Jason laughed. They both laughed, releasing a bit of the tension.

Victor called George and told him what had happened. "Good God, guys. This needs to go to the police."

"AVP says they will take us."

"Do you need to go to the hospital? This is bad."

"No, we have each other. He didn't touch us, just threatened."

George grumbled, "You don't know how often stuff like this happens. A bartender ignores Gay guys who drop in. A doctor tells the guys to find a new physician in the future. AVP, Lambda, ACLU, Human Rights Commission, hear them all. People are prejudiced, as simple as that. Trump made it okay. All of the minority groups have an uptick in incidents. People are filming the worst that can happen. Sometimes the perps themselves post videos of their criminal attacks. You sure you guys are all right? Do you need help?"

"We are upset, but nothing more physical than threats and shouting happened. We'll be okay."

"I want you to call me any hour if you need to. That's a promise, not an offer." He asked that they call him at his office after they get done at AVP. He'd connect them directly to Lambda Legal's reporting desk person. Jake Benson would guide them better than he could.

They called Mortana. She wanted to come over. She put the phone on speaker; Danny had been asking what was wrong. Once she was assured they were all right, she asked, had they called 911?

"We just wanted to get away from there. We got into the subway in what seemed like seconds."

She was more than furious, cursing up a hurricane of epithets. They told her not to come.

Danny asked, "Are you sure?"

"It's okay. We're okay."

Mortana insisted she go with them to report it to the local precinct.

Putting on her cop hat: Did they have the driver's name? Yes. Car plate number? No, they think Uber will give it to them. They know the car make, etc.

"OK, get the info from Uber. AVP can help when you go there. I'll meet you at AVP, eight-thirty, right? I'll go with you to the precinct. My badge will help get their attention."

"They won't do anything." Jason was disgusted.

"It's a bias attack. That brings double penalties. You can't threaten people with a God-damned machete. No one threatens my brother and brother-in-law."

The city official speaking: "This also belongs with the T&L Commission. And statistics matter." Switching back to big sister: "You sure? Danny and I can be there in less than an hour."

Victor leaned into the phone. "We have each other. I think a shower and bed is in order right now."

"Call us if you change your mind. Call me first thing. I'll meet you at AVP. Promise to call if you need us."

"I promise," Jason swore.

"Victor, listen to us." Danny had taken over. "We are here for the two of you. No brave faces. You change your minds, and we fly there."

"Thanks, but we are safe behind many locks. We need bed and sleep. If that's possible." They ended with expressions of love. "Don't tell the kids, please. Not yet."

"Okay. Sleep. Please try to sleep," Nurse Mortana prescribed.

The men planned their Monday in new configurations on calls to their respective bosses.

Dr. Shakira Bailey, Jason's boss, asked how she could help. Yes, of course he could have tomorrow free. She'd post his office hours cancellation. If he needed Tuesday, she could cover his lectures. She had had her own incidences; being Black, your skin attracts bigotry. She expressed her sorrow that they had to have it happen. "I'm here, if you need to talk." Jason couldn't bring himself to say it was their family's engagement party for them.

Victor's editor was furious. Gil Krier rhetorically asked how many times they had to expose these crimes against the community. "People need to stop chalking it up to city life and Trump. *Do* fucking something. Ignoring verbal attacks, threats, and things like getting thrown out of cabs even without threats of violence fuels worse. Murders against LGBTI people are up. Trans women especially. Black Trans women particularly." Gil almost couldn't stop his anger. "You've been writing about the latest. Take tomorrow, get Jason's sister on it. We publish on Friday. Have copy to me on Thursday."

"Thanks a lot, Gil," Victor replied, expecting more sympathy.

Gil ordered, "Put the anger you feel in the piece. Put the fear you feel in it. Put Jason's feelings in it. Put the experiences you have wherever you report in it. Plan at least one more piece next week. If the politicos see it as useful, we'll have a long run with you doing the main writing."

Gil shifted back to disturbed friend, "Really, guy, are you okay? Jason okay? Need company? I can hold your hands. Or any other parts you want me to."

"Gil, you're a dirty middle-aged man. Love you for it."

"Not kidding, guys. Do you two need a sitter?"

Jason had been listening to the whole thing. They had both used speaker setting to not feel alone in these conversations. Jason appreciated how nice an offer it was. "Maybe tomorrow, when we have a better handle on what just happened."

They ended the conversation with an assurance from Gill he would be forcing himself on them then.

Vic felt calmer. He could see how to take back a semblance of control of his life after talking with his boss. He formulated a plan, thinking out loud to Jason.

Jason thought it time to be harder on the police. "I know my sister is a police officer. I think that she needs to see what happens to people like us when they need justice, response from the cops." He had participated in a fair amount of activism in the past, seen police indifference, once even hostility, when trying to report a crime. "Should we call the boys?" he asked Victor.

"No, I'm exhausted. They would not take no for an answer. In the morning." Victor poured them more red. "Here, it's not blood, yet."

Jason started crying. On the couch they'd been using as crisis central, Victor, arm across Jason's shoulder, pulled him closer still, trying to meld into him, kissed Jason's cheeks and forehead. Rubbing his shoulder, he looked at him and said firmly, in an *I'm taking control* voice, "I know. We'll get that bastard. You know I'll never let the bastards win, at least try not to. I am not letting this damage you or me." Victor knew it was partly bravado on his part, but one of them needed to be the strong one this time round, and hugged him. They sat holding each other for a few minutes more. "I love you," Jason said, and kissed him.

"Ditto." Jason smiled wanly at Victor's occasional adoption of Jeremy's love expression. "Get up." He pulled Jason to his feet. "Let's wash this crap off us." He guided them to the shower. They undressed, scrubbed each other vigorously. Dried off.

In bed, Victor almost growled into Jason's ear, "I love you so much," aggressively seeking intimacy. Jason responded equally. It was releasing, reassuring, reconfirming, restorative, rearmament sex.

It was make-up sex with the City that had betrayed them.

Spent, exhausted emotionally and physically, they curled into their puppy pile.

20

NOW, NEW YORK CITY

HENRI, WE WILL STAY HERE for another two weeks. Just because I'm exonerated doesn't necessarily mean the police have given up on me entirely. You know my caution. I think a full six weeks will be sufficient. We'll return to Brooklyn when Mr. Beyer boards his plane to Switzerland."

"Very good, sir. Can I get you dinner?"

"Not tonight, I'll be going out. A snack perhaps. I'm meeting Mr. Virlus and his fiancé in Chelsea."

That raised an eyebrow.

"I'll be home around midnight. If any later, I'll call you." I always feel Henri should not wait for my return uninformed.

"Tomorrow starts your weekend. Any plans?"

"Thomas and I are going antiquing in Connecticut. Did you forget? You said we could use the Infinity."

"Of course. I'm sorry. There have been a few distractions. I'm using the Tesla, so the Infinity is all yours. Are you two looking for anything in particular?"

"Thomas has started a collection of porcelain dogs. I'm interested in Native American jewelry and objects, as you know. You admired the Maria Martinez pot I got last year. We are just hunting. Nothing specific. God knows we have more than enough things."

"Well, have a good time. Perhaps you'll have something interesting to show me when you get back. I do love seeing your finds."

Henri has exquisite taste for rare objects in the areas of his interest. His Japanese phase filled a vitrine with beautiful ceramics. He helped me to find the Nori Sashida plate I had used with Elio.

"Could you lay out my burgundy outfit? Immediately. Thank you."

After he puts the clothing on the silent butler, laying the jacket on the bed, I nod approval.

"Anything else, sir?" I shake my head, sipping the aperitif glass of my favorite red that Henri has poured.

"I'll let you know when I'm leaving." I like to treat Henri more like a roommate than an employee. His formality melts away when we're in Brooklyn. I suspect the Victorian mansion brings out his Victorian butler side.

"Very good, sir." He quietly closes the bedroom door.

I find it much easier to have my clothing arranged in sets. My dressing room is the size of a small boutique on Fifth Avenue. This burgundy set consists of a burgundy shirt, black jeans, black loafers, a black leather jacket this time of year, and a burgundy Barbour for the winter. I choose my underwear and socks on whim. I like interesting prints. They make for interesting conversation. Everything is computer catalogued.

I'm a bit miffed that my exoneration hasn't been as well publicized as I had hopped.

V2 didn't even write the piece; the editor did. I guess I'm more annoyed about that, actually. The editor devoted the editorial page to my exoneration and letters to the editor about crimes against LGBTQI people during Covid. An op-ed piece was about community cooperation with the authorities.

I found Mr. Virlus intriguing. Rather attractive, actually. Crusading to save the people. Good writer. Physically nicely appointed. Winning smile. Long neck. Exotic face and coloring. I took inventory when we met at the FBI conference.

His new series about the unfortunate Uber event got me thinking about meeting him on a more personal level. I would like to write my memoirs, and that would take cultivating a co-writer. My peculiarities would take a special kind of ghost writer. This dinner is just a preliminary social engagement.

Interesting but logical that Jason Lemures is his fiancé— the second of the pair my agents identified who started this whole affair. More so that his sister is who she is.

I easily reached him through his newspaper. I offered my condolences for his and his future husband's near violent episode. He was cordial but cautious, a good thing to be if you are a newspaper reporter.

I complimented his new series, noted that it had stirred up the city. The mayor and the city council had already set up a special committee to investigate and make recommendations about police reforms in response to Black Lives Matter. His reporting widened the public's awareness to the dismal reaction to LGBTQ lives.

I asked him and Mr. Lemures to dinner. My treat. Just to be social. He said he would ask Jason.

We tentatively agreed on Thursday night, around eight. From his articles I was able to glean which was their favorite restaurant in Chelsea. I said if it wasn't invasive, we should go there. Were there to be a next time, it would be to my favorite. He confirmed on my private line via text.

I THINK HE'S LONELY, VICTOR TEXTED JASON.

Okay. Nothing like having dinner with a super-rich ex-murderer. Jason added a winking emoji.

Don't joke about that. I know he wants that far away from himself.

Ur right. Dinner is fine. CR is OK. We won't need to get dressed up.

"I KNOW THIS IS PECULIAR, BUT I'M GOING to have desserts only. I developed a sweet tooth in Bavaria and rarely indulge it. But tonight I feel celebratory. I haven't had a night out since I came upon mister, may I call you Victor?—" a nod from Victor— "Victor's sketch article of me."

"Fine with me, Mr. Beyer."

"Please call me Augustus. My father was Jonathan also, so the family called me Augustus, my middle name. I never got a nickname that stuck except for Sailor, which is another story and allowed to only one person."

"I've always been Jason. Victor and I sometimes call each other Vic or Jay, but that's for us. And some cutesy lovey-dovey stuff."

"Charming. V2 isn't a nick name?" I asked, looking at Victor.

"More of a reporter's shorthand."

The server brought the bottle of red that I had chosen from their wine list. Jason noted it was not the most expensive but did approach that. The server uncorked it and asked whether he should let it sit. I indicated my glass.

He poured enough for a taste. I approved, and he poured for each of us.

"Nice simple bouquet. A friend of mine has interests in the winery. I've had it a number of times."

I reminded them, "Remember, my treat. Without sounding gauche, cost is of no concern. Please, let's make this a release-from-almost-house-arrest party."

Victor knew from the post-Albuquerque Bio-Killer police conference that I could order everything available on the menu and consider the total a decent tip for the waiter. He had, I imagine, appraised Jason of that fact while they dressed.

Jason ordered his favorite—seafood salad, chicken marsala, a side of spinach with garlic.

Victor had a pear-and-gorgonzola salad, lobster Fra Diavolo, and stuffed mushrooms. Jason thought, Well, he didn't hold back, but had no regrets over his choices.

I asked if the restaurant had Italian-style creampuffs. "Bring them when my friends' entrees arrive. And a bottle of sparkling water. I will be having another dessert later. Think of what you would consider your most enticing. I'll leave it up to you when these gentlemen order theirs."

We discussed the duo's backgrounds. Jason's current position at the university. Their Covid experiences. I told them about my time in Sicily. "I was twenty. A gap year after college. I was advanced. I loved to sail and would go to these little islands in the Ionian Sea between Riposto and Taormina. To my regret, I often sunbathed in the nude often. My Italian skin let me turn a golden brown, which helped my love life immensely but ended up poisoning me. As the years have passed, sun exposure increasingly causes me pain at best and often damages me in ways that take many Swiss doctors and huge numbers of francs to cure. That is why I'm a night dweller."

"That sounds awful," Jason sympathized.

"Almost as awful as your recent experience. Victor's account was hair-raising. They caught the perpetrator, did they not?"

"Mr. Basil Black is facing six months to four years of incarceration. Double for a bias crime. Using a machete as a threat comes under the criminal law." Victor said it would be in his next column.

I turned to Jason. "Having a prominent police officer as a sister must have been most helpful."

Victor laughed. "Once she stopped cursing. She was in the Marines. When we called her, the list of expletives she spewed was bracing. Some in Pashtun, maybe Urdu, I'm not sure. As she put it, no one threatens her baby brother and her brother-in-law."

"I had a woman in my past who could do the same. Women are not the delicate flowers foisted on us be in the past."

We spent the rest of the dinner talking about the duo's wedding plans. I spoke of my need to fly to Switzerland shortly. They finished their desserts plus two American coffees, and I mine with one double espresso. I paid in cash.

We had our jackets on in the cool November air.

They walked with me to my car, a dark blue Tesla. "How's it drive?" they asked almost simultaneously.

"Very nicely. There are a few limitations, a few kinks, but considering the advance in technology, it's brilliant."

They were almost drooling. "I usually hate cars," said Jason. "But this one I could love."

"Let me drop you off."

"We're at Jason's tonight, a very short walk," Victor said, flirting without realizing it.

"Soon expanded, we hope," Jason confided. " I have a neighbor who's considering selling her apartment. A studio, next to my one-bedroom. We could just put in a door between them and have a place for home offices. All our married friends say two bathrooms make relationships happier."

"If we can afford it. I rent right now. No capital gains." Victor's revelation spoke pages about his salary.

"I'm sure you'll work it out." I restrained myself from offering financial assistance.

"Thank you for this lovely night. It was most generous." Jason held out his hand.

"My pleasure. Definitely a good release party. I hope the first of others." I climbed into my car. While I drove silently away, they waved good bye.

"THAT WAD OF CASH!" VICTOR EXCLAIMED.

"One Mr. Beyer has the hots for you," Jason observed. "Do I need to be jealous?"

"Don't be silly."

"He couldn't take his eyes off you, maybe you not taking yours off him?"

"He eyed *you* enough."

"You gave him a hard-on," Jason teased.

Victor was a bit pleased by that idea. "Get a grip." Victor grabbed his arm. Released it.

They did not hold hands on the way home. Uber Astoria had done its damage.

"HELLO, MR. COCHRAN, IT'S ME. Yes. I have a name I want you to vet. Mr. Basil Black. He has been in the news. Bias incident, anti-Gay. Drove for Uber. Yes, correct, a machete. Tomorrow is good. Use the encoded address."

I click on my drive gate opener a block before I arrive, turn in without stopping. Pull the Tesla into the garage. Everything locks when I click the car key. Mr. Black, shortly, very shortly, I roll in my mind.

The door between the garage and manse opens. "I'm back before twelve, Henri." Almost a teen early for curfew.

Henri smiles. "Was your engagement pleasant?"

"Most. Two charming men. Mature but young. Delicious. I promise myself not to eat them up. Could you draw me a bath? I need to think. Some red, please. Then get yourself home to Thomas."

21

THEN, SICILY

I HAD MADE WAX IMPRESSIONS OF THE KEYS on Circe's chatelaine when she had me lock up Vincenzo. She spent the night caring for Lucia. I returned the keys in the morning, saying I had thought better of disturbing the two women and the baby.

The next day I waxed Vincenzo's keys when I gathered his things for his purgatory month. For money, the foundry in Taormina asked no questions to sand-cast them.

Those gave me a chance to assess the cash stored by the Tartus men—more than enough to restore the fortune I was lending to Paulo to bribe loyalty to him, some before, much after, our plan was finished. Circe had all the keys necessary for the security of the compound, an obvious advantage when setting the plan in motion.

Vincenzo's disappearance would be of little consequence. With no heir, the fiefdom would be ripe pickings when the Don died. The child was not a consideration. My dilemma was that I wanted both of those beasts to know it was *my* plan, *my* execution.

I wanted Vincenzo to know he was an incestuous bastard. He was horned by Lucia, his son Paulo's. I wanted Don Deimos to realize he and his bastard had been doubly betrayed by his own bodyguard. I wanted Circe's silence.

Paulo and I agreed Circe would stay in the Riposto compound until I went back to the mainland, giving him legitimacy. I would see her to my mother's care. Most deliciously, I would dump her secret on my father and expose my mother for the liar she was, revealing the incestuous nature of his in-laws. He would not be able to send Circe back because Deimos's successor would expose her and see her shame spread to Milan.

The whole missing heir and murder of the Don would be staged as a Tunisian smuggler raid. The last deal had gone sour. Deimos had felt cheated and sent agents to Tunisia. The agents had not slain the intended victim. They'd confessed under torture. One had been returned by the attackers with a warning knifed through his heart.

In the Tunis underworld, the corpses would have their hands removed. Only one of Vincenzo's hands would be found, his body dumped in the sea but giving the impression that he was kidnapped and tortured to satisfy the insult. Eventually, all knew those Arabs would send his body washing up on our beach.

The smuggling would be damaged, but money would eventually repair that—that and a whisper of the truth. The Tunisians wouldn't care who was Don, only who would pay. They appreciated a climb to the top.

Paulo thought the only way to make my plan effective was to drug the two beasts.

"Do we just barge into the apothecary and ask for the latest knockout potion?" I asked sarcastically.

"My mother is an herbalist. Her mother was a midwife and herbal curer, *her* mother a midwife and witch. I'll see if she will be willing to help. When I tell her about what Deimos did to her uncle, the truth about Deimos and Circe, I think she will want to help erect those headstones. But that will have to wait until Deimos is back. I can't leave my post before. We don't want to raise suspicions. And I need to make the request in person. We can't chance Circe's spies."

We were on the beach where my boat was docked, out of sound range down the cliff, reviewing our plans. It was about 9:00 AM. Paulo looked intently at the water. He pointed—all tiny, jumping waves. Vibrating. "Etna, Vulcan, is hammering!" he shouted. "We need to get off the beach!"

He grabbed my arm, and we started rushing up the path to the compound at the top of the cliff. Halfway up we were knocked off our feet. I looked at the beach. It had grown by one hundred feet.

Paulo picked me up as he yelled, "Run!" We reached the top and watched the hundred feet and more disappear under a huge wave. It came about a quarter up the path, higher than the highest moon tide. We get knocked down again. The ground was quivering. Part of the path disappeared. We scrambled to get away from the cliff.

Another shock. We were flat on the ground. We both lay there. Now ash was falling on us. Paulo covered his nose, indicated I should, too. We pulled up our shirts and headed to the compound and into the main house.

Circe was tending to Lucia, who had a cut on her head. It was dark— Circe had closed the shutters to the ash. No lights were available. The baby lay in a woven basket on the floor, under the table.

Paulo rushed over to the women.

"She banged her head on the edge of the chair when the second one hit," Circe told him, pressing on the wound with her apron still tied on her waist. Nyxos started wailing. I picked him up and tried to soothe him. Paulo undid Circe's apron and took over helping Lucia. Circe collapsed onto a chair she had righted.

"That second one was bad," she moaned, badly shaken. I went to her, found water, poured her a cup, wet a towel to wipe the blood from

Lucia's face so Paulo could better access the wound.

Lorenzo and his son, Mikel, came running in. "Two workers are trapped under the cantina's back wall. We need help."

Circe stood up and took over from Paulo. I put Nyxos back in the basket, crying but not the wailing as before.

"I'll take care of them. You two go help." Before I left, I looked around the kitchen and saw that damage was all loose things; the walls and roof looked solid.

Paulo, Lorenzo, and I headed to the cantina. He told his son to get the horse from the barn. "Bring ropes. Block and tackle."

The wind had changed by then, and the ash was blowing somewhere else. Thank God.

As we rushed to the cantina, it was necessary to cut through the vineyard as the road had sunk, creating a pit no wheeled vehicle could traverse. The horse had strength we would need.

Paulo and Lorenzo took command. Many of the workers were already tearing at the fallen bricks. Some had quenched the fire started by the stoves having been overturned. The cantina was not as sturdily constructed as the houses seem to be.

The roof beams seem solid enough, though. The rest of the walls were standing. Mikel threw a rope over the beam. The men tied it to the cross brace that a solid part the wall was still attached to, covering the men trapped below. It had twisted and fallen inside the building. We were able to attach the brace to the plow harness on the horse. Slowly, carefully, they raised the bit of wall. Three of the workers grabbed the arms and shirt of one of the men trapped, pulled him out. A group of women gathered him up and away from the cantina. The other man had not been as fortunate. He had been crushed. The men pulled out his bleeding body, lowered the wall, and eased the rope on the horse.

A circle formed around the dead man. The rescued one insisted the women help him over to the body.

"He pushed me aside when the wall cracked at the first tremor. He ran to the wall to hold it up. He put his back to it. He must have braced it enough to keep it from crushing me. I owe my life to him."

"Valentino will be well remembered and honored for this. Take his body to the dorm. Jacobo, please ladies, help Jacobo there also. Mikel, supervise the horse. Lorenzo and Marco, check the vineyard and orchard. Sebastione, come with me to the dorm. The rest of you listen to the nephew here. You organize a cleanup, please." Paulo was talking to me.

The men looked to me. "First," I said, "anyone hurt, cut, please wash up. Unharmed women, can you see to the wounds? Anyone else who is uninjured, see if any of the food in the cantina is salvageable. We will need to eat if we are to work. Find tables and benches. Set them up in the orchard. Bring all useable things there—food, dishes, everything. If we can't use the stoves, we will cook over campfires. Everyone pitch in."

Two of the women had been hurt badly enough that I sent them to the dorm. One of the men had to carry one. The other was able to walk on her own.

"Our children?" Some of the women and men were very concerned.

I picked two to go to Father Assisi's school and bring them. "Please ask the good Father what his situation is. How much damage has his property had?"

The rest of the men I put to work clearing the debris.

"Who has building experience?" I asked. Two men stepped forward. I asked them to see how solid the cantina actually was. Then they were to go to all our other buildings, especially the homes of the workers, and do the same. If anything was locked, they could speak to Madame Circe—she could unlock anything for them.

By afternoon everything had been righted that could be. Food supplies were adequate for three or four days. The children were unhurt.

One house had collapsed. Two had roof damage. The rest seemed to be structurally sound. Vincenzo and Lucia's home had a crack in the kitchen wall, which, like all farm kitchens, was an extension from the main building. So the rest of the house was safe to use.

Santa Maria Del Mare, the wooden church, had swayed but was fine. The good father's home had been spared. I was greatly relieved. I could not run to my Admiral to hold him, but the news was comforting.

The ash was slight. We would go into the vineyard the next day with rags and brush as much off as possible. The olive trees would have to wait. Hopefully it would rain and wash them. The ground didn't even have a solid layer. We would need to till it in as soon as possible.

Valentino's family lived in Catania. His oldest son ran a laundry there. We would send to get him. Paulo said we would pay for his funeral and some money to the son. Valentino was a widower and had grown children, which was a terrible blessing in its own way. Jacobo didn't seem more hurt than bruises and cuts, one big one on his arm. His days off would be paid correctly. The women the same. Celia, the one who needed to be carried, had a bad bump on her head but seemed clear-headed. Rest would help.

Paulo sent for the doctor, who would come when he could. There had been many injuries throughout the area.

Thankfully, Etna was quiet once more.

Lorenzo took over the supervision of the cleanup. The head gardener had commandeered as many men as could be spared. The tsunami had wrecked the dock. A temporary path had been made using planks across the washed-out gap, because there was a blessing for us, if not the fishermen: tons of dead fish tossed up on the coastline. They would make excellent organic fertilizer for the plantation. Marco was making piles of compost of them. Waste not, want not.

My boat had been tossed up onto the path just above where it was washed out. The mast was snapped but the hull was safe. I would be able to get that repaired. Some of our men probably could do it. I found the sail, ripped but patch-worthy. It had blown into an olive tree, probably from the wave's crashing wind, Paulo speculated.

Over the next day we would hear about the rest of Riposto's environs. Two others had died; the damage in general was moderate. Father Assisi would lead a pilgrimage to Etna on Sunday with all the other parishes in the region. The bishop in Catania had ordered it. Paulo said I should attend. He had seen one years ago as a boy. He said that one had been splendorous. Better than an opera, he imagined.

When we returned to the main house, Nyxos was sleeping quietly. The ladies had made a huge supper. Paulo, Sebastione, Benedicto, and I sat at the table. I had sent word that the other three would be with me. Lucia was wearing a bandage around her head. She had a gash above her right eyelid. As any boxer could tell you, they bleed like a dagger wound even when shallow. Paulo restrained himself from doing more than asking after her.

"Aunt, how are you? We have had quite a day." I'm solicitous of Circe.

"Etna is the devil in our paradise. Earthquakes and ash are his curse. Lava at least renews the soil. It has never spewed in this direction since before my grandmother's time. Vulcan be damned." She makes a spitting gesture. "I'm sure there will be a procession. The Holy Mother will hear our prayers and put Etna to sleep."

All descendants of Rome are superstitious. Throw in Greeks, and you get Sicily, a veritable pagan culture.

"Well, we will make that pilgrimage together," I surprise her by saying. My plan is to be Assisi's censer carrier. I will go to him tomorrow to arrange it, if possible.

Deimos returned the next day. He began figuring the costs of repair, the new home for the worker's family that had collapsed, Vincenzo's kitchen. Procuring food came first. He sent Antonio and one of the men toward Messina knowing it had been little affected. He told Vincenzo to return immediately.

The day Vincenzo came, Lucia got word that her mother had been hurt, her foot broken. The earthquake had struck as far away as Trapani. She asked to go to her. Vincenzo was happy to see her go. Deimos said, "We can't spare the men to accompany you."

Circe, who wanted to get as far away from Etna as possible, decided out loud, "Monday, after the procession, I think I will go to Trapani with my daughter. Mikel, Lorenzo's boy, can come with us. Anna has not seen her grandson since his birth. We will be safe on the road. Mikel can be our protector." Deimos had been spoken to.

Paulo interjected, "While everyone is praying at Etna, I will go to Taormina to check on my mother. I should see her. I can be there and back in one day."

Deimos approved. No one would work if there was a procession to be watched, no matter the disaster.

Sunday I saw Paulo off. "Will this be an herbal visit?" I asked.

"Etna has given us many opportunities here. We will strike while the women are gone. I leave it up to you to finalize the plan. My three cousins are on board. They have no other details other than I plan to be Don within the month. Most of the other soldiers will be happy with bribes and guarantees of better pay."

"You have greased the wheels?" Was my money being spent wisely, I wondered.

Paulo reminded me that Sicilians expect disasters to bring change. That we would confirm.

"You did well, finocchio. The workers were impressed how you cared for them first before the plantation. They've started calling you 'the Good Tartus' behind your back."

"I am neither good nor a Tartus, but if it helps the cause, I'm okay with it. Pray, why do you use that word?"

"Okay, okay, from now on, I ban it. Goodbye. . .Sailor."

I was, as the English say, gob-smacked. How did he know that? What else did he know? He truly was worthy of being the Don.

22

NOW, NEW YORK CITY

"WHAT'S UP? WHERE'S DAN?" JASON, CONCERNED, asked his sister.

"Dan's not coming. He's in the hospital."

"*What?* What happened? Is he all right?" they both asked, almost at once.

"Bit of a story. He'll be all right. I hope."

The waiter set their coffee and pastries down on the table. They were in the Columbus Circle complex, the windowed wall to Central Park. Mortana suggested it as a place where she was sure none of her neighbors would show up.

"I don't know why I ordered this. I can hardly eat." She stared past the balcony, out to the column, with Columbus still offending by his presence.

"Sis, you're scaring me. Tell us what's going *on.*"

Victor silently handed her the miniature milk pitcher. Danny had proven to be such a great guy in his life that he was extremely worried, more than just for a future in-law.

"Okay. Try not to interrupt. It's going to be hard enough." She took a deep breath before going on.

"Danny isn't in a hospital. He's in a rehab center in Hudson County. He is addicted to oxycodone, shooting heroin."

"What the *hell!*" Victor gripped Jason's arm indicating silence.

Mortana continued. "During his second tour in Iraq, he and some buddies got addicted to opium. The scenes they saw drove them to try all sorts of things to squelch the nightmares. The Corps, being somewhat more enlightened than in the past, sent him to Germany for rehab. When that was over, he had a short stint back in the States, visiting the kids who were with Tia and Abuela. He then re-upped for a third tour. Some kind of Marine macho thing to prove his manhood. That's the only reason I took a second tour in Afghanistan."

She fiddled with her cup, eyes on the rim. "He was good from then on. Then, four years ago, he had a minor car accident that messed up his back. The docs put him on oxy. Since then, he's been on and off it. He has been doing therapy."

But two weeks earlier, she had found a needle and syringe. "I confronted him immediately. His psychologist has connections with the rehab center. His ex-Marine status got him near the head of the line."

She had transformed her cloth napkin into a twisted bread stick.

Victor groaned, head in his hands, resting his elbows on the table, his eyes filled with tears.

"I didn't want to upset anyone. Eva knows. Probably Juan. We kept it from the kids and Abuela all along. They think he's in Los Angeles, doing a script repair. But that's not going to fly much longer. He doesn't seem to have time to answer their texts. They're worried. I can only lie for so long. His mom is a whole other story." She sighed, stopped, looked down at her hands, then from man to man.

Jason stood up, came around behind her, and bent to embrace her, kissing the top of her head, the only gesture possible under the circumstances. Victor reached to squeeze her arm. Jason came behind Victor. His hands trying to comfort his fiancé, gripping Victor's shoulders, he asked, "What can we do?"

"...Nothing. It's all up to him until he gets home. Then it's still up to him. We just need to let him feel our love. I know you guys love him. He's always admired you, Jason. He talks about Victor as much as you these days. . . . I needed to let you know before I tell the kids. *That* is something I'm terrified of. They worship their father."

"And their mother," Victor blurted. He had tried to drink his coffee a number of times but kept putting it back on the table. It never seemed to reach his lips.

Jason, seated again, folded and unfolded the paper remains of a sugar packet. "When are you doing it?"

"Tonight."

"Would you like us there?" he offered.

"No. This is my and Danny's responsibility. Since he can't do it, I need to."

"How about we come out tomorrow? We can take the twins to the park on the waterfront. Walk around. Go to the weekend food vendors. Maybe the flea market. Calyce likes old costume jewelry. Jeremy will find something. Talk. Sound them out. Help them process it." Victor wanted to be there for the teens and Mortana. Danny would have to wait while he got freed from the danger.

"I think that's a good idea." Jason added.

"What about Abuela? Danny is her shining star," Jason fretted.

Mortana explained that she and Eva were taking Mrs. Santos to the cemetery on Sunday to visit her favorite cousin's grave. It was the fifth anniversary of her passing. Abuela always felt that her cousin enjoyed her visit. It actually lifted her spirits. They always went for Filipino food afterward. That was when Mortana would try to explain. Abuela had lived through a lot. She was tough. As long as the person was alive,

Abuela believed everything could be fixed.

"How long will he be there?" Jason needed to know as many details as possible. Details always had a certain amount of comfort in them for him.

"It's a month's program. We are so fortunate. My city medical insurance is good, covers most of it. So another three weeks. He'll be back before Christmas."

"He's doctored two movie scripts while still waiting for the PBS thing. That was a lot of money. My salary covers the monthly bills." Mortana was obviously reassuring herself that their lives would not completely crash.

They barely drank their now-cold coffee, poked at their sweets. Jason paid the bill. They walked Mortana to her subway.

"Wish me luck tonight." She kissed them both.

"We'll be there tomorrow. What time is good?" her soon to be brother-in-law asked.

"Mass is at nine. Eva will have brunch afterward. Do you want to come?" she asked, her tone almost begging.

"No. We don't want to burst into flames." Jason snarked.

"No church, you heathen—brunch." Mortana shoved him in the chest. Smiled a bit, the first today.

"No, we can sleep late and come out about twelve. Will the kids be home or with Juan?" Jason asked for them both. He only entered a church for weddings and funerals. Victor had refused to go to weddings until recently, when Gay people could marry.

"Home after brunch to change out of their Sunday jeans." Mortana sighed.

"Okay, if you leave before we get there, we'll see you later. We'll take care of dinner with the kids unless you want us to wait."

"I'll be eating an early dinner with Eva and Mama."

"Okay, we'll check in in the morning. Get home safely. Love you."

Jason hugged and kissed her. Victor did too, as always.

"We got your back." Victor called to her as they watched her go, adding thoughtfully, "When you speak to Danny, tell him for me how much he is loved."

"Ditto.".

THEY HAD SLOWLY BEEN MOVING VICTOR'S THINGS into Jason's apartment. The neighbor had not made any decisions yet about selling to them. They had gone to Victor's studio for the rest of his clothes after leaving Mortana.

Furnishings would be next. Jason loved Victor's king-size bed. It would occupy most of the bedroom, but they agreed they could live with that. The father of one of The Boys had a van to lend them the following weekend.

Finally home, they had time to talk about Danny over the Chinese food they'd called in, sitting at the small table against the window in the kitchen.

"I hate this. Heroin killed my father before I knew him. Then my mother when I was eight." Victor looked as if he had spent two days awake.

Jason, stunned, put down his chopsticks. "Oh, my God. I knew they died, but you never said how. Oh, Vic, I'm *so* sorry."

Victor had tears running down his cheeks. "I just can't have another person I love get eaten by drugs. I just can't."

Jason scrunched down, enveloping him in his arms. "Honey, he'll be okay. He's surrounded by people who love him. You didn't have that. But he has." Jason kissed him on the forehead.

"You've joined a family of absolute huggers. We never let love go. Why, my sister and I still keep in touch with the Wicked Witch of the West." Jason straightened up, groaning, "These knees are not that young any more."

They both laughed. Victor blew his nose, went to the sink to wash his face, dried it with the dish towel. Smiled weakly at Jason, back at the table, he said, "Pass me the dumplings."

Jason left him to his thoughts. They did the dishes and watched TV. "Kids tomorrow."

23

NOW, NEW YORK CITY

I DON'T THINK IT PARTICULARLY FAIR they put a man in jail for making a threat he didn't follow up on, especially a God-fearing Christian." I'm speaking to Basil Black's public defender, having tracked him down, passing through many agency departments.

"I most definitely do *not* want to be identified. A courier will bring the money to you by the end of the day. After the trial, it will be returned in the same manner. How long will his release take?" The caller sounded like a person who enjoyed people's subservience.

"By tomorrow afternoon or Wednesday the latest," the lawyer explained.

"Fine. Please text this number to let me know." The connection dropped.

THE DIGITAL FILE SENT BY Mr. Cochran was exactly as expected:

Mr. Basil Black: a typical religious extremist. His rants on social media were prejudiced against many people, LGBT people at the top of the list. Each justified with Bible quotations. He is five feet six inches, weighs 180 pounds, is forty-four years old, has a Russian mother and U.S. father, is divorced, and has no children noted. His address is 425 Jerome Place, Astoria, Queens 13749, telephone (516) 542-6969. He lives alone.

Previous employment: Uber driver, longshoreman, handyman for an apartment building in Long Island City, school bus driver, short order cook, cane field worker—Puerto Rico, etc. Some fired from, most left on his own.

United Synod of the Resurrection of the True Cross is his latest church affiliation. There have been six others. He was asked to leave the last two, amid conflict over the correct interpretation of the Bible, and made threats to those who disagreed. He carried a machete to services in the last one.

Police record: Two bar fights, convicted for domestic violence against his wife and a girlfriend. Spent six months total in Rikers, then branch of the Brooklyn House of Detention on Second Avenue and Thirty-fourth—Thirty-fifth Streets. Hangs out in two bars, The Beaten Rooster at 1629 Roosevelt Street, Astoria 11091; and Harry's, 4278 Himrod Avenue, Ridgewood 10017.

Details: In the addendum.

Mr. Cochran has an idiosyncratic way of presenting his findings.

"HENRI, I WILL BE BUSY FOR the next three days. Please follow our regular schedule. I will be unavailable. You can text the W phone. As you know, leave messages. I am quite sure we are done with the police. Next Sunday we will send Mr. Beyer on his way and return to Willow Street on Monday. You will arrange his departure, please."

"Very good, sir. Are there any things here that you wish transferred to the Willow Street residence?"

"I'll let you know. Monday arrive after 4:00 PM. You will bring the

Infinity."

"Yes, sir. Anything else, sir?"

"No, I'll be gone shortly. I'm taking the Tesla."

"Be safe, sir."

"Your good wishes are always welcome. I will see you next Monday."

"Goodnight."

"Goodnight, Henri."

All business, Henri knew the voice that said, "No social inquires, please."

I love the way all these electronic gadgets do manual labor. I press the button, and voilà: The garage opens, the gates open, the car opens, starts. Silently I ride across the Queensborough Bridge. The GPS brings me to Jerome Place in the most efficient time possible. I dial (516) 542-6969. Mr. Basil Black lives alone. He answers. I know he is present, one flight down, in the basement apartment.

"Mr. Basil Black?"

"Who wants him?" Gruff, cautious, angry before the conversation even begins.

"I'm your bail officer, Johnathan Greene. I am making my first un-scheduled visit."

"What the fuck is a bail officer?" Black has never had one before and is confused. Suspicious, he threatens to hang up.

"Wait! The company that lent your benefactor the complete bond appoints an officer in each case. I am yours. I can explain all this to you. Let me in. Normally we do this at our offices, but your ankle brace-let precludes that. You know you have only approved places you may go to. Our location is not one."

"Why you here so late?"

"Because I'm only available now. Look, either we get this face-to-face over with, or your bail gets rescinded and you'll be sleeping in Riker's Island again."

"Shit, all right. My door is on the side of the driveway."

"I'll be there in five minutes."

Since the Tesla is virtually silent, I pull it in. Snap open the trunk lock. When Mr. Black answers the door, as he turns to lead me in, I grab him, cover his nose with my prepared mask, etherize him. Our business is going to work differently than my usual kill. I have my Covid mask on; a pulled-down baseball cap hides my hair so he cannot identify me.

I easily snap the ankle bracelet apart, toss it onto his living room chair, and close the door. I pack him into the trunk after hog-tying him with the ever-utilitarian duct tape. Silently my electric vehicle's GPS finds our way to Vernon Avenue, over the Pulaski Bridge, along McGuiness Boulevard to the BQE, the Brooklyn Bridge exit, left under the overpass, right onto Henry Street, right on Orange to Willow, left onto Willow, left through my automatic garage doors. All spectrally soundless.

As I have said, I am quite strong. My Sicilian year's muscles have been maintained since, fixed by physical labor, exercise, and time. He may have been a bit of a weight, but once in the secret passage Mr. Black is on the ancient trolly that is there to transport him to one of the two chambers—pleasure or horror. Perspective is like that.

I stamp in the code, provide my thumb print and retina scan. The door, designed by a vault company, lifts inward and slides to the side. Black is wiggling all over; he looks like a beached sea lion (ears, you know.) I drag him into the room. Hooked to a winch, he hangs in the air while I inject him with propofol. Once he's quieted own, I cut the bonds, lay him on the table, strip him, and attach his wrists and ankles to two cross bars. I use the winch to raise him for transport to the wall and easily hook the bars into cleats on it. Some time will pass before he regains consciousness. Lights off, I lock the door to go upstairs.

Entering the ideally regulated wine cellar with my cache of special red, I make my selection. Up, out of the underworld, the house, as closed up by Henri, is covered in sheets. The kitchen contains non-perishables only. I climb the stairs to my sitting room to avoid ruining the silence with electronic elevator sounds. Liking the solitude, I keep the lights off. I turn off the window's electricity so I can look out the sitting room glass into the garden. I undo the bar panel, open my red, let it come to room temperature, and stand it on the zinc bar. Removing my favorite crystal glass from the adjoining vitrine, I caress the cut design with my fingertips. I don't bother decanting the liquid. Carrying both to my chaise, I place them on the marble side table.

In my greenhouse, the night blooming cereus has opened. Two blossoms have already passed their prime. The night-blooming jasmine looks ready to break its buds. I'm glad I came in time for that. Tomorrow night it might flower. When it does, I'll let the fragrance flood my sitting room. Abundant with sweetness, last year the whole house was filled. For now, the green house smell of earth, humidity, plants' green tang envelop me in soothing comfort. I leave the door open, pour my drink and settle on the chaise to drowse. The experience for Mr. Black will progress when my glass is drained.

Rousing myself from my delicious thoughts, I change into my work clothes. A set of medical scrubs, mask, shoe coverings. Having watched all eight seasons, ninety-six episodes of *Dexter*, I have gleaned a few ideas. Not that I lack a rich imagination of my own. The writers were most creative. I have no need to copy his use of plastics any longer. When I designed my Willow Street pleasure chest, I installed a self-cleaning system that will wash the rooms in the manner of a dish washer; a special boiler heats the water to sterilizing temperatures. The rooms are made of surgical steel. In the center stands a customized autopsy table with restraints. On one wall, a workstation of knives, saws, weapons, surgical equipment, reproductions of simpler inquisition accoutrements. A sliding panel protects fabrics, ropes, gauze, drugs, electrical equipment, and such.

Mr. Black is attached to a flexible bolt array on the third wall. The electronic winch is on tracks in the ceiling. I'm sure I will add more interesting equipment as I expand my hideaway. The second room is under development as an S&M dungeon for a playmate, not prey. I have only kept a subject for at most two nights.

Over the years, I've developed a philosophy similar to that of Dexter's father. *Prey on the evil.* Recently I narrowed that category, as you know, now suspended. Partly. In general, the authorities are less pressured to find the dregs of society who go missing. My spontaneous killings do violate that. But in general, I'm selective.

Mr. Black's religious extremism would not usually have attracted my attention. However, his attack on Victor and Jason has. I feel those two should be my friends. I may not be able to share my peculiarities with them (we shall see), but a social relationship would be fulfilling.

So let us begin.

I enter the room from the midnight hallway. He can hear the door open and close. The room is blacked out still. His mouth is taped. He is screaming through it. I stand in front of him, not one photon of light available. I speak. This startles, terrifies him. He cries, screams, makes quite a commotion through his taped mouth. "Mr. Black, my dear fellow, we have Biblical business to do here. You do so like that. I thought we might replicate one or two stories from the Good Book. With my interpretations, of course."

I am caressing his naked body as I speak. Touching his face, running my hands over his neck, his shoulders, up his crucifixed arms, my fingers slide through his, back through his arm pits, chest, nipples, using the back of my hand down his rubber belly over his genitals, now fingers grasping his scrotum, finally down his legs as far as my arms reach without me bending. He is quivering, ranting, doing his best to avoid my touch. The inch or two he can move is inconsequential.

I switch on the light. Bright and blinding. I am a minimum of five inches taller than him. My surgical mask, surgical skull cap, hide my face and head. I am unrevealed to him in this light.

"You will get to choose occasionally between incidences." I feel choices are good for pilgrims on this Via Dolorosa.

"Let's see. Genesis 34 is a good place to start. We'll skip Cain and Abel. Murder would end our play. Genesis 34: It seems Dinah's rape can be assuaged by marriage and the circumcision of Shechem's men.

"I have zero desire to marry you.

"Mr. Black, I feel generous. You get to choose— circumcision or rape. I'll give you a minute to decide. Let me take your tape off." His language is simply unacceptable. I put the tape back on.

"Sir, if you can't be civil, we cannot converse and I will be forced to make all decisions. Perhaps a little encouragement. If things go well, you will live. Again, when I take the tape off, civility will reign, or all offers are null and void."

He is loud, has not abandoned the foulness of his words. "Who the hell are you? Let me the fuck go. What kind of faggot are you—taking my clothes, touching me?"

"Stop!" I bellow, striking his face. "I warned you. Language. You will not get another chance."

His lip is bleeding a bit. He looks shocked. Having been used to doing the striking, he is taken aback by having it done to him.

"Your choice? Circumcision or rape. You have a long foreskin. I am no doctor but enough overhang will mean I will probably not cut the head."

Black begins to shout, thinks better of it.

"Rape is not generally in my repertoire, but the verse demands it. You are far from desirable, but I'm sure I could soldier through with help." I'm beginning to feel my excitement build.

"One punishment short-lived, the other permanent. Choose." I increase my intensity.

"Let me go. We don't need to do this. I won't tell anybody. Damn it. You can't do this."

I tap his penis. "I believe I can. I believe I will. Choose."

With deliberation, I retrieve a scalpel, lay it on the table. I do the same with a large dildo, letting it stand to display its length and girth.

"Please, please, *no*." He is crying, gagging, his breathing erratic.

"Choose." I am firm. If he could see my face, he would see growing impatience as well as amusement.

"That," he says, indicating the dildo with his chin.

"Ah, a moment. Nothing permanent. Your choice." Such fun, I am thinking.

Using the winch I keep him hanging, I release the bars from the wall. He thrashes about. I zap him with my cattle prod (not quite as intense as a taser).

"Cooperate, or we will have higher intensities. That was to your leg. We can find much more sensitive areas to play with."

His crying is exhausting him. Resigned to his fate, head on chest, he sags as much as the bars allow.

I flip him over, bolt him now face to the wall. I see no reason to delay further.

While he is calming as much as one could in his circumstance, my own body has responded to these von Pittasching endeavors. I strip off my surgical pants and put on a condom.

Not that one. I promised Elio that was over.

I use Vaseline to make it as slick as possible. The situation has made me more than functional. "It is apparent I am ready. This is your first station of the cross."

After some maneuvering I drive into him. His screaming is so delicious that I feel excited past my lack of attraction, in fact distaste. Basil has no idea how the screams drive me on. When he begs for mercy, it drives me to finish: more scriptural duty than pleasure. He is bleeding a bit. I guess I didn't used as much lubricant as I thought.

A few minutes pass for my recovery; no need to wait for him to stop sobbing. Re-application of the cattle prod has gained Mr. Black's submission, and I've released him from his restraints. Ordered to climb onto the autopsy table, he obeys, and the straps are easily applied with his compliance.

It looks as though he may have soiled my wall with his own ejaculation. That does happen to some raped men. Not out of enjoyment but due to extreme physical stimulation and emotional distress. Human beings are complicated.

Basil has evacuated his bladder and bowels on my floor. I needed to sanitize. A hidden hose allows me to wash him, the table, wall and floor. The floor slants to a central drain. The effluvia washes into it.

I adjust the nozzle to clean him. I wash the dried blood off his face, spray his dripping genitals. The blood dripping out of his anus is not excessive. The water washes away any offal he has excreted. The table drain at his feet lets this shower run to the floor gutter.

"Well, you seemed to have enjoyed that. You impregnated my wall." I enjoy making this abuser feel humiliated. We are in for a number of long von Pittaschings.

"The dildo. You didn't." His words fragment through his crying. Moaning.

"I'm sorry for your misperception. It was merely a visual aide for your decision making."

"God help. . .I'm bleeding."

"Wait." I get a hand mirror and hold it so he can see what is dripping.

"Please, I don't want to die." Basil's speech is clearing.

"I told you, if things go right you will survive." He can't see my smiles, perhaps in my eyes.

I've discarded my full condom. I have an incinerator for ruined clothes and such. I pick up my pants, go to the door.

In full Schwarzenegger mode, I declare, "I'll be back," switch off the light, lock the door, and go to shower.

No tears can be heard through the vault. It's the silence of the sanctuary.

I THOUGHT I MIGHT WAIT TO THE NEXT NIGHT to continue, but that act requires its own singular performance.

Twenty minutes later, I am clean and refreshed.

"Mr. Black I've returned." No lights for now. A nice element of surprise. "Tell me, how do you feel?"

"Damn, how do you *think* I feel?" He's defiant as ever, even through his emotional exhaustion.

"Language. Again, cooperate and you will live. How do you feel?"

Lights on. I hold the cattle prod so he can see it. A zap to a tender sole clears up any misunderstanding of my intent.

He opens to his experience with a sufficient description to satisfy me.

"Very good. When you describe your experience to others, do so with as much detail as you've just managed." One must compliment better-than-average recapitulations of an event.

Feeling a warm rush, I introduce our next station of his cross.

"We now open our Good Book to the New Testament. No crucifixion. . .yet. This comes from Luke, Chapter 12, The Parable of the Unfaithful Slave. You know this, I'm sure. The slave betrays his duty to his master, and the master cuts him up. Jesus's own words are softened in most translations. In the original Jesus seems a bit extreme, but *c'est la vie.*"

"Please, no. What are you talking about? Let me go. Please." He goes on and on. His voice a bit strained from his previous caterwauling.

"Let's try to unfold the meaning of this in your life. Your last job was as an Uber driver, paid to drive people from one location to another. Isn't that so?"

I don't wait for an answer. "While you were not a slav, you were duty-bound to do your best. Instead, you betrayed your passengers for planning their wedding in your hired vehicle."

"It was a mistake. They were. . ." He halts, having learned that lies have consequences in this transcendent temple.

"That mistake may get you eight years in the slammer. And it has attracted my attention. We never know the consequences of our unbridled actions, do we?

"To finish this parable we must cut. . .you. . .up." I proffer each word as a dwelling point.

Now our Mr. Black is decidedly upset. If I hadn't locked the table to the floor cleats, he could have turned it over. But my design took such actions into account.

"I was once employed in an abattoir, slaughtering pigs. Those skills have stayed fresh over many years. I promise, you will only be a bit inconvenienced after we execute Jesus's teaching."

The master fulfills his scriptural duties. Poetically, Mr. Black's ring fingers are no longer offended by same sex marriage.

The blood is confined in the table and flows to the drain. I have a container under it to catch it. After a bit, I cauterize the wounds. My chapel is well appointed. His ululations cannot penetrate the six surfaces of our sacristy.

I remove the bloody container.

We have been at this for a number of hours. I have not included all of our conversations or lesser von Pittaschings. Some things are mine to hold dear.

I insert an IV for fluids, antibiotics, and sustenance into Black's right arm. I turn down the lights to low. Put a pillow under his head, a sheet over his body. I turn his altar to face the wall of instruments, hoping he will meditate on the possibilities of coming atonements for his misdeeds.

At 4:00 AM, I murmur, "Sleep well. You should rest. Tomorrow we will conclude our pilgrimage. Rest Mr. Black."

"TIME TO WAKE UP, BASIL." I turn up the lights. "Did you find your accommodations adequate?" He should know this room cost more than many homes. I'm trying to be a good host.

I remove the sheet, wet from his urine, and detach the IV. The cleansing hose is necessary again.

His eyes follow my every move. He pleads for release. I have punished him enough, and so forth. Black would never be a good lawyer. He makes no coherent argument to support his case.

"Our last Biblical station on this road to Calvary. A desire written in a letter by a disciple, the one who fell off his horse. Or was it a jackass? A message from Paul, the first real Christian. Before him, your religion was just a cult inside Judaism. Now he has taken it full-blown evangelical. He brooks no dissent."

"Galatians 5: Paul wishes that his opponents would castrate themselves."

"Dear God, no! *No*, you stupid fuck. You can't. *Please, no!*" His parched-lipped expressions barely audible.

Before he says another word I stuff a cloth in his mouth. Today there will be only one bodily intrusion. The cattle prod is in its recharger.

"That language will not get you freed. Be careful. Your cross on Golgotha is ready. I admire your quick apprehension of our final ceremony. It would be a bridge too far to ask you to complete Paul's desire. I will humbly be your Simon of Sirene."

I need to hear his reactions. I remove his gag. Chastised, he tries bargaining.

"Please no. I'll do anything," he says, and repeats, repeats, repeats. I interrupt to suggest he remember to appeal to God. Beginning the Lord's prayer, Basil picks up my lead.

Like the eminent director Alfred Hitchcock, I present the MacGuffin, placing a machete on his stomach. The clue is not missed. He replicates the hounds of hell in his howling.

I tape his penis to his stomach. I want it uninjured to remind him, every time he uses it, that he lives due to my mercy. A wooden block raises his scrotum. His true cross. A wide leather band squeezes the junction of jewels to perineum, his crown of thorns. His testicles stretch his scrotum.

I step out of his view and contemplate for some time. His breathing gurgles through cries for mercy.

My meditations completed, I ask, "Ready? At the count of ten."

Picking up the long blade, a metaphor for the Roman soldier's lance, with Gregorian intonations, I chant, "We sing in praise of the Lord and his disciple Basil. Mr. Black's sacrifice cleaves his sins from his soul. Lord grant him peace . . .or pieces."

I can be such a wag sometimes.

"One, two, three—" I'm sorry. I couldn't wait. He faints as he exceeds high C.

Mr. Black's somewhat incomplete naked body is found on the corner of the Astoria Street he ejected my friends at. A rosary of scrotum, testicles, and fingers graces his neck.

His language was better measured when he awoke from his faint. He is alive as promised.

As the light began to break the darkness, I'm sure Basil Black realized how untidy he was for Sunday services.

24

NOW, QUEENS, NEW YORK

J EREMY WAS STANDING ON A TOOL that looked like a pogo stick. He lifted it up. Calyce dropped a bulb into the hole. Jeremy held the tool over the hole, pushed a release on the handle and the plug of soil fell into the hole. Calyce used her boot to finish the job. They moved on to the next one. And the next. And the next. They needed to plant two hundred tulip bulbs before the ground froze. Global warming was being a friend for once. It was late, but the uncles' wedding would be in April. Their mother needed the tulips planted for that. Jeremy thought she'd lost track of the seasons.

He saw his father at his office window. He waved to him. Calyce turned her back to the house.

"Like you never made a mistake," Jeremy said.

"Don't start with me, Jeremy. I'm in no mood." Another hole, another bulb, another plug, another trod boot.

"Calyce, he didn't do it to *hurt* us. He was trapped in pain. He said he was sorry. He promised never to let it happen again. You cutting him off isn't helping."

"Just dig the hole." She was angry. She had no ability to hide it. Nor did she wish to.

"WHOEVER IT WAS, HE ACTUALLY MAILED Black's clothes back to him," Mortana said to the other three. The Santos and the duo were out to dinner to sort of celebrate Danny's return from rehab.

"Still, what was done to Black was gruesome." Danny almost blanched with this reflection.

Victor had written a number of columns prompted by the vigilante attack on Black. He wrote how people understandably might want revenge on the man for his religious prejudice and threat of violence, but lawless vigilantism was a dangerous thing to start. Someone innocent always ended up hurt.

"There is a certain poetic satisfaction, though," Jason observed. They were finishing the guacamole dip. Their Mexican entrees would follow shortly.

"We all missed you at Thanksgiving. Christmas will be so much better," Jason said to Danny.

Danny was not comfortable with the carefully curated conversation, avoiding the common knowledge permeating the pauses. "I need to clear the air," he said quietly. "I hurt the whole family. I want to apologize to you two for what I did—for using oxy, heroin, for being an addict. I'm apologizing to the whole family."

"We're starting family counseling Tuesday," Mortana said. "We each need to figure out what's going on."

"Calyce is having real problems with me," Dan said in deep sorrow. "I can't blame her."

"There's no need for an apology, Danny." Jason was nervous and uncomfortable. He had avoided thinking about what might come up at dinner.

"Well," said Victor, "you did upset us all. I accept your apology. I appreciate it. You made a mess of my nicely constructed perfect family head story. I was angry for the family, me included. I was pissed. Also sorry for you. . . . If you really have a handle on this, you will call one of

us if you get tempted. Don't struggle through on your own. No shame.
No judgement. If I'm joining in this family, you're going to have to put
up with my mouth on occasion."

Jason was silent. He thought Victor was being harsh but agreed with
him, embarrassed that he had not had the courage to express how angry
he was for his sister, the kids, and himself.

"Well said, brother." Mortana grabbed Danny's hand.

"I'm ashamed I didn't trust in you guys. I really hurt Mortana, our
kids. My family at Eva's. But I want you to be honest with me about
your feelings. I want to do the same. I'm continuing therapy. I'm attending Drugs Anonymous. I have a sponsor. I need to know you love
me enough to call me on my shit."

"I have my own history." Victor did something Jason found almost
shocking: He talked about his parents. Mortana and Danny expressed
their sorrow.

"What I want to know. . .what I would like you to tell me," Victor
said in a whisper, "is why you let it get to where it took you? You had a
lot of people around you who cared about you, loved you." He thought
his mother had loved him, his brother and they her. Her death to drugs
had shattered that.

"There's no simple answer." Danny said, and continued with some
of the things Mortana had already spoken about, facts, revealed his feelings. Describing various stages of his deepening addiction, the conversation went into areas none of them had expected. Anger, depression,
betrayal, physical pain, mental pain, war. . . .

Two hours later, they left a large tip, payment for occupying the table
so long.

The men walked Danny and Mortana to their car and exchanged
conventional goodbyes, all grateful to have lifted the heaviness.

Mortana was wrapped in her brother's arm. "It's getting cold. You
think we'll have a white Christmas?"

Victor hoped so. He had turned into a complete romantic despite his tough exterior.

"Love you, and don't forget that," Jason said to Danny.

"Ditto," Victor added.

"You sound like Jeremy," Danny chuckled.

"A good teacher."

"Who's keeping the house from burning down, tonight?"

"The kids," Mortana said proudly.

"I need to learn to trust," Danny said very simply. "They're more than capable of caring for themselves. . .and, we hope, our property!" he added with a chuckle.

They climbed in their car. Everyone waved.

Jason held Victor the way he did his sister. "God, baby, you were incredible tonight. I'm so proud of you."

Victor just smiled. They walked arm in arm the six blocks home.

25

THEN, SICILY

"WE HAVE OPTIONS." PAULO EASES his full knapsack onto the floor of the kitchen, speaking softly. The lunch bell has not rung. With the women away, it has fallen on the Gay man to cook, as if a desire for men somehow makes you a domestic. I fix a vegetable soup; bread was bought from the baker, and there's olive oil, meat, cheese, olives, water, wine.

"What are they?"

"My mother has developed a clandestine herbal practice she didn't tell me about. She supplies potions to the surrounding towns—the kinds of things that induce love, cause vengeance. My sweet mother's lived in Riposto too long. Like all good entrepreneurs, she saw a need and filled it."

"Get to the point, man. They will not like lunch late. Options?"

"She gave me tinctures of herbs she mixed. My bag is full. We may need a lot. One, given in enough quantities, may cause a heart attack. The other is a relaxer, sleep inducer, again depending on the amount. She explained how to do the one over days so it looks like heart trouble appeared before the heart attack. She warned that some of the side effects could alert a person who knows herbs or their extracts. So we must not let a doctor get involved. Or a gardener."

For future reference I ask what the herbs are. He only remembers opium, witch's glove, belladonna, and mushrooms whose names he can't remember. I ask what witch's glove is. He thinks it's called nightshade but isn't sure. When I get to a more civilized place, if I need to, I can find sources for them. Calming prey would make my abductions easier.

"If this works, I'll send a letter of commendation to your mother. Let's meet tonight and finalize our plans. The women will be away at least a week, maybe longer. As you said, that gives us a better opportunity to rid Riposto of the Tartus pigs. Let's meet at the ancient tree near the cliff on the east side of the orchard after sundown."

"Time to ring the bell."

"DEIMOS WANTS US TO REBUILD THE DOCK. Stop work on this wall. Take that crew to the beach." Paulo is ordering one of the builders at the cantina.

Donato asks, "Where will we get pilings? Planks? Nails?"

"None were salvaged?" Paulo is incredulous. Nothing gets wasted at the plantation.

"Not to my knowledge."

"Check and see. If not, go to Catania. See Deimos's ally, Gregor. His lumber yard is across from the wharves. Tell him what you need. If he can't give it to you today, tell him Deimos will expect the supplies tomorrow, no later. Gregor has ways. If need be, the planks can come from the new roofs and building being worked on."

"I'll need three men at least to go with me. The same for building it. That will take away from the rebuilding here and the homes."

Paulo sighs, "I know. We do what Deimos says. People will continue eating in the orchard, living in tents."

"The weather has not been good—storms twice this last week. People need housing. My family needs more than fabric over their heads." Donato would never complain to Deimos.

Paulo commiserates with him. "I agree. I feel badly too, but the Don orders, we obey. Money is more important."

Donato goes to spit on the ground, thinks better of it. "Arabs before Sicilians, not good."

"I'm sorry, my friend. We are at Deimos's command, his mercy. The quicker we get the dock in, the quicker we go back to rebuilding. Be on your way. Hopefully, we have salvage. If not, leave the best workers here. You only need mules to cart the wood. Quickly, now."

Donato tips his hat in a sign of respect, "Don Paulo." Donato has given Paulo a title that could be dangerous if a Tartus overheard it. Paulo is, however, pleased with the sound. Pleased with the discontent.

"Go any further and you'll fall off the cliff," Paulo warns me in the moonless night.

"If I can guarantee you of one thing, my life always comes first. I know this tree well enough."

"Why? Who do you meet here? I see how you look at Mikel."

"Paulo, a gentleman never kisses and tells. Let's get to our plans. Enough with my love life."

Paulo proposes that we start giving the heart medicine to Deimos. Since I am the cook, I can hide it in his food when I serve it. We discuss how that will be tricky since we all eat together. That needs to be resolved. Vincenzo will be taken care of as in our original plan.

"I want to do Vincenzo. I have been thinking. If, when the Tunisians arrive, you can get him to be rude or even in an argument, the next night we will put him to sleep. I'll take him in my boat. When he recovers, I will reveal all the secrets to him. Out to the current that goes toward Catania, I'll cut his hand off, throw him overboard to drown."

"Can you do that?" Paulo is incredulous.

"Have you seen me butcher a boar?"

"Perhaps we take no chances. Cut his throat. Do both hands. Tie them to his body like a necklace." Paulo is caught up in his revenge.

"Fine with me. We will need a loyal guard on the dock gate. Whoever it is needs to be willing to be knocked out or something so he is not suspected of helping the Arabs. When the body washes up and Deimos sees it, we give him a fatal dose in his next meal or, more likely, cup of wine."

Paulo tells me of his conversation with Donato. "Gregor had pilings but no planks. We will need to use the new roofs. The workers are already grumbling. This will piss them off. The more discontent, the less resistance to a new Don."

"Which soldiers are loyal? Who needs higher bribes? Will any be a major problem?"

Paulo answers all that I ask. "Beggio is not going to be easy. Perhaps I'll put him on the dock gate and slice his throat—then Vincenzo can be carted away."

"Can you afford to lose a soldier?"

"Once I take over and start buying the men not already in our pay, I will have young bucks knocking at my door." Paulo speculates, "I can take care of Beggio while you gag and truss that pig. You'll need my help carrying Vincenzo."

"I will be here just two more months. Then I'll be leaving. I'll take Circe. Although, if our plan is strong, she may welcome you." We couldn't admit that we know her shame. It's a price I'm willing to bear; my father would not hear of Circe's denouncement.

"The head capo almost always takes over the family if there are no heirs. I could be Nyxos's regent. Marry Lucia next year, be confirmed in the leadership." Paulo dreams.

"Get the dock done. Figure out a way to anger the Arabs, so your men can see the conflict. I'll start poisoning Deimos's food."

"One more thing. Just a matter of curiosity. How do you know about 'sailor'?"

Paulo smiles in the dark, "Ah! my friend. The new curate. The Viking. I figured out that your information could only come from Father Assisi. I approached Father Tomaso. That man is tall. This bishop has a thing for tall priests. Anyway, I donated a nice sum of cash for where to find family histories that were probably not in the regular records. Assisi had told him about the secret book's existence. I offered some extra cash to let me see it. He used 'Sailor' when he told me Assisi had shared it with you."

"Your money gave me your name." Paulo laughs, hands me a bottle of wine. "Have a drink to seal the deal." We pass it back and forth until it is drained. The wind has picked up. Rain will fall before morning.

DEIMOS DOESN'T LIKE MY COOKING. I bring him food from the cantina cook. That trip allows me time to spike it. Vincenzo decides he wants the service also. I make sure to keep the meals separate. I start putting sleeping potion in Vincenzo's dinner to see how much it takes to knock him out. Paulo and I take our meals in the orchard with the workers.

The men finish the dock. Two nights later the Arabs arrive. Paulo, who speaks some of their language, causes a misunderstanding between Vincenzo and the crew leader. The Tunisian pulls a knife. Paulo steps in, prevents bloodshed. He disarms the Tunisian. Later, admiring the weapon, he offers a swap and money. The man is astonished. He could buy five new, better, in Tunis for that amount of cash—but he accepts the trade, suspicious of the reason but not caring because of the profit. Vincenzo is definitely on his shit list. He tells Paulo that, in the future, "that one" needs to be elsewhere. Paulo doesn't tell him that "that one" is the Don's son. He and the man grasp arms in the fashion of allies.

Deimos has been having weakness and dizzy spells.

The next night the plan is put into effect. Sleeping potions to father and son.

"WHAT THE FUCK?"

I have poured a cup of the Ionian Sea over Vincenzo. "Awake. We need to talk." The boat mounts the low waves. Ionia is calm but not quiescent.

"What the hell are you doing? Untie me, you cock-sucking fag." He does have a way to charm the vultures out of the trees.

"Dear cousin, you have spent the last ten months making my life as hellish as you dared short of dismembering me. Tonight I will be sending you to that actual realm."

The man is so dense that I need to wait for him to understand my meaning. ". . . You wouldn't dare. My uncle will flay you alive, rich bastard or not."

"You have just made two misstatements of fact: 'uncle' and 'bastard.' I am not a bastard, but you are. You do not have an uncle, you have a father."

The excrement flowing from his mouth far exceeds his mother's.

"No one likes to hear his mother and father are brother and sister unless they are Egyptian pharaohs, which you are not. Oh, another thing. Nyxos is Paulo's son. Lucia has horned you, much to my delight and admiration."

"Liar, I'll cut your tongue out." He spits at me because his head and its parts are all he can move. I have learned much about immobilizing pigs this year.

"Cutting. . .you speak of cutting. How is *this?*" I cut his right wrist through the bone. Hold up his severed hand to his astonished eyes. I have bound his wrists and arms so tightly that no blood is flowing in them, wishing the mess to be minimal. I tied the hand to a cord. Dangle it in front of him. His screams are empty to the night.

"Calm down. I have more to tell you." He is babbling, crying. I lean next to him, pull his hair so his left ear is near my mouth. I whisper, "Your father is to be poisoned to look like a heart attack. Arranged by Paulo's mother to avenge her uncle, Messina, Deimos's first kill. You must remember that story. Your father and you had such fun about my manhood that night. Is this manhood enough for you?" I take off the other hand.

He faints, so I baptize him a second time.

"I planned to throw you overboard and let you drown but Paulo made a request—that I slit your throat." I pause to let that sink in. "To satisfy both our wishes I will make a slit from which you will not recover. You will still be alive when I throw you over to drown. A little detail. I will stab you in the chest close to your heart but not in it. We have the Tunisian's knife. Your death will look like revenge for the insult last night."

I haul him to the side of the boat. Dangle his shoulders over the edge. Tie the handed cord to his neck. "I have done this five times already, so you have a professional, no amateur, sending you to hell." I slice his throat, cut the bindings. He is gasping, gurgling.

"The salt is going to burn like the devil." I thrust the blade between his ribs. "Goodbye, you worthless bastard of two demons from Hades." Over he goes. He kicks for a minute, treading. He curses me one last time and sinks, the stars more scattered for his thrashing.

I have brought cloths to clean up the blood. There is quite a mess but no trace remains when I am back at the dock before sun up.

The senior gardener raises the alarm when he finds Beggio's lifeless body. Next, Deimos.

26

NOW, NEW YORK CITY

AUGUSTUS IS BACK IN TOWN NEXT WEEK," Victor tells Jason. "He would like to have lunch. In his new home. Saturday. He would enjoy seeing us." He reads the text. "There's a picture of Bern, Switzerland. His car on an overlook. Another Tesla."

Jason has taken Calyce out for lunch, just the two of them. He's listening to Victor's message while Calyce uses the bathroom. He texts back. *Okay to see, Augustus. New home? Where?*

Calyce returns to the table.

"How about dessert? They make great pastries here."

"Do they have ice cream?"

"I'm sure. They have a dessert menu. Look on your phone." Since Covid, Jason almost never touches a menu.

The view of Central Park and the statue of Columbus are as clear as they were the last time he was here with Mortana and Victor. The leaves have already dropped. Nights have finally gotten cold enough.

Lighted giant snowflakes color the air between their balcony cafe and the windows on the outside world. At the cross-walk, a huge one hangs high, celebrating the season.

Calyce asks if she can have coffee.

"How about half regular and half decaf?" Jason isn't sure what the Santos's rules were around this.

"Sounds OK. They have vanilla ice cream and chocolate lava cake. What's that?"

"It's sinful. Try it. I always think it's better to try. If you don't like it, no tragedy. If you do, it goes on the list of things to have again some other time."

A waiter comes over. Jason indicated that Calyce will order. When she finishes, he does. "I'll have the same, but a double espresso for my drink."

The twentyish waiter smiles and says, "I'll be right on it."

"He's been flirting with you ever since we sat down."

"I know. Fun, isn't it?"

"Victor would be jealous."

"No, he would be 'He's mine, you can look but don't touch.' We share the same interests in men and enjoy it when someone appreciates a catch we've made. Does that shock you?"

"A little. It certainly isn't the way girls think boys should act. My friends all want boyfriends to be jealous if someone even talks to them."

The conversation about teen love life continues until the dessert arrives. Calyce does not have a boyfriend. She does not want one.

The waiter comes with their desserts. He eyes rove over Jason as he puts the plate and espresso in front of him.

Calyce asked the waiter, "Do you have a boyfriend?" Jason looks startled. So does the waiter.

"Calyce?"

The waiter replies, "No—do you have someone in mind?"

She responds matter-of-factly, "My uncle is getting married in April. Was he flirting with you?"

"Calyce, that is quite enough."

The waiter says to Jason, "I hope I didn't offend you."

"No, I told her it was a compliment for me, and that my fiancé would not be bothered. My niece is being a very rude teen. And she had better stop."

"To answer your question, young lady, *I* was flirting. He wasn't."

"When you have a chance, we'll have our check."

"Of course." The waiter dashes off, beet red.

"Girl, you are in danger. Your get out of jail free card just got used up." Jason was embarrassed by his niece.

"You said today I was to speak my mind. So I did." She was pouting but smiling at the same time. Was that even possible?

"Okay, enough teen word games. You promised me you would explain your behavior toward your dad by the end of the meal. We have dessert, that's the end of the meal. Truth time, my soon-to-be fifteen-year-old favorite niece."

"*Only* niece."

The waiter sets down the check and disappears, hardly noticed. "Ball's in your court." Jason stares at his hesitant niece.

"He was always so strict, go by the rules. Military correct. Expected us to be perfect. Wouldn't even let his fourteen-year-old kids stay home alone for a night. And then he blows everything up with drugs. Not just drugs but shoots up with heroin. What the fuck?"

Jason ignored the last line, "You're absolutely right. But neither of your parents was unreasonable. They just wanted to keep you safe. I know that's from their being in wars. I'm not making excuses, just talking reasons."

"You sound like you sat in on the family therapy last week. Did someone say something? We all agreed that nothing left there except between us." She is gearing up for a full-on battle. Another betrayal would be the absolute end of her forbearance..

"No, no one said a thing, except that you refused to talk. Look, you're almost a woman. In a lot of ways, you are. In the 1800s we'd be shopping you around as wife material. So I'm telling you this is not the only time you'll find that adults have feet of clay. You'll have them too at some point with your kids if you ever have any."

"Now you sound like Jeremy."

"Smart boy."

"Like I'm not."

"Unless you're gender-fluid, I think you are one smart young lady who needs to look at her father as a human being, not Superman. For that matter, your mother and the rest of us adults, too. Have you said any of this to him?"

"We are not speaking." Stubborn as a two-year-old.

Jason laughs. "I've seen that face before. When Aunt Eva refused to let you climb in the washing machine."

"Good grief, give that story up, puh*leeze!*" She's all teen, rolling her eyes.

"I will when you give up pouting and start using that very smart head of yours with your very warm heart and show your father some compassion. He loves you." Jason said what the whole family would say about her character.

"He has a heck of a way of showing his love." This, he concludes, is stubborn but revealing. There it was: Victor's very concern. The betrayal of love, cutting deep.

"Well, he *does* love you. He didn't stop loving you because of the drugs. He loves you as much as ever. He is *suffering*. Maybe he deserves it a little, but this response of yours has gone on long enough. Give him a bit of a break. An early Christmas present."

He hopes he has gotten her to think at least. They've finished their deserts, and he holds the bill and his credit card up to the waiter. The waiter has brought the Star Trek Tri Corder, too. Jason curses Mortana,

"I'll never get that out of my head!" and completes the transaction.

"You know," he tells his niece when the waiter has one, "you just cost me extra money. I put a super-large tip on the bill because of your bitchy young woman act."

"Uncle Jason!" She exclaims, shocked and demure. How does she *do* two emotions at once, Jason asks himself.

"What? If you can say fuck in front of your uncle, you can be treated as a woman. I'm starting now. As your dad has said repeatedly to all of us, I'm calling you on your shit."

"I'm telling Mama on you. No, better yet, Uncle Victor!" she declares operatically, letting her light-hearted side slip through.

"Go ahead. I'm too old to stand in the corner. My question is, are you?" It's a challenge he wants her to think deeply about.

They leave to catch the subway back to Astoria. She holds on to his arm, the cold late fall wind seeking entrance through their buttons. While they wait to cross at the third corner, she reaches up on tip-toe to kiss him on the cheek.

"HONEY, I'M HOME!" IT'S THEIR RECENT JOKE. Jason gives Victor a kiss. Victor waits for him to come out of the bathroom. He leans on the bedroom door frame while Jason changes.

"I called Mortana before to see how things are going. She said to ask you where you got the alien you dropped on her doorstep yesterday."

"That's good. I'm a regular Svengali." Jason, in his sweats, hangs his slacks and shirt away. The tie goes in the dry cleaner basket.

"Not exactly, but things are less frosty. She thinks family counseling might be better tomorrow. I told her we both hope so." Victor picks up Jason's shoes and puts them on the closet rack.

"Did you start dinner? What do you want me to do?"

They head to the kitchen. "Make a small salad," Victor says. "I have veggie burgers on English muffins. Do you want fries?"

"They make such a mess. No." Jason usually does cleanup.

"Okay, but I might start buying frozen," Victor threatens.

"Julia Child would be horrified. . . . Did you answer Augustus?"

Victor nods.

Jason unloads the salad makings from the refrigerator. They work around each other in their kitchen. It might have a small table to be stationary at, but it was not designed for two grown men milling about.

"He texted back. His place is in Brooklyn Heights. I have the address. Saturday at 1:00. His "man" is a superb cook. I requested vegetarian. We went back and forth on that. Ovo lacto will do."

"What about his UV problem?" Jason wondered.

"I don't know. We'll find out, won't we? Jason, my dear, why haven't you made us fabulously wealthy?" Victor is joking in the reflection of their new friend's extraordinary riches.

"Didn't you get my memo? That's your department."

"Screwed, we are so screwed." They peck each other's lips, proceed with their tasks.

"He said the first house next to the driveway."

"A driveway in Brooklyn Heights! Talk about wealthy."

"Forty years ago you could buy one of these brownstones for one-fifty K. That's almost the price of a parking space in some new buildings." Victor is playing real estate agent. "Now a run-down one is five million."

They've walked down Pierrepont to Willow and turn right. The view of Manhattan from Pierrepont is filtered through the trees lining the entrance to the Promenade, the wind slowed by those and the ones lining the street.

"This is too much. Looks like some of Chelsea's streets without the noise, people, and traffic. Buy me an apartment here."

"Buy lottery tickets. We will never earn enough. Here we are. So beautiful." Victor is entranced.

They come to a stop in front of one of three brick buildings with black trim, the third a story higher than the others, set back from the wrought-iron gates. There are small front gardens. A half story below ground, the windows are at ground level. The carriage house to their left has a cobbled driveway to that deep-set building.

"Close the gate. We don't want to be gauche," Victor murmurs.

"Seems a bit small for a man used to multi-room mansions," Jason whispered to him.

His "man" opens the front door decorated with a Christmas wreath before they can ring the bell. He's fifty-five to sixty, gray haired, more butler than a Hollywood version. They climb the five steps up to the doorway, "Gentlemen, Augustus is in his sitting room. He'll be right down. My name is Henri. These are lovely," he adds, noticing the flowers they brought. " Please give them to Augustus yourselves. There he is now."

The elevator door slid open. I came out into the entranceway, dressed in a pair of black jeans, a powder blue vee neck tee, and suede shoes, powder blue as well. No socks. Filling my clothing very nicely.

"Henri, take our guests' coats, please. This is Jason, Victor." I nod to each. "We don't stand on ceremony in my home, gentlemen. We use first names in Brooklyn. The flowers are lovely. Come into the living room while I put them in a vase. Then I'll show you around.

"This is like the Tardis, bigger on the inside than the outside." Victor is referring to *Dr. Who* of BBC fame.

Instead of sitting, they stand at the island as I manage the flowers. The living space has a gold-and-cream-striped patterned couch against the windows. A set of matching sea foam upholstered chairs each has a narrow rectangular wood-and-glass end table. Lamp tables and coffee table are glass and blond wood also. All low and pale. A deco side table stands between two closet doors. A painting—a Lucien Freud portrait—

hangs above. Bronze statues of satyrs stand guard on the table.

The walls are Mandarin yellow. The floors are light cherry, with soft-colored Chinese rugs defining the sitting space and dining area. The long entrance runner is similarly designed, with a matching one along the other wall down a hall. Discrete overhead lighting modules create intimate areas.

"Yes, indeed," I reply. "I had two of the houses completely combined. The third's two upper floors are Henri and his companion's. Their apartment allows access to the attics and roofs. Other staff live elsewhere and come to clean, do the gardening and so forth, on a weekly schedule. I lead a simple life. Luxurious but simple. Henri, here, supervises everything. I am so lucky to have such a wonderful amanuensis."

Having cut and arranged the flowers, I place them on the dining table. Henri begins working in the kitchen, carpenter's apron over his vest and tie.

"The kitchen can be masked behind sliding screens cleverly hidden into the two opposing closets. It forms a cube with the elevator and half bath down the other side. The half floor below has the mechanicals, washing machines, gym. Storage space. An office space for Henri to manage things."

Below that was not open to discussion.

"There's a guest bedroom with a bath, and my office, on the first floor of the third building. They're hidden behind those closet-looking doors. The entrance hall goes straight through to the garden. Stairs to the downstairs. This door is the elevator. The beautiful open stairs also take one to the sitting room and my bedroom. Please, let's go up to the bar and sit for some catching up. Henri will call us in a few minutes for his fine food. . . . Henri, do you need me for anything before we go up?" I call out.

He emerges from the kitchen into our line of sight. "No, sir, all things are set. Enjoy your reunion."

"Gentlemen, come let's elevator up. I love this totally unnecessary toy. My renovating these buildings with old age in mind is silly. I almost always move every five or six years. New interests, new dwellings."

The cherrywood-paneled elevator barely fits three. I apologize for crowding in. Jason and Victor joke it's like trying to work in their kitchen.

The door slides back. I invite them into the sitting room. "Come, sit. I'll get us drinks. What would you like? Wine, spirits, perhaps? Henri has bought an IPA."

"Red wine for me."

"And me." They stand together, taking in the deceptively simple luxury of the setting.

"Perfect. I'll join you. Three reds. Please look around while I pour. I decided not to have Henri put out hors d'oeuvres. His meals deserve our full attention." Taking three Swedish modern wine glasses from the vitrine, I press the button to open the bar panel and retrieve a decanter that Henri has prepared with my second-favorite red.

"Is that a Basquiat?" Jason, spellbound, whispers to Victor. "Christie's just sold one for over a hundred million."

"Yes," I say. "Isn't it dramatic? Full of energy, forces you to look at every complexity. The sleeping screen below will be changed for winter. It's one of four for the four seasons. I must say, the summer one is filled with naughty goings on, frolicking in the warm waters, open pavilions of multiple couplings. This one starts the calming. Bedroom scenes. Pregnant women being examined by midwives. Winter gets more pregnant. Spring has the births. If you look, the artist has not missed our kind. The summer one is more filled than the other three. Sixteenth century."

Victor was looking at a family portrait. "This looks a lot like you."

"That's a Botticelli. One of my ancestors. We have strong genes. My brother is an outlier. Blond to the rest of our Italian colorings. He is our French line. Every two generations one pops up."

I explain the special UV glass. Demonstrate the electrification. Show the greenhouse. Look out to the terraces and garden. "If you're here at dusk, we can go out. . . . The green house takes the whole top floor of the carriage house. I had to build a bridge to it from the sitting room. Up until two weeks ago, Henri informs me, the night-blooming jasmine filled the house with the most delicious perfume. Too bad it's over. We can open the door. The earthy smell is delicious on its own. The glass is UV-protected. Plants do not need it, a common misconception. So I can putter at any time. The gardener supervises.

"This is the bedroom."

The bookcases open, a set of gray panel doors slide into the wall pockets, revealing a gray-and-white room. The door frame and trim are painted in cream white. A dropped ceiling dart-and-egg border is tied a cream-colored ribbon around the room. A king-sized bed on a gray-wood platform with a gray- upholstered headboard dominate the left wall. A small table and chair covered in soft gray fabric sits on the opposite side.

I open a panel on the wall next to the sitting room exposing drawers, with cabinets above. The cabinetry matches the bed's gray. Another panel reveals shoes. Pants, shirts another. Sconces of gray-and-cream fabric with Japanese metal cranes hang above where bed tables should be, the only wall decorations in the room. I press a rectangle under the sconce, and a shelf pops out. One matches on the other side.

At the end of the wall with the table, there's a Restoration Hardware steamer trunk desk, gray with brass fittings, diagonal to what should be the street window, with a closed tablet on it. There is a panel in the wall that hides a huge TV and other electronics in the center. The remaining side is a panel that hides the street window, with a gray upholstered bench in front. A panel behind the desk matches it, all in soft gray; when closely examined, the walls are covered in linen fabric. The floor is covered in gray Berber. There are traditional gray Tibetan rugs on either side of the bed. The cream bed linens, I mention, are specially woven in France, the gray silk comforter above them woven in India a paisley pattern in a slightly darker thread.

"My brother wore a similar vest. I hope he doesn't object to my copying it." I like to give credit where due. Using someone's find for myself is deserving of recognition.

"When all the panels and doors are closed, the room is basically a sealed cube, an island of silence and darkness," I sigh.

To the left of the bed, a walk-in closet door is seamless to the wall. The bathroom door is to the right of the bed contains aa sunken spa tub, a shower that is also a sauna big enough for four, a heated toilet, a bidet, heated towel bars, and there are radiant floors in gleaming white tile, some with designs, randomly placed. I call them "little surprises." There's a rare white granite sink, and there are no mirrors. I tell Victor and Jason that they are behind a tile panel so they don't steam.

Returning to the sitting room, I find Henri standing at the head of the stairs. "Gentlemen, lunch is ready."

I ask them to bring their drinks. "Henri, grab the decanter, please." We use the stairs.

"Your home is so beautiful," Jason begins.

"Adopt us," Victor adds cheerily.

I laugh. "You're far too grown to adopt as anything other than friends. I hope that is happening." They are deliciously charming in body and minds.

"My Manhattan mansion is my official residence, much more formal. This is home to me."

We sit at the modern glass-and-sculptured steel dining table. Henri serves delicious poached eggs with truffled hollandaise and creamy polenta to the side. The wonderful breads he has baked including miniature croissants, which he serves with French butter. A salad follows of tender peaches on a bed of baby bibb, watercress, leaves only, sprinkled with the largest capers either of the men has ever seen, apricot vinegar, and olive oil from my family farm in Italy. Later, a delicious *tres leches* cake with whipped hazelnut cream. Coffee, wine, still water throughout. Conversation about Bern, Italy, their work, family. The neighbor not coming down in her price. Some hints of a family crisis being managed.

We return to the sitting room.

I request, "Lao Tzu, Sailor." A piano performance of a romantic Schubert sonata begins—soft, clear, distinct but unobtrusive. The windows darken slightly to a dusky blue sea not quite opaque. The lights create pooled areas of light flesh tones over sitting areas in a sea of soft, creamy white. Sensuous.

The duo exchange impressed glances. I anticipate a coming sealing of our friendship.

We enjoyed a fragrant Portuguese port. As dusk deepens, I open the glass doors to the terrace. They sit on the heated terrace while I lounge on the chaise inside. At some point I refer to the vigilante articles. Victor and Jason, alcohol relaxed, share more details than what has been printed.

I am enthralled.

27

NOW, QUEENS, NEW YORK

HELLO, MORTANA," HE SAID. She immediately recognized Agent Brown's voice on the other end. She was just getting ready for bed. The two-hour time difference meant it was 9:00 PM in Albuquerque.

"Hi, How are you? How's Albuquerque?"

Danny mouthed, "Who is it?"

"Agent Brown," she whispered to him.

"I'm good," said Brown. "Cold and dry. They have a winter thing here called Watermelon Sky at sunset. The red looks just like a ripe watermelon. Nothing I've seen anywhere before. How are you?"

"Doing OK. What's up?" She settled next to Danny.

"The case out here is as dead as in New York and everywhere else. I think our guy has gone to ground. If nothing happens— not that I want it to, but if nothing happens—headquarters will shut us down by the end of January, if not before. I have a hunch he may be hiding 'til the heat is off. I'll be back in D.C. then."

"What are you up to for Christmas?" She was trying to catch the thread of his emotions. Something was not right.

"Seeing my daughter, grandson, son-in-law."

"You never mentioned her before." So the grandson belonged to a daughter.

"You know me. On the need-to-know kind of guy. She lives near Baltimore. I can drive from my apartment and be home the same day. Richard, her husband, is with Langley. She teaches at a community college, Spanish and French. Both language whizzes. Ricky, my grandson, speaks Mandarin, Farsi, French, and Spanish. Nine years old."

"I can see he's got a career path going for him." Come on, Brown, she was thinking. Let's have more. I know the good person in there, you can trust me with him—her mind reaching for a deeper connection.

"How are your kids? Husband? What are you up to these days? Where have you been reassigned?" Brown asked in an uncharacteristic stream.

Mortana explained that Danny hasn't been well, not touching on why. She had taken a position with Public Liaisons, which gave her a regular working week. Good for Danny and the kids. They were looking forward to the holiday break. As she was talking, she began to suspect that Brown had been drinking. Sounded a bit down. Certainly more talkative than ever before.

"What's your daughter's name?"

"Beverly, after her mother. She died six years ago. Beverly my wife, not my daughter."

Definitely been drinking. "I'm so sorry. That is hard. Christmas with your daughter and her family will be good for you. Will you stay with them?"

"They want me to, but I like being alone." He sounded depressed.

"Agent—no, I'm not going to call you that for this conversation. Charles—" she chose to be bold, to chance it, sure by then that he needed some hand-holding. His reticence was loosening. Mortana had encouraged him to spend time with his family. He was alone too much— "Charles, I've seen what a wonderful person you are." His family deserved to see more of him, his kindness.

"You're probably right. Anyway, I just wanted to say hi. Catch up a bit." She was coming too close to his emotional limit.

"Nope, I'm not letting you run away." Her mind snapped to attention. She brightened with an idea. "How long will you be on the East Coast?"

"A week, ten days. December 23 to January 2. Why?"

"My kids would love a holiday trip now that Danny is doing better. I could book us into a Washington hotel, do the museums, historic sites. We could have lunch so you could meet them. Maybe a dinner just for the adults the next night? How would that be?"

"Are you sure? You don't want me to scare them." He seemed interested.

She pressed on. "You aren't scary to the good guys. I'm going to text you with dates. Let me know what's good for you. I'll need to book things ASAP. We could use some fun."

"Okay. Mortana. . . ." After a bit of silence, he told her she'd made a good choice going into public relations. Always put your family first. When his daughter got to be a teen, he got a series of promotions. He lost those next years. His wife was sick for three of them. He refocused on her, the family. It wasn't sunny times, but those three years were some of their best. And obviously the worst. But he didn't care. He had them to remember now.

"I agree, absolutely. Promise me, promise yourself to spend a few days with your daughter and her family. We'll plan the visit on our end tomorrow. I'll send you a text. I really want my family to meet you." She felt good about this.

"I think you're right, I need to get to be with Ricky more. Beverly and Richard, too. See you soon. It's a date." He signed off.

"Merry Christmas. See you in two weeks. Take care." Mortana especially looked forward to seeing him.

28

THEN, SICILY

A BODY HAS WASHED UP ON THE NORTH BEACH, close to Riposto. It can't be Vincenzo. The current I cast him in goes to Catania. The distance guaranteed at least three days in the water.

This man has drowned. Everyone is in an uproar.

"What's going on? Who is it?" I grab Mikel, who is almost collapsing in tears, by both shoulders, shaking him to break his sobbing.

"It's Fra Assisi."

"*No! Liar!*" As I am turning to run to the beach, he holds me back, tells me they have already brought him to the church.

I gather myself. I burst through the church doors. They have placed him on the raised floor at the steps of the altar. I cannot contain myself, fall to my knees next to him, uncontrollably hysterical.

Father Tomaso sends everyone away except me. He tells me to look, lifts my dear Admiral's shirt. He is covered with bruises. He has been beaten.

"What does this mean? Who would do this? Why?" Tomaso is now crying. I wonder who has a vendetta against my Admiral. I only saw goodness in him. Lusty and pious. A true lover of life. My heart aches like never before. I think I may be sick. Rushing outside, I leave my meal on the side of the walkway.

Mikel comes over. "I am in danger. Maybe you and Tomaso, too." That straightens me up. I look at him, confused.

"This is about his sex. I think it may be my father. Pietro taught me more than arithmetic. I know about you and Tomaso, too. My father beat me when he found out about Pietro and me. I was saved from worse when Dona Tartus took me as guard to Nyxos's grandmother."

"Your father would kill a priest for having sex with you? He knows that, in Sicily, priests top Mafia Dons almost." I am a fool to think this. Male honor is above all things in this island of violence.

"I think it was actually Don Deimos. I saw those bruises. I saw them once before on one of the gardeners who had offended the Don by complaining about being under paid. Two soldiers held him while Don Tartus beat him with brass knuckles on both hands. Used him like a punching bag. Took weeks for the man to work again."

No, Lorenzo may have complained to the Don and the beating done as a result. The drowning was for more. The only thing I could think of was he wanted information and Pietro wouldn't give it. The drowning was an ultimate threat. Pietro took whatever the Don wanted to his death. Or maybe he told and was removed before he could warn anyone. Or was simply dumped after death.

Jesus, I have to get Paulo.

"Mikel, find Paulo. Bring him to the church. Make sure you and he are not seen. Do this immediately. Steer clear of the compound and your father. We may have to flee."

I turned to Tomaso. "Where's the secret baptismal?"

"What's that got to do with our friend's murder?"

Everything. I believed the Don has gotten wind of it. But how?

This has little to nothing to do with Lorenzo. This has to do with the Don feeling threatened. Why attack the priest except that he must be at the center of that threat. Knowledge of the secret baptismal was all I could think possible.

Tomaso returned with the book. I tore out the damning pages, took the book to the caldron used to burn the palms for making Ash Wednesday ashes, douse it with brandy from Assisi's room, and set it on fire, a complete incineration.

Those two pages I will send to Elio for safe keeping. Will I need to escape? How do I get my money out of my room? Paulo either needs to strike now or run. Our plan may be in jeopardy. There is more to my Admiral's torture and death than reprisal for a worker's son's virginity.

Paulo slips in the sacristy door. I show him Father Assisi, the bruises. I tell him what I have done with the book. Should we not flee?

Mikel asks what is in the book that someone like Don Deimos might fear. I tell him and Tomaso the secrets. Lucia is in danger, too. They piece together the scenario.

"This is a way to flush us out." Paulo's calculating the known behavior of his murderous Don. "The compound is carefully watched. You and Mikel are known lovers of the good father. Tomaso we all suspect also. There are no secrets in Riposto. You three are in the most danger. He may decide to torture any one of you. If Deimos knew anything certain, we would be in the sea already. He is biding his time. We will go about as though nothing is going on, just an unfortunate drowning. There is, of course, the possibility it has to do with the missing Vincenzo. But Vincenzo has had nothing to do with the church or the good father since my boy's christening."

I am to tell Lucia of the failed plan at lunch, when I can get her alone. Tell her to empty Vincenzo's treasure chest. Put an equal weight in. She will need my keys. Vincenzo probably hid his when he got back, or gave them to Circe. We'll send the money to Paulo's mother with instructions to go to Palermo. We'll meet her at her brother's house or let her know it is safe to return within the month.

"Mikel, you will do this for us tonight?" Paulo both asks and orders.

"I'll sneak to my house and tell my mother. I am too afraid of my father. I will be sleeping elsewhere. She doesn't need to know where."

The women and Mikel had returned the night before Father Assisi's body came home. Two days earlier than expected.

"Good boy. Now everyone back to your regular duties. Sailor, wait. No more drugs. Circe would surely know. Get the money from Lucia today. Do you have a bag that will hold it?"

"I have one I got in Taormina." How I got it is none of his business.

I help prepare Pietro's body. We are horrified to find his right-hand fingers have all been broken. His torture was immense. I will cry in secret for months. Tomaso does the service in the morning. We bury him with mostly old women attending. Mikel arrives, stands in the back as we finish.

The next two days go on as usual. The family worries about Vincenzo. Deimos has sent out feelers through all of Sicily. Is any other family after his fiefdom? Has anyone been offended by Vincenzo to the point of murder?

One of the smuggler dock men tells Deimos about the Arab pulling a knife on Vincenzo and how Paulo intervened. Deimos is aroused. Why didn't Paulo mention this when Vincenzo went missing? He sends a message to the Tunis smuggler asking if his man has had more to do with Vincenzo. He doesn't expect the truth in any case but the way the Tunisian reacts to the insult will tell him the truth. Or as near as possible.

The next day, three after Assisi's corpse washed up, word comes from Catania that they think Vincenzo has come to a beach about five miles down the coast toward Riposto. They report the Tunisian knife and severed hands. He and Circe are besides themselves in mourning. Lucia puts on a good act.

Vincenzo's body is brought home. The Border Guards accompany the body. They tell Don Tartus and his sister that all the evidence points to Arab pirates. They hand over the body—what's left of it. Five days in the water, the fish have eaten much. But the ring on a secured hand was definitely the Tartus signet.

A day and a half later, Tomaso is altar boy to the bishop, who has been called in for the service. Father Assisi did not get that honor. His casket, made of expensive cherry wood, was paraded from the plantation to the church, then to the family cemetery in a procession of every man woman and child in the district, commanded to attend by the Don's henchmen.

After the mass and burial, everyone is invited to a meal. Given the day off, most attend the tables laid out in the olive orchard. Circe and Deimos seclude themselves in the compound. Lucia sits at the head of the table—the mourning, widowed madonna. The Bishop excused himself to meet with Tomaso, presumably to discuss a new monsignor for the three parishes Assisi has left unmoored.

Paulo instructs Mikel and me to meet him at the ancient tree. There he gives Mikel a good deal of cash to get him, Tomaso, Lucia, and Nyxos to his uncle in Palermo. A priest and a woman with a child would be suspicious, but having her sixteen- year-old brother with them will be more acceptable. Transportation must be arranged. In two days, they must be gone. We will follow as best we can.

"Our fortunes are over here. I plan to kill the demon, but if that doesn't go well, you all must promise to get Nyxos and Lucia to my mother at my uncle's for safekeeping. The Don has hired outsiders; paying more than Deimos for their loyalty is impossible. Our plan has been scuttled."

"Why not just run? Why risk your life when a baby and woman need your protection?" I ask, astonished by his statement.

"Honor."

These Sicilians have very slanted views on life. My aim is survival at all costs. My reputation does me no good if I'm in a shark's belly. I don't understand honor above all. Besides, dead means the wrong headstones sit on the wrong graves.

Later in the day, Circe sees me in the courtyard and orders me to clean the kitchen. The cantina women will cook a private meal for them and the Bishop. His business with the curate did not take long. A Neapolitan will arrive in some days to temporarily take over.

I am to set things sparkling. She and Deimos are going to visit her son's grave. They will say a rosary and expect dinner when they are back. Lucia will do the prayers in the morning. The custom is repeated for a full seven days, both ends of the day.

I cannot believe the luck. I expect it's a trap, but such an opportunity will never come again. I raid Deimos' treasury, replacing each emptied purse and box with rocks to fool the weighted feel if not the eye. Secured in my backpack with my valuables, the heft is more than Nyxos's pounds. Clothing can be bought.

I am in the kitchen, setting the dinner dishes. One of the new hires rushes in. At least I am presuming he is one of them. "You look tired. Here, have some water. Wine? Food? Why the hurry?"

"I just arrived from Tunis. Where is the Don?"

Instantly understanding the circumstances, I say, "Cantina," which is in the opposite direction of the graveyard.

I grab my treasury, run to Lucia, and tell her all has gone bad. We must run. I'll take her and the baby in my boat to Catania. We can buy our way to Palermo. She hands me the baby, his pack she had readied. We run to the dock.

She says "Go, I need to get something." She goes backup the cliff. I'm halfway down the path. Mikel is coming up from turning the fish compost. There is a God.

"Run to Paulo and Tomaso. We flee now. Go to the uncle in Palermo. Lucia and I will go to Catania and there to Palermo. Warn Paulo."

I have my boat ready to go when I hear Lucia screaming. I see her climbing out the back window. Circe has her by the hair and slices her throat right there. Her body falls limp over the sill. The whitewashed wall has an enlarging stream of dark flowing down it.

Men are running toward the cliff path. Mikel has already disappeared toward Paulo at the home rebuilding. Tomaso will be warned as the church is on the way. I put Nyxos in the fishing basket, tell him to hold on, and push off. The wind is coming off the shore: another blessing from God. I sail as far from land as I can, hoping they think I will go to Taormina to get to Messina, then the mainland. The sky is gray. I hope there is no squall. I pray that Pietro Assisi, my Admiral, can captain us to safety from the other side.

It will be weeks before I learn of everyone's fate.

29

NOW, NEW YORK CITY

"MERRY CHRISTMAS, MOM." MORTANA HAD already called their mother for Christmas, at an hour that would limit the conversation, so the older woman could get dressed and have time to drive to 9:00 AM mass in Scottsdale. She used to go to midnight mass but driving in the dark had become too difficult.

"Jason, Merry Christmas! Have you been to mass this morning? It's 2:00 PM your time. Did you go with your sister and her brown family to midnight mass?"

He had difficulty ignoring the racist sarcasm. Saying no to mass would be a fight before he got to tell her his news. He anticipated what her reaction would be but he was always hopeful his mother would move into the twenty-first century.

"Mom, I've got exciting news to tell you. I'm getting married!"

She was instantly off and running. *Who is the lucky girl? I hope she isn't related to your sister's brown in-laws. Where is she from? Is she Catholic?* Those and a half dozen more questions flew from her lips before she stopped to take a breath.

"I'm marrying Victor Virlus, a news reporter. He asked me. I said yes. Mortana is planning the wedding. It'll be in April. We want you to come."

Silence was not what he expected. He had never been able to stun her to silence before.

"...Mom? Are you still there?" More silence followed.

What came next was more what he expected. Much more, actually. The burning in hell wasn't new. The bible quotes weren't new. The blaming it on a distant father wasn't new. She'd always said that because she'd heard some quack psychologist say that that caused homosexuality. If anyone was distant, it was his born-again Catholic mother.

He couldn't resist, speaking over her tirade, "New studies show that homosexuality tends to follow the *mother's* line. Your mother was a big old Lesbo in her later years, I remember."

That stopped her again, but only for a moment. She went on with her latest condemnations. Such a marriage was a farce. God would punish them extra in hell for the mockery of the sacrament. "Pope Francis encourages people like you to think you're not a sinner. He's the false Christ who has bent over backwards for the fag molester clergy, in order to protect them. He—"

"Thanks, Mom. You'll get an invitation in the mail. Merry Christmas." Jason hung up and sank onto the couch. Semi-prepared for the onslaught, he still needed a moment to recover.

Victor had heard everything, though it wasn't on speaker phone. "Well, that was awful. Can I get you anything? Alcohol? A hitman?"

Jason laughed. "Just what I expected. I told you. How'd you like the big Lesbo line? I've been holding onto that since I was fourteen. I passed it by Cate and Barb."

Their Lesbian friends thought it would be offensive to *them*, but they knew what his mother was like, having gotten whipped by her tongue when she met them in his freshman year of high school—their only concern, was it true? It was. That was another story. In fact, all of his friends had been the target her religious rants until he left for college. He only introduced friends to his dad after the divorce.

"God, we all know people have parents like that, but she really aimed to hurt you. I'm so sorry you had to grow up with that." Victor had been lucky in a way. His aunt, who rescued him, had no judgements to speak of except, "I just want you to be happy and. . .safe."

Jason thought it was time to give the whole picture to his fiancé. "She said something horrible to every friend either of us brought home. I think she read *Carrie* as a Bible study guide. Dad was 180 degrees different. He saved me especially. Mortana got it worse when she met Danny—never mind getting pregnant without a ring."

Jason leaned into Victor, who had begun massaging Jason's neck. "Dad would say, 'She is *horrible* when she's on her religious kick. Otherwise, she's a good person. You're *nothing* like what she says.' I didn't tell you this because I didn't want to scare you away. The twins even know."

Jason had decided to rid himself of the whole sordid story, telling Victor he saw no point in carrying it around any longer. His and Mortana's father had told them everything the day that he filed for divorce.

He couldn't stand their mother's rants. He'd asked her for a divorce when the kids were eight and six. She'd sworn she would take the kids from him, wreck his career.

She had manufactured false stories to her church friends for years about his beating her and the kids. More than once she'd photographed the kids' bruises, and her own, from routine accidents, and shown them to people to back up her stories. She had told him that she'd have people willing to testify to his brutality. He hadn't wanted the children to live without a buffer, a reality check. When he went on deployment, their lives had been hell. As far as he and Mortana, were concerned she remained certifiable. If she hadn't been so constantly, intentionally hurtful, they could have felt sorry for her.

Dad had had papers drawn up. The day Jason graduated high school at seventeen, he'd filed them—the happiest day of his life after their births, he had said. She worked in the parish office, had an income. He gladly gave her the house. Without kids to get child support on, he was completely free of her. Their college expenses and support came directly to them from him. He'd bought a condo in Brooklyn with three bedrooms—one for each of them. If he was away, they had lived there on their own. They'd both gone to college in New York City. He'd trusted them. They had only had one bad party. Luckily, he's been away for another two months. The neighbors had forgiven them. They'd sold it after he died. Their friends had all loved him.

"You would have too," Jason told Victor. "Nothing like a typical marine officer. At home he was a pushover pop," he added with a tinge of sorrow. "We were lucky to have him. Other men would have rightfully run. What you just heard was an average conversation. We've had worse. Mortana has had terrible rows with her. I learned to do what I did today when I came out to them at fourteen—cut it short."

"God, I'm so sorry. I thought *I* had it rough." Victor petted his lover's arm.

"We all have our stories. You and I are going to make much, much better ones together. Promise."

"Promise." A quick peck on the lips.

Shaking off the miserable last half hour or so, Jason patted Victor's leg and got up from the couch to get their coats, "Okay. Gear up. You have never experienced my sister's extended family's Christmas. I didn't let you eat lunch because, at four o'clock, a three-hour meal starts. Those three women, Juan, and the twins have been cooking for three days. Danny made his cookies last week."

"What are we bringing?" Victor asked, realizing no food shopping had been done.

"We sent a case of wine and one of sparkling water. We could never bring all that *and* these presents. Our jingle bells Uber to Tia's will be here at 3:00. Fifteen minutes. Purge if you're smart." Handing him his coat, Jason planted a kiss on his lover's dark head.

THE UBER DRIVER WAS A YOUNG GUY, maybe twenty-two. He packed their presents in the trunk. The food packages that had been thrust on them, they decided would be safer between their feet. "I feel like I ate Astoria." Victor was careful to burp silently.

"I told you." The car was filled with the sweetness of chocolate chip cookies. "Danny's cookies are the best. When Sis married into that family, holiday food hell broke loose. Four adults and two kids who live to cook. We just ate our way from Queens to Manila."

The Uber driver asked, "You two married?"

They both cringed. They know that more than one Mr. Black was out there. Victor cautiously said, "Not yet. April."

"You act like you are. My brother married his boyfriend two years ago. They were together ten years. Expecting a boy. Bill's sister is the surrogate, Rama the sperm donor. I'm so happy I'll finally be an uncle!"

No, he didn't have a significant other. They continued a pleasant discussion of Christmas customs. The driver went on about his Bengali family: Christian for three generations. Grandparents came to America in the Sixties. Grandfather was nineteen, his bride seventeen. They wanted to leave the old world completely behind.

Except for the cooking. Grandpa opened an Indian restaurant on Lexington Avenue in the mid-Fifties. Grandma helped. Named their kids George and Martha. Obviously, they'd never seen the movie. Their children had gone to public colleges. Dad had met his Bombay-descended wife there. The first-generation children had given their kids Hindi names. Dad had become an optometrist. Mom a dentist.

"Wow. That is a real story. Are you in school?" Jason, ever the academic, was always ready to encourage people to a higher education.

"Baruch. I want to be a lawyer. Rama is a dermatologist. Four years in private practice. What do you fellows do? Don't answer that. I pry too much. My mother tells me I'm perfect for a lawyer or a detective." The driver giggled with a Bollywood lilt.

"I don't mind. I'm Jason, and this fellow is Victor. I'm an epidemiologist, a college professor. Vic is a newspaper feature writer. You might know him—V2 is his by-line. He writes for *Gay Nation Press*."

"Wow, I read you all the time! I'm Del. Nice to meet you." A few minutes passed. Looking in the rear view mirror, he chanced, "You guys are just the type I'd like to meet. I'm into daddies."

The pair in the back seat exchanged glances as the car slowed on their street.

"We're here. I hope I didn't bend your ears too much." He turned to them between the headrests, smiling with the same brightness as his spoken come-on. He had parked in front of their apartment building.

Jason offered, "We're giving you a great review, and I changed the tip." Dipping into his bag of cookies, he wrapped three in one of the napkins and passed them forward. "You'll love these."

Del put them on the passenger seat, got out, opened the trunk, and helped them get their bundles to the curb.

"We could add milk to those cookies." Jason metaphor-ed as he handed Del his card, the double entendre well taken.

"Really. I can't tonight, but—"

"Not tonight, we're stuffed." Jason playfully patted his belly. "I'm free for Christmas break. Call tomorrow. We can set up a date to have you. . .over."

Victor wished he had not had thirds. His own appetite for a sub-continent dessert was becoming apparent.

"I'm free tomorrow night." The driver was beyond himself— V2 *and* his husband to be.

"Call, we'll set up a time." Jason made eye-contact. "Merry Christmas, Del. Thank you for a lovely ride. More tomorrow."

"I agree. You gave us a nice closing to a great day. Tomorrow. Merry Christmas!"

Well, if you ignored Mrs. Lemures, which Jason had done better than Victor.

"Merry Christmas," Del waved out the window as he pulled away from the curb.

Victor turned to Jason, leering. "Pint size. Easy to toss around."

"Fun size." Jason laughed, grabbed some bundles, and headed to their doorway.

30

THEN, SICILY

DEIMOS LIES BLEEDING, HAMSTRUNG, on the kitchen floor. Circe is next to him, her intestines visible through her slashed stomach. Paulo's body lies at Deimos's feet, knife in his back. Paulo's long blade has been kicked across the floor by one of the henchmen.

"Jackass! Don't *stand* there, get the doctor!" Deimos yells as best he can at one of the new men. Another comes in to help stop his bleeding. He pushes the man away, dragging himself to his sister.

"Circe, don't leave me. Circe, darling, please hang on. The doctor is coming." He is propped up on an elbow, caressing her face. She is staring ahead, breath smooth, shallow, making no effort to maintain life. The blood on the floor, a bath for her body, is moistening his, mingling their lives. She sighs, and is gone.

"*Bastard.* I'd kill you a *thousand* times!" Looking at Paulo's cut-up body, Deimos falls back.

The man who tried to help kneels down and starts to bind Deimos's wounds. Deimos looks at him from a faraway place, lays his head next to his sister's, and closes his eyes. The man looks to see if he is breathing. Deimos opens his eyes, raises his head. "I will not die," he gasps, "until I see every one of them dead, including his bastard." He lies back down, passed out.

FOR TWO DAYS, HE IS UNCONSCIOUS. The soldiers are starting to consider who will take over such a luscious prize as the plantation. Deimos, to everyone's surprise, then recovers his senses. The doctor is called, rushes to the plantation in disbelief, is almost servile in his attentiveness. "Don Tartus, you are fortunate to live. You lost much blood. You must rest. Eat. Let the cook feed you. You need to regain your strength. I will tell her what to cook for you."

"Get me up out of this bed." The patient struggles to rise, anger the sole source of his energy. He is physically too weak to do so.

"Don Tartus, I am afraid you must brace yourself for bad news."

"Moron. I know Circe is gone."

"No, my friend, almost as bad. . . . Your legs are useless. The tendons and muscles have been cut to shreds. They cannot be repaired."

Deimos feels his legs. He can feel them. But when he tries to move his feet he cannot. "Fool! Tell me who *can* fix them. I'll pay. I have money."

Noting the rising panic in the Don's voice, the doctor sighs. " No amount of money can buy new legs." The Don will need to content himself with a chair on wheels.

"Get out! Go away! Be glad I don't cut your *tongue* out." Deimos does not intend to accept such a fate. Always blame another for your circumstance. Never think how your life led to this or that predicament.

The doctor takes the woman who has been caring for the Don outside. He stops by one of the guards and asks for the head man to come to him also.

He tells the woman the ingredients that must be made into a soup that will help restore Don Tartus' blood and strength. They are to be careful not to upset him. Change the bandages every day. He himself will return every other day to clean the wounds. Most of all, the Don needs rest to recover.

Caputo arrives. He takes the head man to the almond tree. They sit. The sun is weak, and a storm is brewing. He asks one of the men milling about to bring wine. They wait. The wine is poured.

"My name is Dr. Santini. I have been Riposto's doctor for thirty years. What is your name?"

"Guido. Caputo. What do you want?" The head man is busy shoring up his control over the new hires, sidelining the Don's loyalists.

"You are head man, no?" The man acknowledges himself. "The Don will probably recover. He has a strong will. He can never walk again. However, his condition can always turn for the worse. It is in God's hands. I thought you should know."

Guido did not become head man of the new hires without being able to take advantage of a situation. He assesses the doctor. He notes the conflicting prognoses the doctor has had time to spread about.

"You will do as best you can. We will pray to God, but as you say, we never know. You will be paid whatever the outcome. Thank you for recognizing my position." Guido will need to find a consiglieri in his loose new band. No man can capture such a prize as this plantation without a good right-hand man.

The doctor says his goodbyes. Guido accompanies him on the path to the main road, their continued conversation out of all possibility of being heard.

When the woman returns to the bedroom, Deimos says, "Marta. You are Marta?" She nods. "Tell Sebastione to come immediately."

She goes to the cantina to ask where she can find Sebastione. Lorenzo tells her he was at the new house this morning.

Sebastione is not happy to be summoned by Tartus. He was to be one of Paulo's capos. If Tartus knows this in any way, he is fish food.

Doffing his cap when he gets there, he says, "Don Tartus, it is so good to see you awake. You must rest." Standing next to the bed, he thinks, Why is this man alive? The Don looks like a ghost in the graveyard.

"Get four of my loyal men. Let me speak to each, then station two at my door. Two more at the house entrance. Well-armed. Immediately."

Sebastione is relieved, even encouraged that the Don has no suspicion. He needs to plan how to handle things when the Don is more clear-headed and starts to think about the plot that must have been in the planning. Sly, cunning, the Don may not be smart, but he is a ruthless survivor who never forgets or forgives.

Sebastione gathers four of the old guard. The Don has realized that the new men have loyalty to money, not him. Their headman, Guido Caputo, impressed Deimos as someone who was as trustworthy as Etna, ready to blow at any minute.

The bought men see a weakened Don who is vulnerable. He needs to guard his position. Pay them off. Get rid of them. Without Circe or Vincenzo, his life is in utter danger. The old guard is all he has. Trusting in them offers the only possibility to stay alive and regain control of his fiefdom.

He calls Sebastione into the room. "Besides the four, who else is trustworthy? Bring me a list. Count the number of new hires. Keep everything you do secret. Who has disappeared besides that bastard son of my Milano sister? I need to know it all." He is tired, lies back on his pillow. "Ask Marta to bring me the food that that quack ordered. Come back as soon as possible."

Sebastione speculates he could be consiglieri or more if he plays his cards right. He leaves to perform the duties he has been entrusted with.

I arrived in Palermo a week after the collapse. Almost a week of rain made travel slower than usual. I delivered Nyxos to his grandmother and gave her some money from Deimos's treasury, enough to compensate for the child's care and education when added to the trove entrusted to Paulo's mother.

She has had word that Paulo is dead, Circe too, and that Deimos is crippled, a prisoner in his compound. Guido Caputo is claiming the compound and fiefdom. The neighboring Dons are hesitant, unsure what will be done. Legally, all of Deimos's property is still his. His grandson is his heir. He has not publicly disowned the child.

Father Tomaso and Mikel were there but have moved to the cloister of St. Michael the Archangel, outside of town. It is closed to the world, safer than the city. They have not mentioned money.

Deimos has no way of seeking revenge, but Nyxos is in danger from Caputo now. The wheel of fortune is not just turning, it is spinning like a top.

I RING THE BELL AT ST. MICHAEL'S GATE. A small faceplate opens. I tell the friar that I seek an audience with my friend Father Tomaso from Riposto. Perhaps my nephew, Mikel, is here with him. "Tell them Sailor is here to see them." The man, nearly inaudible, tells me to wait.

After a long wait, the door opens, and I'm admitted to an empty vestibule. There is a door on the other side. I am locked in. Through that door's faceplate, I am told by the same friar that I must leave any weapons in the basket. I must submit to a search. The friar watches as I disarm, placing my weapons in a basket that is pulled through an opening. I'm uncomfortable without protection. The friar enters the vestibule. The door behind him locks. He pats me down, then knocks on the door in a short pattern. The inner door opens. He indicates a bench for me to sit on in the small courtyard, and he leaves through another door. I am isolated and simply wait, staying out of the hot sun. A week of damp has changed to heat.

Not much later, Tomaso and Mikel appear. We embrace. "Speak very softly," says Tomas. "The good friars may take vows of silence, but their hearing is better than any wolf's." He turns to Mikel. "Tell him."

"We had to buy our way here. Much of the money Paulo gave me is spent. We are sorry that Nyxos will not have much."

"Don't worry about that. Paulo did not give you everything. Nyxos has enough for now. But Caputo is a real danger." They were present when Dona Geraldi was informed of the results of Paolo's failure to eradicate the Don.

"What next should we do?" Tomaso asks me. He has no desire to be a friar. Mikel either. Sebastione is the one who brought word to Dona Garaldi that her son was dead. He came also to try to raise a force to take the compound back, not for Deimos but for Nyxos. He would make himself Don, leave the fiefdom to Nyxos. He would formally adopt Nyxos. Lucia's mother would approve.

This is obviously not a good plan for Nyxos' survival. Too many would profit from his demise.

"Well," I say, "I have no interest in any of that except to see that Nyxos is safe." I do have some loyalty to Paulo and his son. You cannot abandon your responsibility if you can be confident of your own safety. Away from Riposto, that confidence grows.

"Sebastione said that, when you arrived, if you did, he wants to see you. I'm sure it's about money." He tells me where to find him. I know exactly where to avoid, thank you.

"With your permission, I would use some of the money Paulo gave Mikel and get to Zurich. My mentor is there and could help me get to my home country. My family will help me find something better than this priest's life. Mikel can come with me if he wants."

Mikel says he would rather be in Italy, on the mainland. Tomaso's northland sounds too cold for him. He would not mind traveling with me. I tell them to split the money. I can see them both to Naples, but after that I don't know if we should be together. I need freedom once Nyxos's life is assured.

"Tomorrow, I will come for you." We hug, not sure what tomorrow will bring.

I ask them to ask the friar to return my weapons.

I am locked in the vestibule again, the basket pushed back in. I arm myself and am let out.

I step into the sun light. One step later, I am seized on both sides, and a hood is put over my head, a knife to my back. "Be quiet. We are not to harm you. Sebastione wants to see you."

Damn, damn, *damn!*

31

NOW, NEW YORK CITY

AGENT BROWN WAS BACK IN ALBUQUERQUE. "Hi, Mortana, how are you? The family? . . . Yeah, it was nice. I received word that I'm being called back to Washington. They're closing this down by mid-February. If anything happens anywhere, they'll reassemble the team. Three months of nothing."

He'll be reassigned to a case on human trafficking. He can't say anything more. Mortana tells him that everybody in New York is doing fine. The kids have finished their exams. Calyce did not do as well as she has in the past. She got her first "C" ever, in math. She may need a tutor. She said her dad's illness threw her. Jeremy did well, "A"s in what he likes, "B"s in classes with teachers who are jerks.

"We keep after him, telling him it's the subject, not the teacher, that should determine the grade. But to be honest, Danny and I see his point. We don't want him to use it as an out, though."

Brown's grandson has been given a scholarship to one of the best private schools in Baltimore. The kid is a language and math genius. Takes after his parents, says Brown, in language at least.

"Did I tell you we thought we caught the bathtub slayer?"

The guy knew things that were never published. Every crime has a certain number of volunteer perps. He was pretty convincing until they found out his uncle was a super in one of the buildings where a murder occurred. Holiday dinner conversation cued him in. He spent three days in the Hoboken General Psychiatric ward. Harmless, not even delusional. Just an attention seeker.

Score: the FBI zero, serial killers thirty-two and four. Not that unusual, actually, and until one of them trips up, that probably won't change.

"Let's make a date the next time I'm in New York. I think the new assignment will get me there in a month or two." Charles' voice betrays an unusual anticipation, anxiousness.

Mortana tells him she will look forward to it.

I'D BEEN CORRESPONDING WITH THIS FELLOW for a month. We finally met. He wasn't anywhere near the age or weight of his picture online. I insisted on a coffee shop. Bartenders have become too attentive, thanks to Victor. I offered him a ride home. When he got in the car, I injected immediately him with propofol.

Into the carriage house, through the tunnel, strapped to the table. I went upstairs to let him recover from the drugs. He needs to be clear of them.

I finished the remains of the second and the full third episode of *Midnight Mass* on Netflix. It was quite good. The master flying away looking like a naked bat was an amusing touch. A whole island of vampires with skewed religious zeal in America could be a metaphor for Washington, D.C., or the financial industry in New York where money is the religion. Writers have such fertile imaginations.

Down into the quiet of my own little chapel. He is awake. Of course, there is the usual begging, threats, entreaties. I hook up an empty plasma bag and drain blood from him. This is so much neater than opening a vein and letting the blood drip through the table drain into a container. It also eliminates waste. I take another. The man is well over two hundred pounds, so he is chock full of the nectar, up to two gallons or more.

As I fill each bag, I hang it on the winch bar over him. His eyes go wide. I talk to him about his terrible politics for a Gay man. He is not interested in political discussions any longer. I tell him his demise will rid the world of one more hateful being. He has the usual repertoire of unimaginative metaphors for me. This is tedious. Today is not about entertainment but replenishment. I'm getting hungry. I hook a second line into his other arm, double my capacity.

Four pints hanging from the bar: He is crying. Two more. Then two more. He is weakened almost to unconsciousness. If he were not lying down, he would have passed out. As it is, he could have any number of medical incidents at any moment. He has just the right amount left in him for me to satisfy my hunger without over-indulging. Fresh from the source, very artisanal. I push his head to one side and sink into him; the thump of his heart vibrates my fangs; draining his remaining fluids, I feel the life evaporate.

I put the eight bags in the "special red" cellar in my underground lair.

Preserving his body with embalming fluid is a lark. I found containers enough for twenty or so bodies when I bought my funeral home the few blocks from here.

I will dump it in the Rockaways tomorrow night. When it washes up, the confusion will be delightful. His weight is of little concern; I am quite strong. One of the perks of the Gift.

"WELL, THAT'S GRUESOME."

"What?"

"Weren't you listening?" Danny was looking at the TV at the foot of their bed. Mortana was reading a book.

"Huh?" she grunted, straightening her part of the blanket.

"A body washed up in Far Rockaway. An embalmed body. No ID yet." Danny scanned Mortana's book cover. "Anne Rice. I haven't read her in a few years."

"I'm almost done. This one isn't very revealing. I mean, she's explored vampires to the nth degree. I do love her stories, though."

"How does a funeral home lose a body? Unless it's a zombie. But that's a different kind of monster than you like to read about." Danny nudged his wife.

"I wonder if I'll have to deal with the press on this. Anyway, I'm turning the light off. Work in the morning. Give a kiss." She kissed him. "Love you."

Danny turned off the TV. In the darkness he answered her, "Love you, too. No biting."

32

NOW, NEW YORK

MORTANA WANTS A GUEST LIST. Start getting one together. I haven't met any of your family. Maybe I should
before the wedding." Jason was prodding Victor over the
sound of his after-work shower.

There was no escaping from it. Mortana would be relentless. Besides, Jason did feel a need to know Victor's family. His fiancé had admitted to a brother and some aunts and uncles. The Korean mother's
family all lived overseas. His mixed-race father's family, White and
Black, were all on his Black grandparents' side. They were all holy rollers
and wanted nothing to do with their sinning Gay relative. The White
part were all dead.

Victor had not seen his brother in years, a heroin addict last he knew,
the family curse, the last they'd had contact a text five years before. He'd
wanted money.

"Maybe he's gotten his act together. Text him. Maybe he kept his
number." Jason would like to see if the distance can be overcome.
Family is so important to the Lemures siblings, he can't imagine not

wanting that for his lover's family.

"I'll think about it. Don't push," Victor called back over Jason's waterfall, sure there would be a problem whichever way he decided. "Actually, I have something much more exciting to talk to you about. I've been holding out to see if it was going to be real." Victor was loud so he could be heard clearly.

Jason turned off the shower and opened the door, drying himself off with the fresh towel Victor handed him. "What?" he asked, impatient for good news as always, but with Victor "exciting" could mean a piece about a dismembered body washing up in Central Park Lake.

"Get done drying off. Let's sit on the couch." Victor wanted Jason's complete attention.

"You're making me nervous." Jason hung up the towel and got his home sweats off the closet hook.

"Good. Maybe you'll leave me alone about my brother." Oops, that wasn't right. Victor did a quick repair. "It's good. Put on some clothes and come sit."

"Do I need a drink?" Jason was still a bit apprehensive. "If it all works out, champagne will be appropriate." He pulled on a tee and sat on the couch. Victor sat with his leg bent under himself, facing him.

"I'm all yours. All ears." Jason adjusted his body to reflect Victor's.

"New York One has approached me to do commentary on their morning show." Victor paused. "We've had two meetings about it."

"That's *wonderful!*" Jason would never get used to Victor's penchant to hold his cards close to his chest. "Why didn't you tell me before?"

"I know, but you know me. I don't like disappointment. The first meeting went well. They called a second and started talking money. So I'm allowing myself to feel it's real. I met with them today." Victor was beaming.

Jason punched him playfully in the arm. "Louse. Never keep good things secret. I'll forgive you this time, but good or bad, we are partners in everything. I'm so happy for you. Tell me all about it. I have a million questions."

"Okay. But promise me, don't say anything to anyone until the papers are signed."

Jason agreed. Victor laid out the offer, what his duties would be. No, he would not have to give up the paper. What about Gil Krier? Victor would be introduced as Victor Virlus of GNP. Great publicity for the paper. It would be a Monday-and-Friday gig. Five minutes. Filming in the community. Get out of Manhattan. An LGBTQIA feature: What's of concern to the community, what's happened, is happening, needs to happen. Political commentary. If all went well, more days might be added. Election cycles definitely would require more airtime. It had the potential to pay as much as twice what he was now making—a huge boost in their resources.

"Wow. My own TV star." Jason gave Victor a big kiss.

"Remember, no one knows until it's a done deal."

"Okay. Get dressed, and let me take you out for dinner." Jason had been taught by his father to celebrate whenever and wherever one could. The Greek love of life was well passed on.

"Not until the ink is dry. But you can order in. I'd say you could cook, but I want to live to sign those papers," Victor concluded with a jibe at Jason's acknowledged lack of culinary skills.

JACK, I HAVE SOME GOOD NEWS. DOES THIS NUMBER EVEN WORK? *Vic.* Victor had decided to text his brother.

Two days later he got an answer: *Yes, it works. Call 7:00 PM Wednesday or Thursday. Text me which day.*

Wednesday night, Jason sat anxiously on their couch. Victor was in the bedroom. He didn't want any distractions. The door was left slightly open. Jason could eavesdrop but if he made one sound the door would get closed. Victor was adamant. He dialed his brother's number. "Hello,

Jack. How are you?" he asked in voice a bit tight. He cleared his throat.

"What is this about?" Jack was fairly hostile. He didn't sound much different than he had in the past.

"Well, I'm getting married and my fiancé wants to meet my brother."

Jack was silent, a humming noise in the background all Victor could hear. "What's that noise?" he asked.

"I'm on my break at work. I work three until ten, four days a week. It's a machine. So who's the fool willing to marry you?" Jack had softened his tone though the words were harsh.

Victor wasn't insulted. It was the first real job he'd ever heard his brother have. The question felt more genuine than any he ever remembered, as an adult, from his brother.

"Jack, I really want to know how you are. Then I'll go into details." Jason made sure his concern sounded sincere not exaggerated.

"I'm okay. Clean four years, March, if that's what you're asking about." The voice was defensive but had a note of accomplishment, pride even, in it.

"I'm really happy to hear that. For your sake." Victor paused then answered Jack's question. "My future husband is Jason Lemures. He's a professor. He's thirty-seven. White. I love him a lot. We're good together." Victor stopped, listened, not sure how his brother was taking this in.

"Nice. With our history, I'd've expected an ex-addict. Although I guess a professor could be." Jack had softened, not only his tone, but the delivery.

"No, clean as a whistle. How about you? Any significant other?" Victor hungered for this connection, more than he had acknowledged to himself.

"Not now. I do date occasionally. My program brings me into contact with some good women. Nothing's clicked so far." Sharing this made Victor see the possibility of a real relationship between the brothers.

"Jack, I can't tell you how happy I am to hear you're okay. Where are you living?"

They caught up on the seven years since they'd seen each other. Life hadn't been easy. Until he got clean, it had been skid row and avoiding arrest. Now he was doing okay, working for a metal shaping company, and glad Victor had a profession. He was OK to meet Jason. They make a date.

Victor shuffled out of the bedroom, blowing his nose. Glistening eyes betrayed his emotional state.

"I guess this makes you happy. We'll meet him in Jackson Heights next Monday night. He'll text me the restaurant's address."

"Yes, it does make me happy. And you?" Jason was not pushing but pretty sure of the answer.

"Yeah, it makes me happy. He sounded good. Like the brother I knew before Momma died." Victor seemed a bit lost in memories and emotions.

"I heard most of it pretty clearly. I'm excited for all three of us."

Victor warned him, "I know you and your family. Give Jack and me a chance to reconnect before you swallow him whole. You guys see everyone as Jonah to your whale. I love you all, but let's be careful. Virlus men scare easy."

"Bullshit. You have been, and will always be, my brave hero." Jason hugged him, a physical gesture to secure the truth Jason had just spoken.

"Are you cooking, or do we order in?" Jason's stomach dictated many of their evenings. Victor was an excellent cook.

33

THEN, SICILY

EXACTLY WHAT TOMASO SAID: Sebastione wanted money. Caputo had searched everywhere. Deimos had no idea where it had gone except maybe with the murderer's cohorts. Torture didn't loosen Tarsus's tongue any further.

Fearing they were next on the rack, most of the old guard had fled. Five accompanied Sebastione to Palermo. Dona Garaldi had no idea about money, only the amount Paulo had sent to get her there. The six had searched her brother's house but found nothing more than a few coins. She had hidden Vincenzo's treasure well.

"Where is the *money?*" Sebastione and Benedicto were taking turns threatening, then beating me. I told them I had no idea. I explained that the whole enterprise up until now had been financed with my money. Part of Vincenzo's cache had been to reimburse me. Lucia was to bring it when we fled. That had been what she ran back for. We all knew how that went.

"Then finance us now. Paulo depended on you. Let us recover the plantation for his son." I laughed. I had no money left. A few hundred maybe. I planned to give most of that to Dona Garaldi to help buy food for the baby. Certainly not enough for a campaign against Caputo.

Tomaso and Mikel had had some of my money to get where we were. Paulo had given it to them. They told me it had all been used up. That is why Tomaso had them take refuge with the monks: no money, no place to hide. I personally thought that Caputo's men had found it and, unbeknownst to the boss, taken it. As far as Don Tartus's treasury, who knew where he had hidden it when Vincenzo went missing? Torture would never reveal that. Tartus had nothing left to lose.

I planned to use what I didn't give to Dona Garaldi to buy passage back home. I had a son I hadn't seen. They laughed at that. I did, too, telling them even I made mistakes. I asked them why would I hold out when I had promised Paulo to care for his son and mother. Lucia too, rest her soul.

They seemed to buy it. They let me go. I knew they would watch me. After a night's recovery, I went to the monastery and gave the friar a note to give to Tomaso saying I planned to leave for my home in a few days. I thought they would understand my warning. I hoped they would be ready to leave at any time.

At the house of Dona Garaldi's brother, I explained her choices as best I could see them. Nyxos was in danger from both Caputo and Sebastione—and definitely from Deimos if some miracle restored him. She could stay in Palermo and take her chances that Caputo would simply take over the plantation and force the mayor to put the land in his name. She could chance that Sebastione would get the upper hand and protect Nyxos until he was of age. But it seemed more likely that Nyxos and she would become chum in the sea. I proposed she flee with me to the mainland, to Trieste. There my aunt could help her find a place to establish an herbal practice and raise the boy. The money she had from Paulo would be a good beginning. My aunt knew how to grow money, so she could take part of it to do so for the child at my behest.

I gave her two days to decide.

The next day, seeing my follower across from my inn, I went to the wharfs to inquire about passage to the mainland. I bought passage to Naples for myself for the end of the week. The next morning, I snuck back to book passage for a family to Genoa—a mother, three sons, and an infant leaving the next day.

I sent a note to the monastery with a street urchin, a coin for him and one for the friar. I watched from a side street. Sebastione's man did not catch on. I told the men where to meet me. "We go where I have bought passage. After that it will be up to you where you end up." I did not dare tell them our destination for fear they'd get taken and reveal my plan. As in all monasteries, there was a secret passage to the outside that they would use to be free of their minders.

Dona Garaldi decided to flee. Her brother's wife would take a bundle to the market in the morning. She would dress as the Dona. The bundle would be Nyxos—a diversion to get her monitors away from the house.

I crossed roofs to the inn where I had rented a room when I entered Palermo before seeking out the uncle's house. There I hid my knapsack. I paid the innkeeper to hold the room because I was attending a wedding and needed a place to return from the festivities in a day or two. My wife's family was known for long feasting parties. After traveling with my son, let his mother care for him. I needed a refuge. Money was more important than reasons as far as the innkeeper was concerned.

We met at the square of the seaman's chapel, Stella Maris. We hid below deck in our cabins for the hour until we hauled anchor. Three days to Genoa. Fine weather the whole way—Tomaso, Mikel, and I to one cabin, the Dona and baby the other. We three like-minded men found ways to entertain our nights, being careful not to disturb others. Mikel was Pietro's excellent student.

The small ship's captain respected my knowledge of the stars. We spoke often in the evening after a meal. He ignored the fact that the three brothers looked as unalike as three strangers could.

From Genoa it was a matter of land passage to Trieste for Dona Garaldi, Nyxos, and me. Mikel decided to go with Tomaso to Zurich after all. He had developed a crush on the blond giant. I gave them more money in memory of our patron, Father Assisi.

"TELL DONA CANNE MILAN VIA SICILY is at her door. I need her ear," I call up to the young woman whose head has come out of the window above the door in the wall surrounding my aunt's castle.

"Who are those with you?" The girl is haughty. I have only been here once before and expected this. It is probably one of the few places in the world where women are superior to men in all the stations of civilized nations. Here I would be twice scorned if not for the fact that Geraldine is dedicated to Sappho, aunt to men of my kind.

"They travel under my protection. Dona Garaldi and her infant grandson, late of Palermo."

"Man, wait there. Dona Garaldi, do you need anything?" The guard at the window calls down.

"Thank you, my dear. Just tell my young guardian's aunt we need to speak with her." Dona Garaldi turns to me when the young woman's head is withdrawn. "It is best not to look like beggars. I would like to get some food in Nyxos very soon." The baby has started to get fussy. It is cooler here than in Sicily, and we are wrapped in capes I purchased at a market in a town we traveled through. The baby is swaddled in many blankets.

The woman appears at the window. "Weapons are to be put in the basket in the vestibule. Someone will search you both. Dona Garaldi, enter with the baby. Man, remain where you are." The door opens. This is identical to the monastery's security measures. The times are dangerous.

After some time, the door opens, and I enter. My weapons go in the basket and disappear. The inner door allows a middle-aged woman to enter who searches me the way a man would. I am admitted into a courtyard where my companions await. The searcher tells us to follow her.

We are brought to a room with a simple table and chairs, and some food and drink. We are told the head of the house has asked us to nourish ourselves. She will be here shortly. If we want, a babysitter wet nurse will be happy to take the baby while we visit. Dona Garaldi is uneasy, but I assure her I never knew my aunt to be anything but honorable—at which point she enters in the room.

"Nephew, what brings you to our home? And who is this honored grandmother? And the baby, surely not yours?" My aunt is attired in a fine damask robe over loose silk pants and a blouse, all in golds and greens. Her feet are housed in fine Turkish-style slippers. She wears a dagger at her waist, gold necklace, and a green gemstone ring. The searcher, who continues to stand by, is also armed and in fine wool and cotton clothing, and is also wearing pants.

"Sit, eat. Gerta, could you ask Hazel to make us hot tea? Perhaps a soup?"

"Geraldine, I would take the child to Matilda, to wet nurse him. Is that alright?" She eyes me with caution.

"This is my nephew, who is, like myself and many of our sisters, not interested in the opposite sex. His desire, as I have too often heard from my brother, is for male companionship. Although the baby is a bit confusing." Turning to me, she asks, "Explain your visit my, nephew. Start with the baby." Dona Garaldi accepts the offer for a wet nurse.

I describe my need of help for Dona Garaldi and Nyxos. I give much of the background but not all, letting her know the child is the victim of a Mafia war, and that his only living relative capable of raising him is his grandmother. Both are targets of the rival factions. Dona Garaldi explains her talents. My aunt is mindful.

"Your mother's family was always volatile. Nyx has made my brother miserable often enough. Deimos sounds like a most distasteful person." Aunt goes on about Lucia having a right to happiness, and that she is sad for her murder. Her child is well away from the Tartus clan. The castle is a refuge for all women and children. No one here will ever be a bastard or a whore.

"Hazel, this is my nephew. This is Dona Garaldi. Madam, I'm afraid we are on first-name basis only here. Can we know your name?"

"Sophia, my dear."

"Geraldine, now we can continue over the hot tea. Hazel, what have you in the pot?"

"A simple vegetable soup, sister." I'm impressed by that term. Hazel is in an actual dress and apron. I wonder if there is a code of ranking that governs how one dressed.

Geraldine goes on to explain the arrangements in the household. Although the acknowledged leader and benefactor of the community, she tries to maintain as much of a democracy as can be allowed. The community will decide if Sophia and the child are given refuge. All matters, including finances that have to do with the community, are decided in council and often by a full vote. They have achieved self-sustenance. Geraldine will decide if she will help Sophia with business and investments. External money matters are her business.

"Nephew, do you have accommodations in the village? You cannot stay here, as you know. Sophia and the infant will be our guests until the community makes a decision. She will need to explain herself to them."

"Aunt Geraldine, I have rooms at the Trieste Gedolfo. I was told it is the best the town has to offer. Shall I send their bags to you?"

"A good idea. Yes. The council will not meet for two days. You may not leave town until we decide Sophia's fate. Is that understood?"

As if I could be contained after escaping Sicily. But I want only what will help the grandmother and child. I wish to be free as soon as possible.

"Of course, Aunt."

"What of your plans?" she asks. My plans. . .are a mystery to me.

34

NOW, NEW YORK CITY

S HE SAYS SHE'S COMING." MORTANA HAS TOLD JASON that
their mother has accepted their wedding invitation.

"Do you think she had a change of heart, or should we hire armed
guards?" Jason joked, not entirely. Their mother's change of heart was
at best suspect, fear-filled at least.

"I'll assign Cate and Barb to guard her. Any acting up, and they will
drag her out." Jason was sure his two friends would be delighted to do
that, considering her disdain for them when they were in high school
with her son.

"The tent place says we should order heaters—April will be cool if
not cold," Mortana told him, and they continued to review the arrangements for the wedding. Even with Danny and Mortana hosting it, it was
getting close to the limit of the budget Jason and Victor could afford.
Victor's New York One gig was on hold. A new administrator was being
hired, and no changes would be made until that was complete.

He and Victor planned to honeymoon in New Mexico. Augustus
had an interest in an inn in Santa Fe that he had offered to them as a

wedding present. Generous to say the least. Neither having been there, it would be a fine adventure.

VICTOR CAME OUT OF THE BATHROOM, TOWEL-WRAPPED. Jason had the paisley bed cover up at his waist.

"Where's Augie?" Victor asked, using their pet name for Augustus.

"Behind you. Here, take your glass." I had gone to the bar to refresh their drinks. The two pop-out shelves were out. I put Jason's drink on the one next to him. Leaning down, I caressed Jason's face and kissed him fully. The shelf nearer me was occupied by condoms and various lubricants. A pile of used towels lay on the floor, fresh ones on the bench at the paneled window.

Victor, who would soon add his towel to the pile, climbed onto the covers next to Jason in the center of the bed. Center of attention. I settled next to him after giving Jason his scotch.

"I know neat is supposed to be sophisticated, but I could never stomach it without water," I informed the two near-naked men in my bed.

The night of their Christmas ride in Del's Uber, the duo had had a serious discussion about monogamy. They both admitted that the pint-sized driver oozed sex. They were secure enough in their relationship to let down their inhibitions. They admitted to finding men outside their relationship desirous. They did not want to trap themselves in heteronormative matrimony. Both were open to sharing their bed and bodies but not their commitment to each other. For the moment, ménages would be the accepted format for explorations. Del was the first adventure, I the second. They hadn't wanted anyone else.

"You two are more than delightful. I haven't had such great sex since the Admiral, and believe me I have had a lot." I had mentioned the Admiral a number of times. My home seduction mode to set the mood is in fact "Lao Tzu, Admiral."

"Tell us more about the Admiral," Jason asked. "You've mentioned him each time we've done this."

After Victor closed the bathroom door, I told Lao Tzu to close the bedroom panels. They slid shut, making the room, as intended, a sealed cube.

"Lao Tzu, something soft. Renaissance. Lute, please. Lights, torch." The room glowed in flaming torch light, nowhere near electric bright—an atmosphere created as a placeholder in my long diary.

I lit a joint and passed it to Jason, who passed it to Victor. A Tiffany ash tray traveled with it.

"I haven't spoken of him in years. You two are like the best of him divided in two. I may get maudlin telling this. He was my first and only great love."

I told them the story of my time with Pietro in Sicily. I guarded against details of time, keeping the tale in the near present.

I said to Jason, "He was taller than you, but you're built like him. Hairy chest. Broad shoulders. Strong natural body. Nice thick member." I had had such wonderful feelings riding both.

Victor peeked under the cover, purred, "Nice isn't the half of it. Nope, whole." Victor was playful, a bit drunk, a bit high, a bit intoxicated with testosterone.

"And you, my delicious petite writer, are his spirit. Aggressive, flexible, top, bottom, everything in between, honest, straightforward, driven to do good in the world. Not that you aren't those things, Jason, but this guy from three continents is those things to the nth degree." I leaned over and kissed Victor, who grabbed the back of my head and gave me an open-mouthed kiss.

"I'm embarrassed. . .*not*." Victor adjusted himself. He had been more than a bit stimulated by the kiss.

"How can I embarrass you after the things we've done in this room. . .and elsewhere." We all laughed.

"Pietro was such a wonderful orator. He gave the most beautiful sermons. Way ahead of his time. Never condemning, always seeing the good to be found. He encouraged people to be better than they were taught to be." My reminiscence had brought a sweet sad sound to my voice. I was leaning on my left elbow. Jason had turned full on his right side to Victor, who had propped himself up on another pillow.

"How did he jibe the whole God thing with the Gay thing?" Jason, being the child of a fanatic, was driven from any belief in the supernatural.

I described how we often had philosophical discussions after our trysts on the islands. Pietro had always said that if you were true to your nature then you were probably good, even if others judged differently. If God was all good, then his creations were. Of course, the fact that there is a food chain is a source of a lot of cruelty. Humans think it applies to other humans. That is a wrong concept. . .and the fatal flaw in all ways of dealing with each other.

"I'm afraid we did not always agree. He would say that, in time, all things be clear if you do your best to fulfill your better nature. I have not come near to his ideal. But then again, who says I'm human?" It was a joke with a bite to it, a move to change the mood.

I lit another joint. We all indulged. I put the ashtray and roach on the shelf.

"Well, I think we have done a fine job of following our nature this evening." Jason purposely added a physical distraction. He stroked Victor's chest with the back of his hand, turning it over and then back, fingertips barely on Victor's skin.

I idly opened Vic's towel. "Well, look here. It's alive." I joked. "You smell so good." I looked at Jason. "May I?" indicating a desire to stroke Victor also.

"Have you noticed, *I'm* here?" Victor asked.

I smiled at him with a leer. "Be a good little sex toy and stay quiet while we have fun."

I followed Jason's suit on Vic's right side. I let my hand cross Jason's. We meshed fingers. I drew Jason's hand to my mouth kissed it, licked the knuckles.

"Hey, watch the 'little' stuff. I may not be tall but I'm not little." Victor, actually , had no issues about his height. His security in himself was the greatest strength that his aunt had instilled in him.

"No, sir, what you lack in height you make up in length." I bent over to lick Victor's nipple. "You do smell good. I swear that soap and shampoo are an aphrodisiac. After the shower, I still feel like I want to do more. I've already had two hefty orgasms." Victor shared this as he was being fondled by his fiancé. Victor groaned, then wiggled, as I playfully pinched his well-moistened nipple.

"We can thank my chemist cousin for that. She is very talented in biological creations. She invented the soap and shampoo we used. They *are* aphrodisiacs. That's why I told you two to use the blue soaps. She made them at my request. I'm not clear what they contain, but a small amount of genetically engineered testosterone is part of it. It has no lasting effect and leaves the body in a few hours. One of my companies finances her."

"We've been drugged!" Victor *sounded* angry but smiled.

"Well, it isn't a roofie. I've been enjoying every body part we've washed. It's like poppers without the burn," Jason mewed as he slowly traced his fingers over Victor's appendage.

Victor pulled open my robe. "What are you hiding in here?" He slid his fingers lightly over my prize. I inhaled in delight, shuddered.

"That tickles. The Admiral would do that before he thoroughly possessed me."

"Do tell. Me first," Jason commanded.

"Definitely, but let's play a bit before I surrender to the two of you." I reached over Victor, skimmed the blanket covering Jason, knelt up, bowed over, engulfed Jason's member. Coming up for air, I called out, "Lao Tzu, V and J." The lights dimmed but became a clear pink over the bed, redder on the walls. The scent of the soap was in the air. Barbara's concoction atomized. The sitar music a low throb, intended to be felt more than heard.

When we were cleaning up after this third session, I provided Ivory soap. A silent joke.

"I CALLED YOU AN UBER. No arguing. It's my treat. It's Paul, my regular driver. He'll be here in a few minutes."

"Augie, you are the best host." Jason hugged me for the sensually mystical time they had spent in physical freedom.

"I'd say you're the best fuck, next to this guy." Victor's voice was sexy as he slid his arm around Jason.

Steering back to reality, I asked, "Dinner a week from Thursday night?"

"Sounds good. How about the bistro?" Jason asked. We had developed a routine of dinner together every few weeks since November. Sex was not included. Passion dates, including this one, had occurred three times since New Years, six weeks before.

"Good, I need to get out—8:00 PM?" I asked, knowing that was their usual time.

"I'll make the reservation," Jason volunteered. They had made a deal with me that, when we went out, it was strictly Dutch treat. They'd let me pay when they celebrated Victor's thirty-fourth birthday. I had taken them to one of the most expensive restaurants in town. They couldn't have paid their maintenance if I hadn't.

My phone buzzed. The text indicated the Uber was outside.

We kissed goodbye. Victor fondled my genitals as a final gesture before they left my town house.

In the car, Victor asked Jason, "What would our family say?"

Jason laughed at the absurdity. "They wouldn't *say* anything, they'd all faint."

"Well, what we have here is a case of don't ask, don't tell." Victor was snuggling up to his husband-to-be.

"I don't think the soap has worn off," Jason noted with an enticing tone, looking into Victor's eyes.

"I know it hasn't." Victor glanced down and placed his hand squarely on Jason's hardening crotch.

Jason said to the driver, "Paul, the quickest way home please."

35

THEN, MIDDLE EUROPE

"ELIO, WHERE THE HELL DID YOU COME FROM?" He has insisted that I come to the door, declining my manservant's invitation to wait in the entrance hall.

"Invite me in." I am at a loss why I had to. My man servant is polite to all who present themselves at it.

"Come in. You look as good as ever." My brother has a way that fills the space with light. He doesn't look forty-two, five years older than me. He looks ten years younger. "What has brought you here? We haven't been in contact for at least ten years since I left Father's business. Come into my sitting room. Have you eaten?" Turning to my man servant, "Franko, wine, water, food."

Elio dismisses the food. "Wine will be fine."

While we wait for Franko to return, Elio reviews recent family events.

He informs me our mother died almost nine years ago. I offer my condolences but feel little regret. She had a fall and never recovered. Cynic that I am, I wondered if my father helped that to happen.

Last time I visited to hand over all the paperwork to the Bavarian trading company, he outright disdained being with her. He had a mistress by then and a four-year-old son by her whom he publicly acknowledged, much to Mother's distress. Elio informs me that father has married Beatrice and has now had three sons by her. They are of no consequence to my life at this juncture.

"Quite a family." I express no emotion. Having no contact for ten or more years will make one feel detached. Our familial relations were always at a distance anyway.

Franko returns with the wine. He has brought some bread, fruit and cheese. I never drink without some food to snack on.

Elio is seated in one of our uncle Loup's fine high-back leather chairs. He does make some of the best furniture on the continent. The Persian rug over the center table cost a mighty penny. I let the tray with the wine and food remain on it. I would not insult a guest, especially my brother, by having it removed.

The lamps are lit. It is a full-moon night. The light of the sun's reflection fills my sitting room even more. The blackened trees are thick through the high windows of leaded panes. Books line the walls of shelves. There are a few clothing chests about, deeply carved Bavarian things that are less to my liking each day. I have had many things other than clothing in the one. It has warped somewhat from the necessary washings.

Franko is gone. My brother rises and closes the door. Reseated, he begins. "You look well. You've kept yourself well. Sicily wasn't all that bad for you." I start to protest. He holds up his hand. "Let me continue. Your time there is really beside the point. We have been watching you. We know about your activities, which many would find abhorrent. They are of no concern to us."

"I HAVE NO IDEA WHAT YOU'RE TALKING ABOUT. Who are *they?* You sound like I'm being accused of something." I do not like where this may be going. I have always been extremely careful about following my rules when I kill: outsiders, travelers, the unconnected. The town I've been in for two years now barely notices me except for the few prominent men I curry favor with. My business is a copy of the family's: investments but no public prominence.

"You are called 'the Slayer' by authorities all over Bavaria. I have watched you kill. You are quite adept. I know you sometimes bring one back here, and that the body is secreted out in a day or two. What you are doing is entirely your business. I am here with an offer from the group I'm a member of, the Eternal Family, the Children of the Gift."

"Never heard of them. How could you watch me do anything? Much less kill? I'm not in the habit of doing such a thing." I try to be indignant with sincerity. My heart is all but jumping from my chest. I hide my reactions, I'm sure, expertly.

"Brother, here is my diary. I've marked a number of places. Read." Elio hands me his journal. I scan what is written. I can't believe the accuracy of it. I read a few thoroughly. He certainly has the family's eidetic memory.

"What of it?" I am brazen. I pull my damask robe shut over my multi-patterned shirt and tights, which are coming into fashion in Rome. I have agents who keep me abreast of such things in this back water of "Barberia," as I sometimes call this mountainous land of near cretins. I stay because hunting is so easy. People disappear on a regular basis. It's a national shame. The duke only cares that he has tax revenues to pay for his next castle or hunting lodge. His loyalty to varying lords is always at the behest of his pocketbook.

"I am here to offer the Gift. You've noted how much younger I look than my age. That is the result of the Gift. Time is stopped. I received it when I was thirty-four. How did I get to record your kills? The Gift grants preternatural senses. I heard, smelled, saw, almost *felt* your deeds. Occasionally we can even glimpse a person's thoughts. Some we can enthrall to our minds."

I don't know what to make of him. I think he might be mad. I fear he is a threat. He knows too much of my life, my hobby.

"Let me show you something." He disappears from right in front of me. The next instant he has his hands on my shoulders from behind. His fine wool Cossack coat brushes the back of my neck. I would have bolted from my chair except that he's held me with extraordinary strength.

"You see some of the Gift's powers, advantages for your peculiar habit. We are expanding the Family. We are calling on those we love first. Now you are a mature thirty-six, thirty-seven years old. Your beauty is still apparent. Stopping time would lock you into the height of that."

We sit. He drinks. I examine him with the care of a jeweler buying gems from a pasha. Still blond, smooth skinned, even from here he has that scent that is sex and saint in one. He has a deep green coat wrapped around his lithe figure. All of his garments are in various hues of dark green. His soft boots look very comfortable. He wears the obligatory dagger at his waist. I sip some wine, eat a bit of fruit. Nonchalance is the cover I present as best I can.

"Before you ask, I will tell you the price. You would tithe yearly to the Eternal Family Council. It isn't anywhere near the trust tithe. You would become allergic to the sun. More than a minute of exposure would set you on fire with no escape. You would no longer be human. You would hunt humans as food—not their flesh, just their blood. The rest of your human habits at first will be lost. Food, drink, would make you sick the first month but that goes away rather quickly. You will not need them but will find them useful so you can be part of civilization, enjoying its many pleasures. It is *entirely* a life of pleasure. Within limits."

He proposes the question and answers himself. "And what may they be? . . . Never expose the Eternal Family by your acts. If you give the

Gift, never give it to a child. Always *offer* the Gift, do not merely *bestow* it—an unprepared recipient can go mad and would need to be destroyed. And never kill a member of the family.

"Oh, yes. . .and you must die." He is especially calming in saying this, knowing my motto is, *Do all you need to do to remain alive.*

I am baffled. He's offering what sounds like eternal life but says I must die. I, like most people of the sixteenth century, have heard the legends, the Dra-kule stories. He is saying that such creatures exist. That he is one. That he would make *me* one.

I've heard enough. "Brother, you are mad. A few parlor tricks, and you think you can get a purse full of coins from me." He grabs me by the throat with his right hand, lifts me ever so slowly into the air, to the full extent of his arm. His strength is no trick (he shows no strain in the act), holding my dangling legs just out of reach of the floor.

And then he's lowering me, drawing me into his arms with a kiss. Breaking the kiss, I gasp to recover my breath, ease the constrained air pipe that I had just feared he would crush.

"Brother, I do so love you. I burn for you to have this gift. We could spend centuries exploring the world. No matter what you decide after accepting the Gift, I would be your mentor the first year. We would be considered a family by the Eternal ones. Any one I would have made, or you would make, would be part of that extended family, our family solely of choice, not flesh. Our blooded family. A family of uncon-ditional love."

"Do I know your family?" Frankly, I want references. Absurd as that sounds. I am not in my right mind, perhaps caused by my near strangulation.

"Three, Gaspar and Mikel." I am stunned.

"But you said no children. Who is the third?"

"Gaspar turned eighteen when he accepted. Mikel was twenty-six. Quite a stunner. When you last saw him he was a teen. His manhood has created a Roman God or Greek, seeing his Sicilian roots. Gaspar looks like his true father, fair in the French way. Fine hair the color of a pale sunrise. Lovely olive skin from our sister. A pleasure to look at but not equal to Mikel. Few are."

My brother tends toward men, but women have always found him irresistible so he had many to bed before I lost track. From experience I can say he is part incubus. He brings out the deepest sensuality in you. If his powers there have increased, he is a danger to all who submit to his lust.

The third was a nun, Margot. He did not expand beyond that.

We discuss some of the ways he has used the Gift himself. He is now wealthier than Father. He manages the treasury of the Eternal Family. The position has never before descended on one so young. Understandable: Father always thought him the most trustworthy and honest in business.

I ask how the giving is done. He describes it all. I am horrified. When I think about it, how different is it from a von Pittasching? I have always had to fight drinking the blood. If I accept, that struggle would end, my most denied desire fulfilled.

"Brother, can one be killed other than by sunlight?" I need a more complete picture.

"Beheading, dismemberment, wooden stakes, fire. Of course the sun. Some say crosses. But I haven't had any problems there. Oh, I left out that you no longer reflect in a mirror. So fix your image in your mind if you accept. Your hair will always return to the style, length, it was at the time of the gifting. Cut it when you rise from your bed, and it is full length at the next arising. It would never be longer. Your features will never change.

"As I've said, I will be your guide. Many of the things you hear in the stories are not true. We sleep in beds, unless you prefer a coffin. As long as some fool doesn't throw open the drapes to let in the sun, we are safe. We can be up but not about during the day. When we travel we need only a stone from our place of gifting to guarantee safety. Again, that may be a fiction. I've met very ancient family members who say they never had one. My mentor did."

"...Who made you?

"That story is too long for now. Some time in the future." He is being evasive, which of course makes me more curious. I listen to my own words, wondering where reality has gone.

"I will be back tomorrow night. Prepare yourself. See to it that you are as you would wish to be seen for eternity. Shaved, hair well done. Manicured. Trimmed down where it counts, just a reminder of how attractively you have always done that.

"Think long and hard. Send your servants away. Pay them off. I and my family will help you figure out everything. We never leave our newest child of the Gift to fend for themselves.

"If you accept, answer your door when I knock tomorrow. Mikel and Margo will be in attendance. Do not open it if you reject the offer. That would mean a sure death." He all but evaporates.

And so I was made a child of the Gift on a Sunday, August 4, of the Christian calendar in the year 1546.

36

NOW, QUEENS, NEW YORK

A ND DO YOU, VICTOR HUGO VIRLUS, take Jason Patton Lemures for your lawfully wedded husband?" Ron West was performing the ceremony although the duo had written their own vows. With the second "I do," he pronounced them wed. "You may kiss your husband," he added, which they did discreetly.

When they turned, he had arranged for them to stand in front of him for a moment, flanked on the left by Jack, Richard, and Calyce, on the right by Mortana, Danny, and Jeremy. He then announced, "Beloved guests, may I present to you Jason and Victor Lemures-Virlus!" They had hyphenated their name at the toss of a coin. Everybody clapped. One or two whooped.

The tulips the twins planted had decided to cooperate, providing the border of beautiful colors Mortana had envisioned.

The men were in white tuxedos, with rainbow bowties and cummerbunds. To lighten the formality, they were also wearing black Converse high tops. They started to walk down the grass aisle in the tent in Mortana's backyard.

Barb screamed, "She's got a gun." Francesca Lemures had stepped into the aisle with a large automatic pistol pointed at her son and his husband. She was ten feet from them.

"Abominations! You are all *abominations!*" The first slug hit Victor in the right chest, and he collapsed. Jason supported him to lower him to the ground. A second shot pierced Jason's skull above his right ear, blowing most of his head off.

She continued to fire. At first it seems random, then more focused. The officiant collapsed. His husband, running to him, was shot in the back. She aimed at Calyce, then her daughter, Danny, Jeremy. Each crumpled.

Francesca was toppled by Barb who had crashed a folding chair into the woman's head, knocking her out. "I hope I killed you, you fucking *witch*." She repeatedly kicked her in the stomach. Someone pulled her back. She collapsed in shock. Cate was holding Victor, screaming for a doctor. People had rushed to the victims. Someone was yelling, "Apply pressure." Two people were trying mouth-to-mouth on the twins. Danny's brother-in-law was pressing his jacket into the wounds in Danny's stomach. Mortana lay unconscious, Charles Brown at her side. Two other people were also wounded.

The guests had scattered. People had fainted when they saw Jason's head burst open. Someone had taken on triage, and a medic from the group of Marine friends was instructing people how to staunch the bleeding. Charles Brown's jacket over Jason's upper body.

The police arrived. Ambulances arrived, faster than thought humanly possible. Hours later or immediately, time was warped.

One of the wounded was a member of the NYPD. The gun held twelve rounds. Barb had prevented two more people from being murdered. The police tried to console her with that information. She was loaded into an ambulance, Cate at her side, shock engulfing Barb only slightly more than Cate.

Abuela, Tia, Juan, and David were not harmed. Tia had passed out. Abuela had thrown herself on top of David. He might have a broken arm. The ambulance EMT comforted Juan. "I think you saved this man's life. I've got him from here."

Juan went with Danny, who lay unconscious, sedated by the EMTs as he yelled for his wife and children. Tia took David in another ambulance.

Charles and Abuela went with Mortana, Jeremy with them. "Daughter, Mortana, hold on. Jeremy, love, baby we are with you," s he repeated over and over, obviously in shock herself.

As soon as the EMTs stabilized each victim, they loaded them into ambulances. Del went in one ambulance with Jack, both holding Victor at one point or another. Ron and Richard were wounded but conscious. Babatunde and his fiancé piled into ambulances with them. The other two guests, friends from Jason's university, had both been wounded and were in serious condition. Their spouses went to the hospital with them. EMTs check out the people who had fainted. The ones with cuts and bruises from the melee of overturned folding chairs were treated on site. All eventually went in ambulances to the hospital. A police officer went in one with Francesca.

The cops interviewed the remaining guests. The videographer had filmed most of it until he got knocked over. In truth, it had taken less than a minute from Barb crying out to her bashing in the murderer's skull.

The street was filled with neighbors. News trucks had arrived. Victor's boss and two reporters were guests. They filed reports to various mainstream newspeople they recognized, emphasizing that it had been a Christian attack on a Gay wedding. The gun had been brought from Arizona, where you could buy one in Walmart. They all knew Jason's mother's story. Victor had told it at the in-house bachelor party they held for him.

By the time it was dark, most of the police action had been completed. All the guests were in hospitals or sent home. I had not heard the radio. I arrived in my Tesla. Jason and Victor had understood why I couldn't attend the ceremony. I swore I would be at the reception.

I pulled over as close to the taped-off street as possible. My preternatural hearing and sight cued into the police and reporters' idle discussions. I hadn't been so heartbroken since the Admiral's murder.

I eventually found one of the reporters from the reception guests, a guy named Ted. He knew about Beyer. He gave me as many details as he could. The man was divorced from his words. Gil Krier spotted us. "I recognize you from the drawing. Vic spoke a lot about your becoming a friend. I can't believe this. The world is fucking nuts. I hope the bitch doesn't die. They say the chair took out her eye."

"Where did they take Jason and Vic?" I asked Krier with some urgency in my voice.

He told me they'd sent Vic to the hospital and taken Jason to the city morgue's crime wing in Manhattan. "Friend, you do not want to see him. I've thrown up more than once just remembering."

He rushed off to the corner litter can to do so again. Ted went to help him. I followed. Ted helped Gil to the curb, dropped next to him, and put his arm around his shoulders. They both began gut-wrenching wails.

Concerned, a cop approached. "Do you guys need help?" I intervened, told him we were all friends of many of the victims. The cop expressed his condolences. I asked where Victor had been taken. The cop murmured for me to stay put. He returned to his blue-and-white and checked its computer. "They transferred him to Langone in Manhattan. It's better equipped for the surgery he needs. Fellows, I'm so sorry. My wife's brother is Gay. I'm really worried about him now." We thanked him.

I ordered the two newsmen to get in my car. They allowed me to get them to Ted's home in Hell's Kitchen. He had a roommate, a former lover, whom he'd called. The guy insisted he bring Gil to stay at least overnight. Gil had no strength left to argue. Ted had lost track of Jessie, the other reporter friend. He finally got him on the phone. "He walked to his mother's house. He lives about ten blocks away, in Queens. His brother and sister are helping, taking care of him." Ted sobbed again.

"Listen, you guys are in shock. Eat something right away. Shower. It will help. Let your boyfriend take care of you and Gil here. I need to see Vic. I'm going over to Langone."

"They won't let you in." Gil knew how these things worked.

"I'll figure it out. Please eat. I know you'll drink. But eat, too," I advised them from the car window as they got out. "Guys, I'm sorry about Jason. Let's all hope Victor pulls through. I'll be in touch. Victor gave me the office number."

Gil, worried for me, asked, "How are you doing? I think Victor and Jason are—*were*, fuck—attached to you. And, I would guess, you to them."

"I love them like brothers. I'm going to Langone. I plan to scream from here to there."

"Do you think you should drive?" Gil needed to feel like he could take care of someone, even if it was this complete stranger.

"Gil, my friend, one of the best things I own is this car. It drives itself. I just have to tell it where to go. I could be asleep and it would be safe. Thanks for asking. Go upstairs. Eat."

They climbed the stone stairs to the tenement Ted lived in. I told the car to take me there. "Shortest route. And call my lawyer." I slumped into the driver's seat, crying so hard my insides hurt for the first time in centuries.

37

NOW, NEW YORK CITY

THE RECKONING THE NEXT DAY WAS HORRIFIC. Calyce was dead. Mortana was wounded in the right shoulder, her clavicle shattered. She would need more surgeries to restore her movement. Danny had severe small-intestine damage. They removed about a third. Jeremy was in a coma, his left ulna shattered, radius broken. He would recover but needed extensive surgery. David's arm was not broken, the shoulder just dislocated—Abuela felt relieved.

Ron had been shot in the left side of his chest. The bullet had broken a rib, deflected out, and pierced his arm. He was in satisfactory condition. Rich had been shot in his back; the slug; going through his shoulder blade, had landed in the muscle in front. Helen, Jason's colleague, had died over night. One of Mortana's friends from the force had also been injured.

Babatunde, Jason's colleague and short-term item, had a wound to his neck. A half-inch to the left, and his carotid would have been severed. He thought the blood was from holding one of the 'Boys'; in the ambulance, the EMT had noticed it. The shot had probably been a ricochet, the angle impossibly oblique.

Of course, Jason was dead, and Victor close to it.

Francesca Latorre Lemures was in a coma. Barb had taken out her right eye, broken those facial bones, and fractured her skull and six ribs. She might live.

Victor had severe damage to his right lung. The bullet had bounced around in his chest cavity, causing more damage. The doctors might have to remove the whole lung, having already removed a large portion. Most of the ribs on that side were damaged in one way or another. He was in a medically induced coma.

By the morning, my lawyer had Jack sign papers to let the hospital admit me to Victor's room. Jack willingly cooperated when the lawyer told him that I had unlimited funds and wanted to see to Victor getting the best treatment possible.

I spoke with Juan, Eva, and Abuela, assuring them of the same for the Lemures. I had my people arrange Calyce's funeral. Mortana knew she was gone. Danny and Jeremy did not. Before they induced the coma, Jeremy kept asking for Calyce. He'd been told his parents were going to be okay. The doctors felt his sister's death would be too traumatic for him. Seeing his whole family lying in blood, the murder of his uncle, Victor's collapse, and others mowed down by his deranged grandmother was more than a fifteen-year-old should be asked to bear.

I visited Mortana in her Queens hospital before returning to Victor in Manhattan. I wanted to, among other things, get her approval on the funeral arrangements; burials would be delayed until Danny, Victor, and the others could attend.

"Danny is critical, terribly damaged. Jeremy may lose his arm. They say we're all going to need many surgeries. How do I tell them? My precious daughter is dead. My husband. . .my son. . . . My brother gone. That witch should rot in hell."

I did my best to calm her. There was no consoling. My tears were as real as hers. "Right now, we need all of you to heal your bodies. I will help as much as possible. My personal medical team in Bern is in contact with all your doctors. They will advise you of who needs to be called in. The world's medical experts are at your disposal. That goes for the other guests also."

Mortana started to thank me. I hushed her, telling her she needed to conserve her energy for her healing.

"No, I absolutely feel utterly helpless. This is only a gesture of my pain. Victor and Jason had become more than family to me." I would never reveal how much deeper our relationship was than mere family.

"Have you seen Victor?" Mortana hit the morphine button for the line into her arm. She struggled to speak coherently.

"I'm so sorry you're in pain. I should go." I tenderly patted her hand.

"No, Victor first. Tell me. It's better I know." Mortana sank back, the drug affecting her.

"He's critical. Touch and go. There's a clinic in Bern with the best chest-trauma team in the world. I tried to get them to fly over. They have too many patients to come here. I'm going to talk to Jack about flying Victor over. I have a private jet. The doctors here are in consultation with the Bern group. It will be up to them and Jack."

"Thank you, Augustus. Everything you're doing is more than we can repay you for."

"The only payment I want is for you all to recover. Think only about the living now. It will help you to find a way through this. Rest. May I give you a kiss?" I kissed her forehead. "Sleep well, dear sister."

I sagged against the wall outside her room. I had not felt as drained since I was made a Child of the Gift.

My Tesla was parked across from Langone; I rushed in.

In Victor's room I talked with Jack. "The doctor was here about twenty minutes ago. He says that it's a toss-up. Victor may not live through the flight. On the other hand, they have nothing more they can do here." I'm at a loss. His brother and he had just repaired their relationship. Now this. Jack slumped back in his chair.

"Jack, the team in Bern is the only chance. We can fly him there if you decide he can go. I think we need to take the only chance we have." Pressing for a decision, I needed action. Only in Bern was there any hope for Victor, one way or another.

"I can't leave the country. I'm on parole until next year. Vic has one fucked-up brother." Jack felt trapped by his destructive past.

I advised him not to be hard on himself. I knew about the recovering drug addiction. The parole could eventually be handled by my lawyers, but that would take time. A decision must had to be made immediately, with everyone in agreement. Jack agreed to the flight. I called Henri to arrange a video conference with the Bern people. I asked Jack to go to the desk with me to smooth arrangements on this end.

I stole a quick trip to the blood bank to renew myself. Unless they slowed down the monitoring tapes, no one would notice my rapid in and out when the next nurse came in for a patient's supply. The loss would be chalked up to a glitch in record keeping. Scanners don't always register correctly when staff is in a rush.

Francesca would have to wait.

THE AMBULANCE REACHED KENNEDY AIRPORT. Jack had found Victor's passport in the apartment. Tia had Jason's set of keys from Mortana. One less paper complication to contend with.

Even with the current April drizzle, because of the sun, I made my airplane my command post the night before Victor's transfer. The bedroom was sealed, windows all UV-protected. The six-seat forward cabin had had three of the chairs removed—plenty of space for the stretcher and special doctor and nurse. I called my brother Elio, going over the past two weeks. Elio was shocked. "I mean, our mother was bad, but to kill your own child and granddaughter, that's a special kind of hate."

I explained that Henri normally arranged the opening of my house in Bern but I had him so busy with the movement of Victor that that would not happen.

"Instead of having my people open your house, come here. I'll host this. Mikel and Margo are here already. We were having a family gathering. Gaspar may come soon also."

"Can you handle all of us?" A family gathering meant a lot of red. Swiss authorities pay close attention to its missing guests.

"I always have a wine cellar full of our special red. If things go as you expect, we will have something more productive than sexual acrobatics for the week." Elio was excited by the prospect of this diversion. Having lived almost six hundred years, tragedy was a departure from daily tedium, even a family orgy.

"The mansion will be all yours, Elio assured me. I'll be off to Quito in a week. The flower industry is taking off again. Time to see to those companies. So just phone me with your ETA, and I'll be ready for you."

WE FLEW MID-MORNING and got to Bern-Belp Airport that night. It was raining at both airports. My jet was directed to a quiet end of the facility. My lawyer and a hospital representative were waiting. The ambulance was there with the Customs people. We had an easy check-through; the lawyer had all the correct papers.

We were driven to the private hospital. It was 9:30 PM Bern time. I had donated a wing there. The one time I survived a sunburn, the doctor there had asked no questions as he soothed my psychic pain. We'd had an arrangement since. Children of the Gift sometimes need a place to rest—more of a sanatorium than a physical hospital. The rest of the facility was exactly what I had said it was: the best thoracic department in the world.

"If you can help him, I will be most grateful. If not, I will take him home to die in my arms. I need my friend conscious and pain-free before he dies, if that is your diagnosis." Dr. Mengele, a great-grandson of that other doctor, even looks like him.

"*Ja.* Let me get him into a surgery where our team can do all the tests needed. You will return at 3:00 AM. I will have an assessment then." Two orderlies rolled Victor from the ER through the double white doors, followed by Herr Doctor.

The New York medical team had been checked into their hotel. They would fly home the following day, after a night's rest.

My lawyer drove me to Elio's villa. I thanked him. He asked if I want him to drive me back to the hospital at 3:00. Not necessary. Elio had my Tesla brought from my less-grand mansion; I saw it parked in the driveway at the guest house.

"Brother, come in." Elio, Mikel, and Margo gathered me up. They were wrapped in towels. My orgy conjecture was incorrect. We went to the indoor pool where the three had been swimming. The servant brought a ewer of special red. After serving us, she left. We caught up.

Mikel's story was for another time. Margo I knew from my making over five hundred years ago. After my drink, I asked to be shown to my room. Elio offered, "The guest house is all yours. Your lawyer dropped your bag off there. Shall I send someone to unpack?

"Yes, thank you. I'll see you tomorrow evening. I need to shower and change. Nice seeing you again, Margo. Mikel, we need more time together." I quickly thought that Elio's description of the adult Mikel was accurate.

WILHELM WAS THE MAN SERVANT ASSIGNED to my care. He was so officious that I couldn't stand him. I thanked him for his orientation to the house, the unpacking of my bag, and shooed him away.

I was up at 2:15 and on my way to the hospital. The rain had stopped. The nurse at the desk directed me to the doctor's office. I waited about ten minutes for him to come in—five for retrieval, five for effect, I'm sure. The German Swiss were so conscious of status, they played these social games without realizing they were.

He took a seat at the desk with a folder of papers. "I must say your friend has an amazing constitution. He should already be dead. Unfortunately, nothing more can be done. His chances are about twenty percent for survival. Although the bullet remained in the right lung cavity, a bone fragment nipped his heart muscle. We only caught that because he went into cardiac arrest while we were moving him. We revived him. If that had happened on his transport from New York to here, he would have not survived. I fear you may want to take him home. He has a day at most."

"Can you take him out of the coma while keeping him pain- free?" I feared the answer.

"Yes, there are drugs a nurse can administer, but it would not be wise for more than fifteen or thirty minutes at most. Even then his psychological trauma will be hard to penetrate."

I thanked the doctor and arranged for Victor's immediate release. I asked him to have all calls directed to my number. Yes, give it to anyone.

I called Elio. "He's coming with me. We will need a nurse. The other professionals we spoke of also. If he says yes, we begin in an hour. There is very little time."

38

NOW, BERN, SWITZERLAND

VICTOR WAS PLACED IN A BEDROOM on the first floor of the guest house. One of Elio's adopted children was a nurse. She kept up her skills in order to have access to the blood bank at her hospital. She works with the hopeless dying. Her kiss is the kiss of death. She's never drained a body. There was no need. A few pints every other day was quite enough. She liked helping people over to the other side.

She administered the drugs to Victor. It took a few minutes for him to stir. I asked him if he knew me. He cried out for Jason. I explained as much as time allowed. He kept saying Jason's name. I offered him the Gift. How much he understood was an open question.

"What about for Jason?" he pleaded.

I had to tell him that was impossible. I described the Gift as Elio had described it to me. I only wanted the best for him. I loved him— Jason, too. I would do anything for them. His eyes began to flutter. I was at his ear. "Yes or no."

He mumbled, "Yes." His most pressing thought then, he later told me, had been that he needed to live. . .that Francesca had to pay.

We took him into the cavern under Elio's villa. There is a passage-way between the two buildings. The professional staff prepared Vic-tor—a complete spa treatment. He would look like this for eternity, the best version of it, the Gift at its best.

When they were done, the room was cleared. Mikel, Margo, and Elio were with me.

Elio stepped back from the stone slab Victor lay on. He had been stripped. "Your child, brother."

I approached this beautiful being whom I had fallen in love with in the FBI office the first time I saw him. I brushed his hair with my fingertips, checking to see he had been completely groomed. I curled over to bite his long, sensuous neck but, instead of feeding, I injected my blood into him.

Elio pulled me off. "Don't drain yourself. We will help." He did the same as I had done, moved away, then Margo came, and finally Mikel.

The process began as Mikel finished. Blood came pouring from all of Victor's pores—the old being driven out by the new. It boiled away as it hit the air. He spasmed violently. The four of us held him in place. His muscles, unlike in the von Pittasching, do not dissolve but became iron bands forged in the heat being produced. His back arched but didn't snap, his new flexibility confirmed. His eyes bulged almost to bursting. He ejaculated a stream of semen mixed with blood. He stopped breathing. We were at this for over an hour. He had a lot of damage the Gift needed to repair.

He opened his eyes. "Stay still," I said. "Do nothing. You're almost there. Another change or two, and you will be an entire Child of the Gift," I soothed him with a whisper in his ear.

Victor gasped, not yet conscious of what had happened. He tried to speak without success. His death throes were upon him. Each cell in his body was dying. It hurts beyond description. Our blood was suffusing every part of him. Next, the marrow in his bones disintegrated. This is the only part of our need for blood, we understand.

He tried to scream. His pain was at the apex. He curved up, collapsed. Snapped up at the waist. Mikel and I laid him down gently. He went into a deep, somnolent sleep.

Elio joked, "Let him simmer for a while. We'll anoint him later." He was covered in dried blood and effluvia.

He and I sat on one of the couches against the wall. Margo had gone upstairs to refill the ewer we had previously drunk from. Gold cups were on a tray Mikel had brought from the mansion bar. They both went to retrieve the bathing supplies and scented oils.

We all drank. Each shared the memory of their making. One never forgets it. Although you appear unconscious you are aware from the moment of your maker's first injection. Victor stirred. We put down our cups. The quartet administered to our new child. He was completely scrubbed, no part left of the old human. We anointed him with the oils. We stood him up, dropped a simple red caftan over his head, and threaded his arms through the holes. Fine slippers—red Prada, like Benedict's—were almost traditional.

"I am *famished*," he said—his first words. They're always the same, expressing the need, just as there are infinite variations in newborns' cries. They are still cries.

I offered him a golden cup. "Drink, my love. There is plenty more." He drained the cup. Margo refilled it as he held it unsteadily.

Elio led him to the couch, stroked his hair, caressed his cheeks, traced his lips. I sat on the other side of Victor. He nestled into me. Elio gave him his official welcome. "Welcome, our child. My brother is considered your maker. But you have had a rare gift. You are made by four powerful Children of the Gift. This one has superior intelligence and cunning. I have a knack for riches and sensuality. Mikel has beauty, charm, and extraordinary courage. Margo...ah, Margo. Having the feminine, especially this woman's, in you with the masculine is rare.

"One can be made by a woman but then it is a hundred percent. Such become more woman than man. You will know the mysteries of women without having to ask. She has extraordinary psychic powers. She can hear your thoughts, even converse without speech, influence your decisions. She's the best enthraller in our family. It's a spectacular gift."

I TOOK VICTOR TO THE GUEST HOUSE to begin his training. We stayed there a month, except for hunting expeditions. After two weeks, I challenged him: He must choose whether to tell the families that he died, or that he's too weak and needs to spend more time in Bern. That would allow him contact with them. He whole-heartedly wanted contact.

After another week, I suggested he call his brother. I had been filtering information to everyone. We rehearsed how to answer questions, and what should not be answered.

Jack was overjoyed to hear his voice, told him he had thought about using since life was such a shit show, but that he hadn't because he wanted to be there for his baby brother. When they got off the phone, Victor was very happy for him, and he almost shed tears proving it.

The Santoses were a different story. Mortana was the one we arranged the call with. The men would get on later. They cried together for a long time. There wasn't much that could be said. They had shared the most terrible tragedy one can. Victor was bereft that Calyce was gone. "Our ring bearer," he kept repeating. They'd buried her and Jason the week before our call, when Danny was finally home. She was sorry that he couldn't be there for it. For Jason.

"I don't know when I'll be well enough to get home. I don't have the strength for seeing his grave right now. Calyce's either. I'm so broken in my mind, Mortana. It sometimes frightens me."

"We all are. We all are." Then they were crying together.

She put the phone on speaker. Danny and Jeremy said, "Hi."

"Uncle Victor, I need to have your hug. Come home, please." Jeremy's voice quavered as he did his best to keep control.

"Ditto," from Danny. Again sadness beyond bearing. They all did a health check-in.

"Augie has made me a new man. I can't come home yet. Another month or two, maybe. I'll be staying with him in Brooklyn for a while. My body is better, but my head is a mess."

Danny offered, "I think we all can identify with that. We do need you here. Augustus has been a Godsend. You two have— you have great taste in friends," he added, Jason as alive in his mind as he had been the morning of his wedding. He shunned the memory of that afternoon.

They said their goodbyes.

"Where is Elio?" Victor asked, trying to get away from his painful phone call.

"He got back last night. We'll have dinner with him in a little while."

"Ari, that sounds *disgusting*," Victor whined. I had told him my true identity, Aristotle Ottaviano de Medici. Yes, a minor branch of that family.

"That's why we can't go back home yet," I pointed out. You need to be able to act as human as possible."

"Okay, but the sooner we get there, the sooner I take care of Francesca Lattore Lemures." He searched his sharpened fangs with his tongue.

FIVE MONTHS LATER, WE HAD OPENED our Brooklyn home when we returned from Bern two months after Victor's gifting. Henri left three days before us to put the house in order. The gardener had been caring for the greenhouse. The regular housekeeper, Tilly, who did the deep cleaning, had come in once a month.

I made Victor as welcome as I could in these new surroundings. I wanted him to feel that this was his home now also. I certainly intended it to be. We have not consummated our relationship since he was made a Child of the Gift. That will come.

We had not told anyone we were back. Victor, like Jason's family, remained devastated by the murders, while at the same time needing to learn the complexities of being a Child of the Gift. Phone calls and Zoom allowed us secluded flexibility.

39

NOW, BROOKLYN, NEW YORK

ORTANA AND DANNY WERE IN RECOVERY. Some additional surgeries might be necessary for both. Calyce's death was particularly debilitating for her twin, Jeremy. His own injuries were repaired by the best orthopedic surgeons I could find. He has long scars on his arm. I tried to encourage him to tell people they were dueling scars. He laughed but not in a good way. His personality has undergone a change. His happy, light-hearted ways had turned dark. He skipped school. His friends tries to support him, but he avoided most of them. Victor was very concerned. Mortana and Danny could barely cope. The DiLangs and Abuela did their best to supervise Jeremy. He loved them but was as difficult there as at home.

Back five months, I decided we should have a welcome-home dinner party for Victor. He was much more emotionally stable. Henri planned it with me to perfection. The family had never been to my—our—home. I also wanted to announce the completion of the paperwork for the foundation I was funding. The adults in those families were integral to its success.

I had registered it under the names of Jason Lemures and Calyce

Santos. It was specifically designed to meet the medical and financial needs of all of Francesca's victims. The law firm of Byron Hall and Associates has become its administrator. Mortana, Danny, Eva, Margo Margoles, and I comprise the Board of Directors. Margo and I plan to keep a tight rein on the administrators, keeping the others well informed but with manageable supervisory duties.

Margo has many attributes. In the human world she is a first-rate business administrator and financial analyst. Elio recognized her talents long ago and saw to it that she had the best training available at a time when women were barely taught to read, much less add. Her guidance early on has helped all of Elio's children to develop vast wealth. She is on the boards of most of my own holdings. This Fund would be an easy addition to her other interests.

SATURDAY ARRIVED. "WELCOME TO OUR HOME," I SAID as I opened our door. There on the steps were Jack and his partner. "Come in. Let me have your coats. This is my all-around assistant, Henri. And Henri, this is Victor's brother Jack and ... ?"

"My partner Alice. Augustus, Alice."

She surveyed the public rooms, "Glad to meet you both. What a lovely home." Jack shook Henri's hand. I handed their coats to him to hang up.

"Thank you. Make yourselves comfortable. Victor will be down any moment."

The door chimed again. The rest of the dinner party arrived. They all kissed me hello. I took the women's coats and asked Jeremy to take David's, Juan's, and Danny's. We put them all on the bed in the guest room. I took the opportunity to speak with Jeremy briefly. "Your uncle Victor," I told him, "needs as much support as you can muster. I hope his living here doesn't upset you. He and Jason were very special to me. Victor needs a lot of attention. I hope it's okay with you that he's here."

Jeremy nodded but offered no reply. We joined the others. His silence filled me with melancholy.

"There's the man of the hour!" Victor had come out of the elevator and down the short hall to the living room. I pointed with my chin to this creature I find ever-lovely, fascinatingly desirable.

They mobbed him. Jack played interference, calmed the rush.

Victor was gently hugged by each one. Jack introduced his girlfriend.

Jeremy had hung back. "Who is that handsome young man?" Victor called out. "Come here, you!" Jeremy and Victor hugged and didn't let go. They held back their tears momentarily, and then, no longer pretending, both cried briefly in each other's arms. The others did their best not to add to the emotionally charged moment.

I waited, then stepped between them. "I think Victor looks almost as good as Jeremy does." I put an arm around each and turned them to the gathering. Victor was obviously robust; Jeremy looked gaunt and worn, almost bulimic, my description a failed gambit.

I tried to lighten the atmosphere. "Let's get drinks started."

There was little actual catching up necessary. We had all been in constant contact.

I took everyone for a house tour. When I turned on the window screens there were oohs and aahs. I switched them from my favorite Ionian Sea to a New England fall—colored leaves, cerulean sky. Juan was agog. "That must have cost a fortune." He got a sharp poke from Eva for that.

I laughed, "To be honest, it did. But money needs to be used, not hoarded. Pleasure and good use need not be in opposition."

I knew that Henri was close to serving. "We'll have a bite shortly. Some of Henri's tapas are on the coffee table and bar. Don't fill up on them, though—his dishes are always a wonder. Later we can sit up here to indulge in delicious desserts. I have a sweet tooth that requires tender loving care. If it's not windy, we can open the terrace doors. It's well-heated."

Guiding them downstairs, I said, "Come sit at the table. Jeremy, sit next to Victor please. Victor and I will sit here." I indicated the side facing the kitchen. Abuela, please sit at the head of the table. Jack at the other end. There's a booster seat for David over there. Juan, if you would." He retrieved it and set it on a chair between Eva and Mortana. Alice sat at Jack's end of the table. Abuela moved next to Mortana. "Too far away," she ventured as she moved her place setting as well, which turned our side of the table into a male bastion. The table sits twelve comfortably, fourteen with armless chairs.

Victor couldn't help himself. "This looks like a sixteenth-century dining hall. Jack, you're the duke!" It took a minute to get his drift. The family laughed. Danny pitched in, "Well, the clothes are a lot more comfortable." We all agreed. Jeremy would have had something to say in the past. He remained sullenly silent.

Henri had engaged the housekeeper to help with the service. "Dear family, you've met Henri. This lovely lady is Tilly, our special house-keeper who, tonight, is helping Henri with this party. We go by first names in this house. Now for the reason we are here—Henri and Tilly, too." I raised my glass. "Welcome home, Victor." Everyone raised their glass and said the same. We clinked with our companions. Eva helped David, who found it all very serious.

Victor lifted his glass again, "To Family, my family and friends."

"To family and friends," came the hearty response.

The repast was magnificent—poached peach salad, roast leg of lamb, roast beef, spinach pie (in case had Jeremy remained a vegetarian), Persian rice, baby potatoes baked in milk and parsley, cheese macaroni for David but plenty for all, carrots with cranberries (sprinkled with mace and honey), almond-toasted long beans, asparagus in lime hollandaise sauce. . . . It wasn't a banquet menu, it was a family banquet.

I had decided not to do a Filipino dinner. No one should challenge a guest with their best recipes. Abuela and Tia had always been praised by Jason and Victor, and by Danny and his kids, too. No competitions are allowed in my house.

Despite my insisting no one bring a thing, Abuela presented a delicious chocolate mousse cake to accompany the delicious pastries made by the cook, who created the Bavarian creme puffs Elio seduced me with. Henri had produced some of his favorites as well. While we had tea, coffee, and dessert in our sitting room, I asked that drivers not indulge in after-dinner drinks but that the bar was open and adults could help themselves.

I discussed the foundation's aims and assured the board members that they could take on more responsibilities when they saw fit. I congratulated Jack for getting into business school. We again celebrated Victor's return to the States, especially to the family.

When they were all gone, Tilly and Henri finished cleaning up. Victor and I went to the restored sitting room to enjoy some special red. We discussed what next step might help the family in their recovery. Jeremy took up a good part of that.

After some time, we sat enjoying each other's company. Henri came up to announce that he and Tilly were finished. "Henri, you outdid yourself. I can't thank you enough. Take Monday off. Victor and I can fend for ourselves very well for a few days. There are some envelopes in my office desk as a special thank you to Tilly and you. Take Thomas on an antiquing adventure. The Infinity is yours if you want to use it."

Henri has made my life, and now Victor's, almost seamless in human comfort. Our association has lasted over two decades. Every child needs an amanuensis. Finding one not needing enthralling is like finding the Hope diamond. His advice, our friendship, has made these years an absolute treasure.

He knows my nature, has never voiced any concerns.

Victor and I retired to our bedroom. "They seemed to have enjoyed themselves." I was more than satisfied with all that had come to pass. Except for Jeremy.

Victor kissed me. "Me, too."

"I promise you, I will do everything to help you to be happy. Them too, if at all possible."

We kissed good night. Chaste as ever, a bit wistful on my part. We would sleep next to each other until dusk on Sunday.

"Lao Tzu," I called out, "bedtime." The house responded as programmed to the command.

Juan drove their van back to Astoria. Eva, next to him in the front, turned to Mortana. "What is wrong with us? We married for love. Next time I want *staff*, too." Mortana laughed at that.

Juan said, "Feel free next time. I'll do the same."

Eva made a fake pout. "Like you would ever leave us. Momma's cooking is too good for you to find a rich cougar."

"Right. Besides, I'd never find anyone like you again, or like my wonderful David." He was loud enough for them to hear him in the back. David was half asleep but laughed at the mention of his name. Abuela and Mortana monitored him in the car seat between them in the back of the van.

Danny put his arm around Jeremy, who sat in the middle with him. Jeremy tolerated it for a minute then shrugged to let his father know it was uncomfortable.

TWO WEEKS LATER DANNY CALLED VICTOR. Augustus picked up the phone to hear, "Jeremy has run away."

About the Author

When Ron Madson is not writing horror/fantasy/spiritual fiction, he and his husband are avid travelers, and collectors of Native American pottery, jewelry, and fetishes. For thirty-three years Ron was an elementary school art teacher, staff developer, and working artist. In the late 1980s he became an advocate for LGBTQ youth and teachers—the first openly Gay Elementary School teacher in New York City. He and his husband, Richard Dietz, as part of a law suit, successfully sued the City of New York for domestic partnership rights (1994), laying the groundwork for Marriage Equality. Ron has had three one-man shows for his artwork, as well as being in numerous group shows. His poetry has been published. Most recently he has had memoir essays published in *RFD Magazine*. He has synthesized a scarred childhood, teaching, creating, advocating, mystical searching, and being Gay in a taboo world, into *Slayer*.

www.ingramcontent.com/pod-product-compliance
Lightning Source LLC
Chambersburg PA
CBHW020541020726
47494CB00006B/1864